MARKED II:
The Resistance

Angela Caldwell

ISBN:0615848346
ISBN-13:9780615848341

For my family

Publisher: 8th Street Publishing
Editor: Carolyn Flournoy
Cover Designer: Lacey O'Connor

MARKED II: The Resistance

Angela Caldwell

8th Street Publishing

www.8thstreetpublishing.com

CHAPTER 1

Keith crossed the California border, momentarily removing his hand from the steering wheel to pump his fist.

"Yes, another state down!"

Keith looked in the rear view mirror at Jacinda. She looked so happy sitting in the backseat next to Kyler, her two-year-old son. In an attempt to make up for the years she had lost with him, she couldn't stop kissing his hands, and lovingly stroking his hair. Jacinda was captivated by the beautiful toddler, and knew she could be totally fulfilled sitting next to him forever. It didn't take her long to learn the tickle monster game. Each time she tickled him, he giggled uncontrollably. As the tickling stopped, he would look at her a moment before saying, "Ticko monner!" Once he said the magic words, the tickle monster would attack. It had always been Kyler's favorite game, and it was now Jacinda's favorite thing in the entire world. Kyler finally had a tickle monster that never tired of playing the game.

Lyla sat next to Keith in the passenger seat. She hugged her knees and rested her head against the window. She was beautiful, and that fact didn't escape Keith.

"Are you getting hungry?" he asked her, in an awkward attempt at conversation.

"Not really," she replied, "but I can eat whenever you guys are hungry."

How can anyone be so passive? He wondered. She hadn't so much as asked to use the restroom since they'd left Oklahoma for California. She simply used the restroom when someone else demanded a pit stop.

Keith glanced back at Jacinda. "I still can't believe you bought a van! Couldn't we have at least traveled in style?" he asked in jest. "I don't know, maybe an SUV made in this decade, perhaps?"

Jacinda met his eyes in the rearview. "You know as

well as I do that everything made in this decade is computerized. I'm not taking any chances of them tracking us down."

"Fair enough, but couldn't you have at least bought one that wasn't all white? I feel like I'm driving a bunch of convicts around! I am. I'm driving a convict van; all we need are bars on the windows. Do you see the way people are avoiding us?" Keith teased.

"Added bonus," Jacinda replied.

Keith looked down at the fuel gauge. "Couldn't you have at least bought a hybrid? We've had to stop for gas every ten seconds."

"It's a good thing you haven't been paying for it," Jacinda quipped, never taking her eyes off Kyler. She dabbed at her face with a tissue, as beads of sweat rolled down her forehead. The man she'd bought the van from had said the AC was in great condition, but the cool air barely trickled out of the vents. The shoddy air conditioning couldn't compete with the scorching July heat.

"Speaking of money," Keith continued, "I still can't believe they let you withdraw that much money at one time! I thought there would be a two-day waiting period or something. It's insane they let you just walk out of the bank carrying that much cash."

Jacinda withdrew every dime the bank would allow. She recalled the overwhelming anxiety she'd felt on the way to the bank just one day earlier. There were so many unknowns. *Would her account be frozen? Would someone at the bank notify The Brotherhood? Would they let her withdraw enough money to live on until she could ensure their safety?* She knew The Brotherhood would do everything in their power to hunt them down. She was fully aware of how widespread The Brotherhood's influence was, and realized that any paper trail would lead them directly to her and her son. Everything had to be paid in cash—everything.

Until The Brotherhood was exposed, Jacinda Kilmeade refused to leave so much as a blip on the radar. Two days ago, she never could have predicted she would be in a twenty-year-old van heading to California with an intern, her precious son, Kyler, and the woman who had raised Kyler since birth. If she had learned anything in life, it was to expect the unexpected. Two years earlier, her son had been kidnapped and her husband killed. She had to start her life over, but had never given up hope of finding her son. She learned very quickly that tragedy could strike without warning. She knew nothing in life was guaranteed, and treasured each and every moment.

Jacinda began to doze off, but was startled awake by the sound of a blaring car horn. She looked up to see a vehicle full of teenage girls giggling and waving at Keith.

"I take back everything I said about this van; it's a total chick-magnet!" Keith announced, only half-kidding.

"Eyes on the road, Romeo! You're carrying precious cargo," Jacinda reminded him, although she couldn't help but giggle. Giggling wasn't something she'd felt like doing for a very long time. She cherished these moments. For the first time in over two years, her heart wasn't aching for her son, because he was peacefully sleeping beside her. Her heart should have been aching for her husband, Gregory, but somehow she managed to block out every emotion but anger when she thought of him. She was still enraged that Gregory had played such a prominent role in her son's disappearance. As far as Jacinda was concerned, Gregory could sit in jail forever. In fact, prison seemed entirely too compassionate.

Jacinda didn't have time to sort through her anger; she was on a mission. Exposing The Brotherhood was the only thing that mattered. It was a feat that no one had ever successfully accomplished. The Brotherhood had messed with the wrong woman—

the wrong mother. Every bit of grief and anger she'd felt over the past two years had transformed into focus and determination. Everything she had left in the world was right there in that van, and she had no intention of losing any of it. A reporter and an intern were about to take on The Brotherhood with a baby and nanny in tow. She vowed to do whatever it took to expose The Brotherhood's wicked agenda. To call it an adventure of a lifetime would be a foolish understatement.

*****

George, the director of *Your Nation Now*, loved his yearly visit to Rhapsody Grove. He loved rubbing elbows with the powerful and elite. He looked forward to mingling with world leaders; it made him feel important. In the grand scheme of things, he did play an important role in the coming New World Order. George was the news director of the highest rated television news program in the country. He had the final say on the stories that aired. George had been pushing The Brotherhood's agenda for years.

While he played an integral role in publicizing The Brotherhood's propaganda, he knew anyone could fill his position. He was merely a pawn. He understood he was expendable, which was why he did everything The Brotherhood demanded. This visit to the grove was different than previous retreats. When *Your Nation Now* had failed to air footage of BARAchip, he had been treated as a traitor upon arrival. Despite explaining the story was complete when he'd left for the retreat, he was being punished for not personally ensuring the story aired.

George couldn't wait to be a part of the action at the grove, which was why he'd headed to the retreat before Jacinda's BARAchip package had aired. It was that careless choice that had landed him in the *sweat shack*. The sweat shack, named because of the sweltering July heat, was where The Brotherhood imprisoned their traitors during the retreat. They didn't let defectors know they'd been discovered until they arrived. Once the traitor checked in, they put a sack over his head, secured it with a rope around his neck, and locked him in the tiny 12X12 foot shack.   Some prisoners described it as a place to think, others, a place to die. Either way, George didn't feel he deserved such harsh treatment after years of faithful service. He'd handled the BARAchip story exactly as they had demanded. He'd even hired Jacinda Kilmeade for the sole purpose of showcasing BARAchip technology to the world.

It wasn't his fault the tape had faded to black right before the story was set to air. Of course, once

Bertha had told him about the tape, he'd known the responsibility would fall squarely on his shoulders. After all, he should have seen the project through from beginning to end. He shouldn't have left D.C. until his mission was complete, and the story had aired. He felt so careless for trusting such an important mission to lackey producers. *Which one of them messed it up?* He wondered. It didn't matter who was responsible; it was George who would suffer the consequences. He feared he was a dead man.

George sat in the sweat shack thinking about everything he'd done to help shape public perception. The scorching July temperature made the air in the shack feel suffocating. The heat of the stale air burned his lungs when he breathed. The stench of rotting wood filled the tiny room, and he wondered if bugs and rats were biding their time to feast on his body. *How dare they treat me like a traitor! Sure, it was irresponsible to leave before the story aired, but I thought everything was handled.* George had believed his job was complete. He'd figured it was in the bag, but the only thing currently in the bag was George's head. Literally. He had never felt such discomfort in his life.

Just when he was beginning to lose every last bit of hope, the door opened. He couldn't see anything, but was able to detect the sunlight that streamed in from the open door. *Thank God*, he thought. *I'm getting out of here.* His hopes were dashed when he heard the thump of a body hit the floor. A man screamed for help. Three seconds later, the room went black.

"Hello," George said. "Who's there?"

"Who are you? Who's in here with me?" the man inquired between sporadic breaths. "How long have you been in here? Will they come get us soon?"

George closed his eyes. Closing his eyes when he felt helpless was a habit. He listened to branches crack as their capturers walked away from the shack. Certain they were alone, he answered as calmly as possible.

"It's George Dittmeir. News Director of *Your Nation Now*." George was far from calm, but knew any outward expression of panic would only throw the man deeper into hysterics. "What's your name? Who are you?" George asked.

"Tony. Tony Randall," the man replied.

George sat a little straighter. "*The* Tony Randall? Louden Records Executive, Tony Randall?"

"Yeah, man. That one. How long are they going to keep us in here?"

"I don't know," George responded honestly. I've heard that some people are put here to think about what they've done, while others say they're sent here to die. Let's hope we're here to think."

Tony remained silent for a moment before asking, "So, what are you in here thinking about?"

"I messed up a story," George confessed.

Tony didn't skip a beat. "The BARAchip story?" George simply nodded, forgetting Tony couldn't see the gesture.

"That's way worse than what I did," Tony said, half chuckling with relief.

"Well?" George asked. "What *did* you do?"

"I fell in love."

"They put you in the sweat shack for falling in love?"

"Not exactly, but falling in love was what got me into this mess."

"So?" George prompted. "What did you do?"

Tony didn't respond immediately. George wasn't sure if Tony was thinking or just avoiding the question altogether. "I guess we're not getting out of here alive, anyway," Tony said. "We might as well confess our sins, right?"

"Right," George responded, although he was holding out hope The Brotherhood hadn't sentenced him to death by way of the sweat shack.

"You ever heard of the Twenty-Seven Club?" Tony asked.

"The what?" George asked.

"The Twenty-Seven Club, man."

"No, I guess I haven't."

"Have you ever noticed how many musicians die when they're twenty-seven? I'm not saying all of 'em made a pact, but a lot of them did. You got the teenagers and twenty-one-year-olds dying to get a record deal. They'll do anything to get signed."

"Okay," George responded, unsure of where the conversation was heading.

"Well, some of 'em, and I can't say for sure which ones, but some of 'em agreed to sign a contract with Lucifer."

"You mean, they signed a contract with the devil?"

"That's exactly what I mean."

"Get out of here; that's just a figure of speech. They

didn't really make a deal with the devil."

"Oh, really? So when the devil collected their souls at twenty-seven, it was just a coincidence? I only witnessed two of our artists participate in the ritual. They didn't really sign their names on a dotted line. It was a little heavier than that."

"Okay, I'm listening," said George, indicating he was still interested.

"Well, my girlfriend, Chyanne, agreed. I signed her when she was only eighteen years old. She was still wet behind the ears. Her career never really took off. She only had one top-forty hit in her three-year career, but The Brotherhood offered her more. They offered her all the fame and success she wanted. She just had to sell her soul. She's only twenty-one, man. She's not even convinced she has a soul to sell, but she wants to be rich and famous more than anything in the world. She'd do just about anything to live that lifestyle. But she didn't know what she was messin' with. She didn't realize that the devil always collects. She came home all excited that she was going to be the *next big thing*. She said all she had to do was show up somewhere and promise her soul. I think she actually thought *she* was conning *them*.

"I couldn't let her do it, man. I couldn't lose her in six years. I love her too much to live without her.

So, I told her. I said, you've got no idea what you're messin' with, baby girl. Once you make this pact, you can bet Lucifer will collect. You can't live on the devil's dime and not expect to pay with your soul. I told her about the two other artists I watched sell their souls. Annette Patrick and Dendy Miller. Both of them were super ambitious kids with stars in their eyes. Both died at twenty-seven."

George took a moment to process the information. "You know, I never really thought about it, but a lot of really great musicians did die at twenty-seven: Robert Johnson, Brian Jones, Jimi Hendrix, Janis Joplin." He paused, trying to think of more, but Tony beat him to it.

"Curt Cobain, Shannon Hoon, and Amy Winehouse. I could go on and on, but what's the point?"

"All of them? They all sold their souls?" asked George.

"How should I know, man? Some of them just died. It could have been a coincidence. I can only confirm the ones I saw. I only witnessed two. I heard about others, but I couldn't swear to nothin'. Once the second artist died at twenty-seven, I knew we weren't playin' games, but I was too far in. I was making so much money. I had houses all over the world. Still do. But not her, man, I couldn't let them take her."

19

"So?" George asked. "What happened?"

"I told her. I told her the truth. I begged her not to do it. She told me I was crazy and stormed out of the house. I figured she'd go somewhere and cool off, but she never came back. That was about a week ago. I guess she told 'em. Why else would I be in this room with this bag over my head waitin' to die?"

The two men sat in silence for what seemed like an eternity. George finally spoke. "Twenty-seven, huh?"

"I'm tellin' you, man, if you ever get out of here, look it up. I'm not sayin' they all sold their souls, but I know for a fact two of them did. Once they turned twenty-seven, the devil came knockin'."

·

CHAPTER 2

Rob Livingston wasn't happy to hear that Keith had involved Jacinda in her son's rescue. He was informed that Jacinda had accompanied Keith after the fact, which left him no time to protest. Once Keith had told him that they were heading to Vega, California to retrieve Gregory's laptop from Jacinda's best friend, Jill, he'd tried to talk them out of it. He wanted to send someone else to fetch the computer, but Keith convinced him Jacinda wouldn't back down.

Keith still hadn't told Jacinda that Livingston was involved. Jacinda had no idea that Livingston was the one who'd sent Keith to rescue Kyler. In order to keep Jacinda out of the loop, Keith had to call Livingston while the girls were in the restroom. It all felt very sneaky, but he didn't want to blow Livingston's cover. After all, if The Brotherhood ever found out Livingston had defected, he'd be killed. Livingston worried that Jill's house would be under surveillance. He feared The Brotherhood would watch everyone who might be able to lead them to Jacinda and her son.

After instructing Keith to not contact Jill, Livingston checked his list of contacts and found Carl—a member of The Resistance who lived In Vega, California. Carl maintained his relationship with The Brotherhood so he could relay their plans to The Resistance. He had agreed to hide Keith, Lyla, Kyler, and Jacinda until they could think of a plan to keep them safe. Carl had asked Livingston to give Keith his cell phone number, instructing him to text when they got to town. The plan was for them to meet in the Shop Mart parking lot off exit 28A near the gas pumps.

After what seemed like an eternity of driving, Keith was relieved to see their exit. "We're here!" Keith exclaimed. "There's Shop Mart. My contact said to just text the guy once we got here."

Jacinda looked skeptical. "Who is your contact? You still haven't told me."

"It doesn't matter. Right now, we just need to follow instructions. He hasn't steered us wrong yet." Keith turned into the parking lot and pulled out the piece of paper with Carl's cell phone number. He picked up his cell phone and shot Carl a text.

Is this Carl? Keith wrote.

It is. Read the return text.

It's Keith. We're here. We're parked in the Shop Mart parking lot now. We're in a white convict van. You can't miss us.

I'll be there in five, Carl responded.

Keith turned to face Jacinda. "He only lives about five minutes away. I told you, The Resistance has people everywhere."

Jacinda looked dazed. "So, The Brotherhood has people everywhere, and so does The Resistance? This is crazy. I feel like I'm trapped in a movie right now. When did this become my life?"

"We're sitting in a convict van, in the parking lot of a Shop Mart in Vega, California. It's kind of funny if you think about it. I mean, this is the last place I would have guessed I'd be a few days ago," Keith said, unable to grasp the gravity of the situation.

Jacinda looked irritated. "There's nothing funny about this, Keith." Reaching over, she unbuckled Kyler's car seat.

"Where are you going?" Keith asked.

"Nowhere," Jacinda replied, "but if we're going to sit here and wait, I'm going to hold my baby. I have over two years to make up for."

Kyler was delighted to be out of his car seat. "Bake up bore," he mimicked.

Jacinda's face lit up, "Yes, make up for!"

Jacinda adored her son. She often wondered how the two-and-a-half year separation would affect their bond, but she couldn't possibly love him any more than she did at that very second. Not even two years could sever the bond between a mother and her child. Kyler had left his shyness back in Oklahoma. He was chatting up a storm. Her son's voice was the sweetest sound she'd ever heard. She had so many questions—so much to learn about her son. "What's his favorite food?" she asked Lyla.

"Well, that changes from day to day," Lyla said, "but right now he loves spaghetti."

"Sketti," Kyler squealed. "I bont sketti." Jacinda's vision blurred as her eyes filled with joyful tears.

"You do, do you? You want spaghetti?" Jacinda asked her son with a smile. Kyler smiled his charming smile and nodded his little head. "Mommy is going to get you all the spaghetti you can possibly eat. We'll eat spaghetti for every meal if that's what my baby wants." The toddler laid his head on Jacinda's chest. She buried her nose in his hair, and kissed the top of his head. "What is his favorite song?" Jacinda asked.

Jacinda continued asking questions until a man in a small, black car pulled up beside them. Jacinda's body tensed and she instinctively clutched her child tighter.

A tall, slim man in his mid-thirties got out of the car. The man's tailored suit was in stark contrast to the grungy clothes donned by the Shop Mart patrons. His confident gait and friendly wave helped Jacinda relax a little. Carl approached the driver's side door. Keith looked terrified as he manually rolled down the window.

"You Keith?" the man asked nonchalantly.

"I am," replied Keith. "Who are you?" He refused to make any assumptions.

"I'm Carl. I just texted you." Keith relaxed his shoulders.

"So you didn't have any trouble finding us?"

Carl shook his head, "You're in a convict van; you stand out like a sore thumb."

Keith laughed and turned in his seat to face Jacinda. "See, I told you we were in a convict van!"

*****

After following Carl four miles to his house, everyone was relieved to pile out of the van. Carl led the group into his home. Jacinda looked around before saying, "It's beautiful."

Carl's house was indeed beautiful. The open floor plan was intricately adorned with expensive, modern furniture and accessories. Everything was tidy and organized. Jacinda decided it was entirely too clean for a bachelor.

"Where is your wife?" Jacinda asked Carl.

"Don't have one," he replied, not feeling the need to expand on the topic. Jacinda looked around Carl's living room and noticed it was decked out with expensive electronics. The house smelled like clean laundry, fresh out of the dryer. The scent was inviting.

Carl motioned to the sleek, black leather couches. "Have a seat. Make yourselves comfortable." Lyla reached to take Kyler from Jacinda's arms.

"I should probably change him," Lyla said. Jacinda shook her head in protest. "I've been robbed of two years' worth of diaper changes. I'll do it myself."

Carl pointed towards a hallway. "There's a guest room down that hall--first door on your right. You can change him in there."

Carl looked at Keith. "I hate to run, but I have to get back to work. You guys make yourselves at home."

Keith looked confused. "But Liv…." He stopped short of saying the name, not wanting to blow Livingston's cover. His heart skipped a beat when he realized how close he'd come to slipping up. He silently chided himself for being so careless. "I just thought we were going to come up with a plan to contact Jill."

Carl nodded. "We can talk about all that later. Right now, I have to get back to work. I was only there thirty minutes when I got your text. I don't want anyone to notice I'm gone. No worries, we'll handle everything when I get back."

No worries? Keith thought. *Does he even know what's going on?* Not wanting to sound frightened, Keith decided to drop the issue. "Where do you work?"

"At a bank," Carl replied, not bothering to get specific. Carl's eyes lingered on Lyla. "I didn't get a chance to introduce myself," Carl said directly to Lyla. "My name is Carl."

Lyla blushed. "I'm Lyla."

And I'm nauseated, Keith thought. *Am I seriously jealous?* Keith wondered. He felt repulsed by his own possessiveness and willed the emotion to disappear.

Carl turned on the heels of his shiny, jet-black shoes and headed towards the door. "I'll be home around noon; I'm taking off early. We'll decide what to do when I get home."

Keith sat down on the couch and reached for the remote control. Jacinda returned from the guest room still carrying the giggling toddler on her hip.

"Where's Carl?" she asked.

"He had to go back to work. He'll be home around noon," Keith assured her. For the moment, Jacinda felt safe. The feeling of safety brought with it the gift of sleepiness. She finally felt able to rest. She looked at her watch and yawned.

"That gives us three hours to take a nap," she said. Without waiting for a response, Jacinda retired to the bedroom with Kyler. It was clear that she had no intention of letting him out of her sight.

Keith decided against turning on the television. He returned the remote to the coffee table. "I guess they're going to take a nap," Keith said to Lyla. Lyla smiled bashfully and twisted her beautiful long, dark hair with her finger.

"You're so shy," Keith said. "I don't mean that in a bad way." Keith was always awkward around women--pretty women to be more precise. He had absolutely no game, and he knew it, but that didn't stop him from trying. "So," Keith continued, "you told me a lot about The Brotherhood, but you didn't really tell me much about yourself. What kind of things do you like to do?"

Lyla had to think a moment. "You are the first person to ever ask me that question, and I honestly don't know how to answer it," she replied.

"You don't know what you like to do?"

"Well, I like to read. I love playing with Kyler. I don't know, during the past two years, my whole life has revolved around Kyler. I haven't had a chance to really explore other interests."

Keith nodded. "So you've had him since day one?"

"I've had him since day two, actually. He was brought to me when he was two days old."

"And you didn't feel guilty? I mean, knowing he was stolen?"

"I felt honored. It was the first time in my life someone trusted me with something so important."

"No offense, but that's a little messed up."

"Yeah, I suppose my entire life was a little messed up. I was just happy to have something to love."

"If you just needed something to love, why didn't you get a puppy?"

Lyla realized Keith could never understand her reasoning. Voicing her thoughts really did make her sound crazy, so she decided to change the topic.

"What about you? What kind of things do you like to do for fun?" Lyla asked.

"Well, nothing really. School and internships pretty much take up all my time. Any free time I have I usually spend on the computer."

Lyla shrugged her shoulders. "Then that's your answer. You like playing on the computer."

Keith nodded. "Yeah, I guess, but that makes me sound really lame."

"Well, are you lame?" Lyla asked, clearly teasing. It was obvious to Keith that she was beginning to feel comfortable.

"I suppose I am," Keith replied.

"Oh, you are not. You're in the news business. I bet most of the time you spend on the computer is for research purposes." Keith knew that was absolutely untrue, since he spent most of his time on the computer chatting with friends via social networking sites, but nodded just the same.

"Yeah, I guess I do research a lot," he agreed, lying through is teeth. It wasn't totally untrue. He spent a lot of time on Facebook researching girlfriends, or, more accurately, girls he wished were his girlfriends.

Lyla removed a rubber band from around her wrist, and used it to tie her long, curly hair into a high ponytail.

"Wow, you really do look like Senator Kilmeade," Keith said. "Especially with your hair pulled back. You could be his twin."

"Thanks a lot. Does that mean I look manly?" Lyla asked, pretending she was insulted.

Keith shook his head. "Actually, I've always found him to look a little feminine."

"He does not!"

"Okay, he doesn't, but there is an uncanny resemblance. What was it like to grow up as a Kilmeade?"

Lyla shrugged. "I wouldn't know. I grew up as a Rockefeller. My mother put Rockefeller on the birth certificate so no one would know that my father was Nicholas Kilmeade. He was a respected politician with a wife and son."

Keith nodded his head, "So, you were a lovechild?"

Lyla pursed her lips while she thought. "No, I wasn't exactly a lovechild, nobody loved me."

Keith wondered if she was unfamiliar with the term. "I'm sorry, I didn't mean to…"

Before he could finish his sentence, Lyla flashed a comforting smile. "I didn't mean for it to come out like that. I certainly don't want anyone to feel sorry for me. It is what it is. That's all I meant."

Keith was desperate to change the subject. "In the interview, you talked about The Brotherhood wanting to sacrifice Kyler to consecrate the ground for the birth of their wicked lord or something. Since you rescued him, and they weren't able to sacrifice him, does that mean the anti-Christ wasn't born?"

"The ground was unable to be blessed, but the baby

still has to be born. The Vessel can't carry him forever," she replied.

"The Vessel?"

"Yes, that's what they call her. She was chosen for her nationality. The anti-Christ needs to be born from a woman of Middle Eastern descent."

Keith gave her a blank stare. "That's it? That was the only prerequisite? She had to be from the Middle East?"

"Well, that and she had to be part of the ancient bloodline, which she is."

Keith's ears perked up. "Mitch wrote about the ancient bloodline; what is that all about?"

"It's a long, boring story. Do you really want to hear it?" Lyla asked.

"Absolutely!" Keith was obsessed with mysteries and puzzles. He was always desperate to know how pieces fit together. He looked at each fact as a puzzle piece to a bigger picture.

"All Right, from what I understand, everything started with the Pharaohs. I don't know how much you know about pyramids, but it all started there—in Egypt. There was a lot of inbreeding, because they wanted to keep the power and wealth within the family. At the time, the Egyptians ruled the world. People either viewed the Pharaohs as gods, or as direct links to the gods. It might have looked like the Pharaohs disappeared, but they didn't. They migrated to Europe, where they continued inbreeding. Originally, they settled in Rome, but quickly spread throughout Europe. They were royalty, and royalty always married royalty. This was done to preserve the bloodline. Eventually, descendants of the bloodline established their global rule in Great Britain. Am I boring you yet?"

Keith looked enthralled. "No, keep going!"

"I don't really know much more than that, except the bloodline is split into thirteen families. They continued to migrate and established power in the United States."

"The symbols," Keith said. "Egypt, and the pyramid—the symbols." Keith's ADD was working in high gear. He remembered Mitch talking about pyramids being a symbol used by The Brotherhood.

It took Lyla a moment to make the connection. "Oh, yes, every symbol has a meaning. None are arbitrary. Pyramids hold great power to The Brotherhood because of the…"

"The sun god," Keith said, finishing her sentence.

"That's right, Osirus, the sun god. How do you know that?"

"Mitch told me. He was fascinated by all that stuff. He said Osirus is also Lucifer."

"Who's Mitch?" Lyla asked.

"He used to be a senator, but he turned on The Brotherhood. He was trying to warn the world about their agenda. I think those cowards killed him before he got the chance to do any real damage."

Lyla nodded. "Yes, that sounds like The Brotherhood. Dead men can't talk."

"So, what do you know about the Illuminati?" Keith asked, finding himself intrigued.

"I know they are all part of the ancient bloodline. They are referred to as The Illuminati, or The Illuminated Ones. They control the transnational corporations, governments, the banking system— everything that controls society."

"Are you part of that bloodline? I mean, are the Kilmeades?"

"No, my parents aren't descendants. My father *is* the lead assistant to Lucio though. Lucio is part of the bloodline. He calls most of the shots. My father is just part of The Brotherhood. He would love to be Illuminati. He just doesn't have the DNA. My father didn't become Lucio's assistant until after retiring from politics. Although, he was a member of The Brotherhood throughout his entire political career."

Keith's eyes looked starved for information. "I can't believe this was actually your life. Did you ever meet Lucio?"

Lyla lifted her legs onto the couch and protectively wrapped her arms around her knees before answering. "Yes, I knew Lucio. He was the one who chose me to be Kyler's maidservant. There's nothing he wouldn't do for power. He spent most of his time studying ancient scriptures and trying his best to bring ancient prophesies to fruition. He's the father, you know."

"The father of who?"

"The anti-Christ, of course."

"Well, of course," Keith said sarcastically. "I mean, how could I possibly not know that?"

Lyla's face flushed. "Sorry, I forgot you don't know much about any of this. I'm so used to being surrounded by members or supporters of The Brotherhood that I forget most people don't know a lot about it." Keith only half-heard her apology. His mind was racing with new questions.

"So," Keith continued. "Since the earth wasn't consecrated with Kyler's blood, does that mean the anti-Christ won't be evil? Will it mess up their plans?"

"Oh, he'll be evil," Lyla assured him. "It's in his DNA. Besides, he'll be raised in the Luciferian church. He'll be groomed his entire life to one day take control of the world."

"Wow, that's a lot of pressure," Keith said.

Lyla nodded, "It is. In fact, he was born today. Well, not yet, but he will be."

"How do you know? Couldn't it change, since Kyler wasn't sacrificed?"

"No, it won't change because of the transit--stuff you probably wouldn't understand. He will be born in Rhapsody Grove at sunset."

Yet again, Keith looked perplexed. "Wait, if a baby is born at the grove, doesn't that mean a woman has to be there, too? I didn't think women were allowed in."

"That's not entirely true," Lyla corrected him. "They just aren't allowed out."

Angela Caldwell

Keith's eyes widened. "You mean they're going to kill her?"

Lyla nodded her head. "It's all part of the ritual. The Vessel knows her fate. She views it as an honor."

"So, how do they know that this baby, this anti-Christ thing, will be born at sunset? Will they induce her?"

"I guess you could say that. They cut him from her womb. She'll be drugged and unconscious when she's sacrificed, so she won't feel any pain. I know it sounds morbid and horrible, but The Vessel sees it as her glorious purpose."

CHAPTER 3

For the first time in her life, Jacinda woke up in bed with her darling baby sleeping peacefully beside her. Her heart ached with happiness as she studied his precious features and watched his chest move up and down as he breathed. She didn't want to leave him in bed, but didn't want to wake him, either. Tearing herself away from him, she walked into the living room. "How long was I asleep?" she asked through a yawn.

"About two hours," Lyla answered.

"What have you two been doing this whole time? The television isn't even on."

Keith shrugged. "We've just been talking."

Jacinda sat on the couch next to Lyla, and tucked her legs under her body. She reached for the remote control and asked, "Do you guys mind if I turn on the TV?"

"Not at all," Lyla responded.

Jacinda punched what seemed like every button on the remote control before giving up and placing it back on the coffee table. "Why does everything have to be so complicated these days?" she asked.

Keith picked up the remote, pushed one button, and the television sprang to life. Jacinda cut her eyes to Keith. "Show off." Keith began changing channels until Jacinda yelled, "Stop! Back up one."

Keith did as instructed. Once he looked at the screen, he instantly knew what had caught Jacinda's attention. It was a picture of Jacinda's mother-in-law, Chandra Kilmeade. The three sat quietly and listened to the reporter:

> *"It appears Mrs. Kilmeade, Senator Gregory Kilmeade's mother, took her own life. She was found hanging from her third floor balcony. While it's still unclear why she committed suicide, it adds to the curious events surrounding the Kilmeade family. Her son, Senator Kilmeade, was arrested after his car collided with another vehicle. They discovered*

*an abducted child by the name of Tommy
Morrison in the vehicle with him. Luckily,
there were no injuries. Senator Kilmeade still
remains in police custody. Although suicide
appears to be the cause of death, an autopsy
will be performed."*

Jacinda covered her mouth with her hand. "Oh my
gosh. OH MY GOSH! NO!" she screamed. Her
yell must have roused Kyler. They could hear him
crying in the bedroom.

"I'll go get him," Lyla offered.

Jacinda was too shocked to respond. She sat with
her eyes glued to the television. "Chandra's dead?
Chandra's dead." Her tone went from one of
questioning to one of acceptance. "Chandra's
dead," she repeated in little more than a whisper.
"But why? Why would she kill herself? Why
would she hang herself?"

Jacinda was too stunned to notice Lyla entering the
room with Kyler on her hip. "She didn't," Lyla
said.

"Didn't what?" Jacinda asked.

"She didn't kill herself. They did it for revenge."
Lyla's eyes moved to the floor as she apologized.
"I'm sorry. It's none of my business."

"Stop doing that. Stop apologizing," Jacinda demanded. It was becoming clear that she was losing her patience. "How do you know they killed her?" Jacinda asked.

Lyla sat on the couch before handing Kyler to Jacinda. "Have you ever noticed how many suicides surround politicians? Sometimes they know too much, and sometimes they just kill for revenge."

"But who?" Jacinda asked.

"The Brotherhood. This is my fault. If I hadn't taken Kyler, Gregory probably wouldn't have been found with that kidnapped child. Between me, Nicholas' daughter, running away with the sacrifice, and Gregory, Nicholas' son, being arrested in such a public way, they had to kill someone. In fact, that's probably how they'll spin it. They'll say something to the effect of Chandra being so distraught over her son's arrest that she took her own life."

Jacinda just stared at Lyla, "How do you know all this? I mean, how do you know so much?"

"I grew up watching them. I heard them. I always knew when someone betrayed The Brotherhood, because I'd hear my mother or father discussing it. Not long after, the traitor would *commit suicide.*"

Keith shot off the couch as if it were on fire. "Like

Mitch!"

Lyla nodded. "Possibly."

Jacinda still looked stunned. "I didn't like her, not at all. But she didn't deserve to die. It's so… It's so…"

"Final," Keith said.

"Yes," Jacinda agreed. "It's so final. I can't believe my mother-in-law is dead."

"They did it to punish my father," Lyla said. "Who knows, maybe they did it to punish Gregory, too."

Numbness swept over Jacinda. It was all too surreal. Maybe she was just shocked, but she felt strangely detached from the situation, registering no emotion whatsoever. She felt numb. Kyler brought her back to reality when he said, "Ticko monner!"

"Not now, baby," Lyla told him, but Jacinda couldn't resist.

"Tickle monster? You want a tickle monster?" The toddler chuckled wildly as Jacinda tickled his ribs.

Carl walked though the door just then and placed his briefcase on the kitchen table. Standing in the kitchen, he said, "I talked to Livingston, and I think we've got a plan."

"Livingston?" Jacinda interrupted. "Rob Livingston?"

Keith raised his hand, signaling Jacinda to wait a moment.

"Yes, Rob Livingston." Carl continued, "Since Jill visited Jacinda, I imagine her home is already under surveillance. More than likely her phone and home are bugged, too. I'm going to have to act like a door-to-door salesman."

"Why?" Keith asked.

"Well, it's simple. After Jill answers the door, I'll stick to the script in case they are listening, but the brochure I hand her will explain when and where to meet us."

Jacinda looked unconvinced. "Won't they just follow her?"

Carl nodded. "If she's being watched, yes. That's why the note says to go to Maggie's Bakery in the strip center down the street. Once she's inside, Maggie will let her out the back door, and Jill will leave with me. I'll bring her here."

Jacinda nodded. "That just might work."

"It better," Carl said. "We need to know what else is on Gregory's computer. Anyway, I'm going to change. I already have the letter written. I'll take off in a minute."

Jacinda stood. "That's it? That's your plan? You're going now? Do you even know where she lives?"

"I do," Carl responded. "I was already given her name, and she's a customer at my bank. I looked up the address. I'll start at the end of the block and work my way to her house."

Keith looked at Carl. "What are you going to tell the people in the rest of the houses?"

Carl simply held up a handful of lawn flyers. "I'm going to hand them a lawn flyer. Everyone has a lawn."

"Wait," Jacinda said. "How does anyone know Jill visited me? She was only there one night."

Carl looked at Jacinda. "Remember Agent Asher? The FBI agent you spoke to about Gregory's disappearance?"

"Oh, no," Jacinda said. "Not him, too."

Carl nodded. "Him, too. He put listening devices all over your condo."

Jacinda buried her face in her hands. "He must have done it when he went inside to secure the condo. It was the only time he was alone."

"Yeah, FBI agents are sneaky; I don't know what else to tell you."

Jacinda's eyes betrayed her. They revealed the exact moment she realized her friend was in danger. "They know she knows! They know she has Gregory's computer!"

Carl nodded. "Yup, that's why we need to do this now. I can't guarantee how much longer she'll be safe in her home. She's married, right?"

"Yes," Jacinda confirmed. "But her husband is in London for the next two weeks. She's home by herself!"

"That's a good thing," Carl assured her. "That's one less person we have to worry about. As long as he's not with Jill, they won't have any interest in him. Once I get her, I'll bring her here. Nobody will look for her at my house. No one has ever had a reason to suspect I defected from The Brotherhood. She'll be safe."

Carl excused himself and walked to his bedroom. He returned wearing an oversized t-shirt, shorts, and running shoes. Jacinda couldn't believe how much an outfit could change a person's appearance. His casual clothes made him look much less intimidating. Carl grabbed the stack of flyers and headed towards the door.

"I shouldn't be gone long. By the way, if anyone wants to take a nap, I have two guest rooms. I mean it when I say make yourselves at home."

Keith made sure Carl was gone before he said, "This is either really smart, or really, really stupid."

Jacinda sat down, curled her knees to her chest, and hugged them tightly. "If anything has happened to her, it's my fault!"

Lyla put her hand on Jacinda's shoulder. "It's okay. She'll be safe. You'll see. He'll be back with her in no time." Lyla didn't completely believe her own words, but she would have said anything to keep Jacinda from crying. After all, Jacinda had already been through so much grief in such a short period of time.

*****

Carl felt ridiculous walking door to door while passing out lawn flyers. He hoped nobody would call the random telephone number he'd put on the handouts. He could just picture some poor guy getting fifteen phone calls about lawn care. As he approached Jill's house, he made sure her note was on top of the stack. It simply read:

Jill,

**Don't say anything. They might be listening.
Jacinda and Kyler are safe. They are both at my
house. There is a good chance your phone and
house are bugged. Leave your cell phone. Please
grab Gregory's computer and go to Maggie's
Bakery on Tolum Road. Once inside, she'll lead
you through the back entrance. I'll be waiting
for you in thirty minutes. You'll have to leave
your car at Maggie's for the time being. I'm
asking you to trust me. You could be in a lot of
danger. Before leaving the house, please set this
note on fire. I will see you in thirty minutes.**

Carl knocked on the door. "Just a minute," he heard
Jill say as she approached. She opened the door
wearing only pajamas. Carl found it odd that she
was in her pajamas this late in the day.

"Can I help you?"

Carl smiled and responded, "I'm just passing out
some flyers, you know, in case you need your lawn
cut. Thanks for your time, ma'am." He waited
until she looked at the flyer. He pretended to be
straightening the papers, stalling until she read the
note.

She looked up from the paper and into his eyes.
"Well, I guess I do need my lawn cut."

*****

Keith busied himself, setting up the camera, while Lyla made Kyler a peanut butter and jelly sandwich.

"I should have figured a single man would have stuff for peanut butter and jelly," Lyla said, before she placed the sandwich on the plate for the toddler. "I can't really talk, though. I have no idea how to cook."

Jacinda sat on the couch while she readied herself for an interview. The interviews would play an important role when The Resistance revealed The Brotherhood's plans to the public. They needed as much first-hand testimony as they could get. She'd done a few interviews on their journey to California, but after resting, Jacinda was feeling much more talkative.

"Are you ready?" Keith asked.

"As ready as I'll ever be," Jacinda replied.

"Then, action!"

Jacinda looked into the camera lens. "The man who is helping us, I won't reveal his name, but he went to find my best friend. The FBI agent who said he was checking my condo for intruders planted listening devices inside my home. They heard everything Jill and I talked about. They know she has Gregory's computer, and they know she's a computer recovery specialist. They also know Keith is involved, because he introduced himself to Jill."

The color drained from Keith's face. "What?"

Jacinda simply looked at him. "Did you not think of that? You're in as deep as any of us, Keith. I'm so sorry."

Lyla overheard Jacinda from the kitchen. "This isn't your fault, Jacinda. You are a victim, just like the rest of us."

"I know," Jacinda replied half-heartedly. "I just feel responsible."

"Well, you're not," Lyla assured her. "But I understand. I feel the same way."

Jacinda moved forward with her interview. "So, here we are," she said, lifting her hands and looking around the room. "I'm sitting in a stranger's living room."

"A really nice stranger," Keith interjected from behind the camera.

"A really nice stranger," Jacinda agreed, "but a stranger nonetheless. We drove from Oklahoma City to California, stopping only to eat and use the restroom."

"In a convict van; tell them about the convict van," Keith interrupted.

Jacinda shot him a dirty look. "Will you stop it? I'm trying to get as much on tape as I can. Who cares if I bought a van? And it's not a convict van. Stop calling it that!"

"The really nice stranger agreed it looked like a convict van."

"Will you stop it?" Jacinda begged. "Why can't you take this seriously?" It was clear to Jacinda that Keith's fear had passed.

"I don't know," Keith replied. "Delirium? Not all of us got a nap."

Jacinda had just finished her interview when Carl and Jill walked through the door. Jacinda sprang to her feet and wrapped her arms around Jill. "Jill, I'm so glad you're safe!" She looked at Carl. "Were there any problems?"

Carl shook his head. "It worked."

Jill turned her attention to Kyler. "Is it? Is that? Oh, Jacinda, he's beautiful!" Jill walked over to pick the toddler up, ignoring the peanut butter and jelly on his hands and face. At first, Kyler looked apprehensive, but quickly warmed up to her. Jill let tears of joy flow freely down her face. "Do you have any idea how long we've been looking for you?"

The tears were contagious. Jacinda and Lyla began crying as well. Keith wasn't going to miss a thing; he was recording every second. He managed to keep Carl out of the shot, knowing he was still undercover. Carl noticed the video camera.

"Shut it off, man. Shut it off."

"I'm not getting you. It's cool," Keith assured him.

"No, I said shut it off."

Keith did as instructed and stopped recording. *He's so serious all the time,* Keith thought. *What's his problem?*

Carl disappeared into his bedroom and reappeared holding a suitcase.

"Where are you going?" Keith asked.

"Rhapsody Grove," Carl responded, remaining a man of few words.

"You're going? Are you crazy?" Keith asked, completely unfiltered.

"I have to keep up appearances. What good am I to

The Resistance if I can't gather information? I have to play the part. I need to be able to tell people what to expect."

Keith nodded his head. He saw the logic. Truthfully, he was green with envy. He would have loved to see Rhapsody Grove with his own eyes. He wanted to capture it on camera and break the story wide open. Carl set his suitcase down, and pointed towards the kitchen.

"There's not much food in the fridge, but there is a grocery store right down the street. That's not where you'll stop. You'll pass that grocery store, and drive an additional twenty-four miles south. Nobody will recognize you there."

Keith seemed entirely too excited, given the situation. "I just wish there was a way for you to, you know, film it," Keith said.

Carl removed a pair of glasses from his pocket, and held them up. "There is."

"How are you going to capture anything with that?" Keith asked.

Carl pointed to the plastic between the lenses before asking, "See that camera?"

Keith looked carefully. "No."

"Good. Hopefully they won't, either."

Keith studied Carl's glasses in awe. "Where did you even get those? I've never seen anything like it."

Carl shrugged. "We've got bad guys in the CIA, and we've got good ones. I got this from one of the good ones." He tucked the glasses back into his pocket. "I have to get going if I'm going to make it by sunset. Will you guys be okay here alone? I left a key on the kitchen table. Just stay out of sight as much as possible, deal?"

Jacinda nodded. She had no idea what they were supposed to do while Carl was gone, but felt out of line asking. She decided to wait for his return before asking him any more questions.

Jill looked down at her peanut butter and jelly-stained shirt. "Well, I hope someone brought an extra change of clothes."

Jacinda and Lyla looked at each other before answering, "I didn't," at the exact same time.

Carl smiled. "The good news is, nobody knows you guys are here. They know Jill lives in town, but for all they know, the rest of you could still be back in Oklahoma City or Timbuktu. I say you take the van, drive south about thirty miles, and go shopping at the outlet mall. You can stop and get groceries while you're out. Jacinda, you should probably pull your hair into a ball cap. I have a few in my closet. Try to look as unrecognizable as possible."

Jacinda nodded her head in agreement. "We do all need food and clothes."

"Don't forget toothbrushes and deodorant," Keith reminded her. "The good news is, we can shop all day, and not even put a dent in your stash of cash," Keith said playfully.

Jacinda shook her head. "You're on a budget, intern boy. You brought a suitcase. Your shopping spree ends with toiletries. Wait, you didn't bring a toothbrush?"

"I didn't have time!" Keith reminded her. "I packed quickly. The last thing I was thinking about was personal hygiene."

Jacinda walked to the guest room and returned with her purse. "Everybody get in the van. This will be good for us. You each get five hundred dollars. Make it stretch. I don't know how long we're going to have to live on my cash, and I don't want to burn through it." Jacinda paused for a moment before tears began filling her eyes.

"What is it?" Jill asked.

"It's just, this is the first time I've ever gone

shopping for Kyler. I mean, I bought a few outfits before he was born, but this is the first time I really get to go shopping for him." She looked over at her precious son. "Everyone has a budget except my beautiful baby boy. You need toys, don't you?"

"Doys!" he said, in the most precious voice she'd ever heard. Jacinda beamed at her toddler. She had never seen anything or anyone quite so beautiful in her entire life.

CHAPTER 4

George and Tony struggled to stretch their stiff muscles. Neither had any idea how long they'd been in the shack. With it being pitch black, there was no way to distinguish night from day, and both had nodded off several times. The burlap sacks over their heads made them feel as if they were suffocating. Having their hands bound behind their backs made their arms ache. The ropes binding their wrists cut into their skin. They were both desperate to take their minds off their discomfort.

"So," George said. "The music industry, huh?"

"What?" Tony asked.

"The music industry. Is it just The Brotherhood or is it The Illuminati?"

"Man, you really have no idea how this works, do

you?"

"I do. I shape the public's perception all the time," George said, sounding offended.

"Oh, really? Do you think the youth of America are watching *Your Nation Now*? No. They're looking up to everyone in the entertainment industry. They're twisting their minds around images they don't even understand. We hide the symbols in plain sight, and nobody seems to notice. Have you ever seen a musician make the sign of a pyramid with their hands? How about covering one eye?"

"The all-seeing eye," George said, not meaning to verbalize his thoughts. He knew the sun god, Lucifer, was often represented with a single, all-seeing eye. At that point, not only did he feel like he was suffocating, but he was sleep-deprived and starving. He couldn't help but blurt out whatever thought popped into his head.

"Yeah," Tony said. "The all-seeing eye. That's not even the half of it, man. It's gotten too easy. Kids don't question the pyramids or their favorite artist covering one eye. They're oblivious to all of it. We got 'em so desensitized, they don't even realize most of the lyrics praise Lucifer."

"Certainly not all of them," George said.

"No, of course not all of 'em. Most of the artists don't even realize they're Illuminati puppets. They're just pushed through the machine. It's a lot of responsibility, you know—shaping young minds."

"That's what my sister says, but she's a teacher. Hardly the same thing," George pointed out. "Do you ever, you know, feel guilty?"

Tony sighed. "No, not really. I mean, not until Chyanne wanted to join the twenty-seven club. Of course, that's not what they call it. Call me selfish, but I don't want to live without her. I couldn't care less where her soul goes, as long as it goes after mine. I don't want to live on this planet even one day longer than her."

George pondered Tony's statement. "So, you don't feel the least bit guilty about sending those poor kids straight to hell?"

"Me? Those kids made their own choices. They had free will. They lived lives most people only dream of. Our musicians had mansions, cash, cars, and fame. They had more in their short lives than most people who live to be one hundred will ever have—combined!"

"Okay," George responded. "Then why didn't you just let Chyanne live her short life to the fullest?"

"I'd miss her, man."

"That's it. That's the only reason?"

"Yup, that's the only reason. I'm thirty-seven. Never been married, and I don't have any kids. Aside from my job, she's my life. I just don't want to lose her."

"So you don't want her to sell her soul *just* because you'd miss her? You're one cold-hearted son of a gun. You know that, right?"

"I do, indeed. Now, what were you saying about the Mark of the Beast?"

"It's called the BARAchip."

"A rose by any other name is still just a rose, man," Tony responded. "You can call it whatever you like; it's all the same thing."

*****

Jacinda, Jill, Keith, Lyla, and Kyler entered Carl's home, completely exhausted from their day of shopping and constantly looking over their shoulders. They had been terrified someone would recognize them.

"Clothes," Jacinda said as she swung the shopping bags back and forth. "Clean clothes!"

Jill turned to Jacinda, "I got so carried away with Kyler and shopping that I forgot to tell you what I found on Gregory's computer! What do you know about the New World Order?"

"Probably not as much as I should. I know it's bad, right?"

"Well, my love, you've always been one to understate the obvious, but, yes, it's bad. The government will try and convince us it's good. They'll convince us it's in our best interest, but it's really just fulfilling some ancient prophecy."

Jacinda looked uneasy. "The government? Politicians? Politicians like Gregory?"

"I'm afraid so, dear. I don't think any one politician sees the whole picture. The scope of their focus seems to be limited to their task. For instance, Gregory's focus was to push the Mark of The Beast." Jacinda cringed when she heard her dear friend state the truth. Jill continued. "But he sees through tunnel vision. He only sees The Mark. He's just as much of a puppet as every other lawmaker."

"You got all this from Gregory's computer?" Jacinda asked.

"No, I got the Mark of the Beast from Gregory's

computer. I also got the plan to…" Jill's voice trailed off. "This is hard to say."

"Just say it," urged Jacinda.

"I saw that he did have prior knowledge of your first husband's murder."

Jacinda teared up. "I knew Jake was killed. They made me a widow, didn't they? They made me a widow so I could marry Gregory and fit into their wicked plan. How could I not have known the man I was married to was so evil?"

*****

Carl made his way to Rhapsody Grove, stopping at every security checkpoint. He noticed there were more protesters at the entrance to the grove this year than last. He was a banker, not a world leader. He was simply a pawn. The Brotherhood needed bankers like they needed people in the entertainment industry, the oil industry, the government, and law enforcement. None of the men knew everything; they simply knew their role. They enjoyed the perks that came with supporting The Brotherhood: money and power. Carl was glad he didn't have time to rub elbows with members of The Brotherhood before the sacrifice. A lot of men viewed the social time as networking, but Carl viewed it as nothing more than necessary.

Carl had an especially difficult time coming to the grove this year. This was the first year he would witness an actual sacrifice, as opposed to the mock ones he'd seen each year before. Luckily, they were unable to sacrifice Kyler, but, tonight at sunset, The Vessel would be sacrificed and the anti-Christ would be ripped from her womb. The very thought made Carl sick, but if he didn't attend, he would draw suspicion. As part of The Resistance, he couldn't afford to draw suspicion.

It disgusted Carl that he had ever been a part of this machine. The Brotherhood hadn't approached him until he'd worked his way into middle management at the bank. He had then been responsible for loaning enormous amounts of money to members of The Brotherhood. That cash had simply been paid back with the interest he charged other customers. He'd never felt completely at ease with those practices, but knew success was about who you knew, not what you knew. He'd realized that if he truly wanted to become successful, he had to play the game. He'd initially thought of membership as a way to fast track his career. It didn't take long before his conscience had led him to The Resistance.

One night after work, he'd had a few beers with Doug, an old boss. Doug had known that Carl was involved with The Brotherhood, and wanted to warn

Carl about his own experience. Doug had defected from The Brotherhood years earlier. He'd quit his job at the bank after The Brotherhood had murdered his wife as punishment for being unable to loan a member of The Brotherhood the two million dollars he had requested. That story was all it had taken; Carl had wanted out. Doug had then introduced him to a group of men who had also managed to escape the clutches of The Brotherhood. He'd recognized many of the men from the grove. They'd explained that The Resistance needed men on the inside. They needed people to go undercover to keep tabs on The Brotherhood's agenda.

Carl continued driving through the campground, wondering how Doug was doing. He hadn't talked to him in months, but knew he was still grieving the loss of his wife. He pulled his car into a large paved lot and made his way to the check-in desk.

"Good evening, Sir," said the old man behind the desk. "I suppose you're here to check in."

"I am." Carl responded.

"Most people checked in a few days ago, but I knew we'd have some stragglers," the man said with a friendly smile.

Carl shrugged. "I wish I could have gotten here sooner, but I had to work."

The old man slid a log sheet toward Carl and handed him a pen, before waving his hand in a gesture of forgiveness. He didn't care that Carl was late; he was simply making conversation.

After check-in, Carl lugged his suitcase to his cabin. The small cabin was far from extravagant. It was little more than a single room. Two beds sat side by side, each with their own wardrobe closet and desk. A depressing energy inhabited the dimly-lit quarters. A door to Carl's left led to the small bathroom he'd have to share with his roommate. He was relieved to find the room empty, and hoped it would stay that way. Of course, he knew better. It was the evening of the anti-Christ's birth, which made the chance of an empty bed slim to none.

He placed his suitcase on the bed and immediately left the cabin. It was getting late, and he didn't have time to settle in. He walked between enormous redwood trees on the familiar path to the altar. He eyed a group of sheriffs in the distance. Carl knew the Sheriffs were paid very well to protect the grove from outsiders—*little men,* as everyone outside of The Brotherhood were referred to. He hated the term *little men,* because it was his opinion that no man was smaller than someone who would sell their soul for money or power.

Most people thought that women weren't allowed

on the grounds, but they were wrong. They did allow women in the food service area, but that was as far as they would ever get to the boy's club.

Tomorrow, Carl would attend a world banking conference, but he couldn't think about anything except the sacrifice he was about to witness. Anxiety coursed through his body as he walked the next mile-and-a-half to the altar area. He smiled and waved at other men as they made their way to the ceremony, but felt as if he were on a death march.

A sense of impending doom swallowed him. He resisted the urge to turn around, willing himself forward. Carl arrived at the altar area to find hundreds of men conversing among themselves, as they waited for the sun to set. Carl found an empty seat on one of the long, wooden benches. Each bench was positioned to face the altar, and the altar was placed in front of an old, 40-foot stone statue of an owl.

The imposing figure represented the demon Moloch. He thought about the history of child sacrifice to Moloch. Leviticus 18:21 read: ***And thou shalt not let any of thy seed pass through the fire to Moloch***. God strictly forbid sacrifices to Moloch, and Carl prayed God would forgive him for witnessing such a blasphemous act.

He recognized the men seated beside him, but was in no mood for polite conversation. Carl likened the buzz of energy flowing throughout the campground to a hive of wicked bees. Tonight at sunset, an ancient prophecy was to become a reality. It seemed every man there was elated to witness such a historic event. Carl was certain other members of The Resistance were present, and wondered if they too were gripped by fear.

Carl felt physically ill. He'd never seen a sacrifice, and didn't trust himself not to vomit. When he'd been a child, he'd watched as his friend fell off the monkey bars at school. He remembered the bone sticking out of the boy's arm, and how the sight had made him throw up. The memory still made him queasy. *That was just a broken bone*, he thought to himself. *This will be murder*.

Men in hooded robes marched slowly towards the altar, as the sun set on the horizon. They chanted in Latin. Although Carl recognized the language, he was unable to interpret the words. When the last hooded man approached the altar, everyone stood and raised their hands towards the sky. "Let him come," the men chanted. "Let him come."

Carl couldn't bring himself to chant. He refused to take part in the evil he was about to witness. His mouth needed to move to avoid suspicion, so he improvised. Instead of chanting, "Let him come," he mouthed, "Lord help us."

*****

Jacinda cuddled Kyler as she listened to Jill and Lyla's conversation. Jill seemed fascinated by Lyla's upbringing, and hungered for more information.

"So you were actually a *part* of the rituals?" Jill pressed.

Lyla looked down. "I'm sorry, I don't really want to talk about that."

"You have nothing to be ashamed of," Jacinda assured her, but Lyla continued to shake her head.

"I just don't want to get graphic. The abuse was horrific, and I just want to forget it ever happened."

Jill refused to let up. "And your parents just watched?"

"Yes, and sometimes they even participated," Lyla said shamefully.

Keith felt ill. He wondered how anyone could abuse a child in such a way. How could anyone hurt this beautiful woman who sat next to him? How could someone not have protected her? He wanted to wrap his arms around her and tell her she was safe. He wanted to tell her he'd never let anyone hurt her again. He wanted to protect her from the wickedness of the world, but how could he? Keith may not be able to protect her forever, but he promised that as long as they were on this journey, no harm would come to her. This feeling of protectiveness was new to him. He'd never thought much about anyone other than himself before. *Look out for number one* had always been his motto.

Now, more than ever, he wanted to expose these wicked men. He wanted to ensure that what had happened to Lyla would never happen to another human being. He looked over to see her delicate fingers slowly twirling her hair. He decided that was her tell. Whenever she was anxious or uncomfortable, she always twisted her hair. Keith was starting to notice things about her that he never took the time to recognize in other women.

Kyler climbed out of Jacinda's lap, and walked towards Lyla. He grabbed her face in his chubby little hands, looked her right in the eye, and said, "Ticko Monner!"

It was as if that one gesture was a gift from Heaven. Lyla's mood instantly lifted. She laughed so hard that tears formed in her eyes. Her laughter was contagious; before long, the entire group was laughing hysterically. Lyla pulled Kyler close, kissed his head, and whispered, "You're such a blessing."

The sun was on its way down, and Lyla felt overcome by exhaustion. She'd gotten very little rest on the way to California, and their shopping trip had completely wiped her out. She liked her new clothes, but they were just material things. Her real treasure was the Bible she had purchased with her $500 budget.

The Bible looked just like the one Marlene had let her read. She missed Marlene. She missed her with her entire heart. Marlene had saved her and Kyler's lives, and was the closest thing to a mother she'd ever known. She wished there was a way to contact her, but knew better. Any further contact with Marlene would put her in danger, and she refused to risk her safety.

Lyla slowly stood from the couch. "I know it's still early, but I'm ready for bed."

Jacinda looked as if Lyla had just said something ridiculous. "Early? You haven't slept for over twenty-four hours; it's safe to call it late at this point."

Lyla smiled. "I'll just sleep on the floor in the guest

room. I saw a blanket next to the bed."

Jacinda shook her head. "You're not sleeping on the floor. Don't be silly. It's a king-sized bed. Sleep there. There's plenty of room for you, Kyler, and me. Kyler will probably sleep better if you're in bed, anyway. Jill can take the other guest room, and Keith…"

Keith didn't let her finish. "I know. I know; I've got the couch."

Lyla felt relieved, knowing she would sleep more soundly with Kyler by her side.

*****

George squirmed, trying in vain to find a comfortable position. He'd become used to the burlap bag over his head, which alleviated his anxiety a little. No longer feeling as if he were suffocating, he began to feel chatty. "So, other than the Twenty-Seven club, what else happens in the music industry?"

"Oh, man, I can't tell you that."

"Why not?" George asked. "It's not like either one of us is getting out of here alive."

"That's true," Tony agreed. "What could it hurt? What do you want to know?"

"I don't know. Everything, I guess."

"Well, I certainly don't know everything. I just know what I saw."

"Okay, what did you see?"

"Man, there was just so much. We had the perfect vehicle to spread our message—music. Everyone loves music. Have you ever met anyone who didn't like music?" Tony didn't give George time to respond. "Me, neither. We had the opportunity to touch each and every listener."

"Touch?"

"Well, not literally, man—figuratively. Once the track was completed, we took it to the temple room. In the temple room, we conjured demons into the track. It's all subliminal man, but it's powerful."

"So, you cast spells on everyone who listens to music?"

"When you put it like that, it sounds crazy, doesn't it? I wouldn't call it casting spells, but it works like hypnotism. The subconscious mind processes the information and it desensitizes 'em. They become tolerant to our plans—our purpose."

"Did all the musicians know?"

"Nah, not all of 'em, but a lot of 'em did. Some even agreed to share their body with a spirit—anything to be successful."

"But aren't those the ones who die at twenty-seven?"

"Nah, not always. Sometimes they're far more useful to Lucifer when they're alive. He's not going to collect a soul that is still serving his purpose here on earth. Look at all the pop stars who've been around forever, man. They promote sexual promiscuity, violence, drugs—everything we stand for. It would be stupid of Lucifer to take out someone who is still serving his purpose by exposing millions of people to his message, and Lucifer isn't stupid. Twenty-seven is usually the age they start regretting their decision. He takes them out before they have the chance to reclaim their souls. Not all musicians know the secret to success. We have to feel 'em out first—make sure they're hungry enough. Once we decide they are, we give them the option of a familiar."

"A familiar what?"

"A familiar spirit, man. We send 'em to a programming facility for three or four months. Eventually, we have 'em participate in a ritual in the temple room. They raise their arms and invite a spirit to enter their body. Go to YouTube. Type it in. *Familiar spirit. Music industry.* It's not such a secret anymore. It's all right there on the internet; people are just too lazy to care."

"I wish I could check it out, but I doubt they'll have YouTube in hell, and I doubt we're getting out of here alive."

Tony chuckled, "You're probably right, man. They probably won't have YouTube in hell. I bet they'll have dial-up modems, though."

George laughed at the ludicrous turn in conversation. "You're probably right. Busy signals, too."

"Oh, yeah, busy signals will be there for sure. But I'm tellin' you, if you *do* get out of here, type in *Satanism in the music industry.* Musicians actually talk about their familiar spirits. They acknowledge they wouldn't be where they are today without 'em. Most of 'em even call the spirits by name. People assume they're talking about their artsy, imaginary alter egos, but that's the beauty—people are ignorant. They're so ignorant they can hear the truth, and still not understand it.

"Anyway, once they invite the familiar spirit to share their body, it's got 'em. Once it's invited in, it refuses to leave. It's just one more artist serving our purpose. Like I said, I just witnessed it twice, but it goes on all the time."

"Do they do that in the movie business, too?" George asked.

"Hollywood? Are you kidding me? Lucifer dominates Hollywood! The best part about actors is people think they're a little nutty to begin with, so when any of them speak out, they're called crazy. Look at that actor Randy Quake! He's held entire press conferences to expose The Brotherhood. Not only was he laughed out of Hollywood, he was laughed out of the country, man! He's been in trouble with the law ever since. Everyone just thinks he's crazy!"

CHAPTER 5

As the sun continued to set, the chanting grew louder: "Let him come. Let him come."

Carl watched the lake, which was about three hundred yards behind the altar. The ripples in the water reflected the light of the setting sun. *It's begun*, Carl thought, as he braced himself for what he was about to witness.

An old-fashioned, river-style boat crossed the lake and approached the boat landing. Torchlight illuminated the boat, making it look all the more sinister. Carl looked to his right, where he saw an old-fashioned, horse-drawn hearse. The hearse was made entirely of glass, which allowed a body to be in full view of the mourners. The hearse was empty, but Carl knew that would change soon enough. As the hearse made its way to the altar, he noticed a horse-drawn carriage approaching the boat landing. It was all very morbid—very foreboding. He was about to witness the birth of one life, and the murder of another. The Vessel was a willing young woman, but a human nonetheless. What choice did he have? How could he be of any use to The Resistance if he didn't remain on the inside?

Although the sunlight was almost gone, Carl could see robed men helping a female out of the boat. Her white robe looked luminescent, almost glowing around her like a halo. The setting sun gave the woman's hair a beautiful appearance. The remaining sunlight weaved through her hair, making it look as though it were ablaze with fire. He watched her board the carriage, and within seconds the carriage was headed towards the altar.

The chanting never ceased; it simply grew louder. The chanting created an almost tangible energy. It was a sinister presence, longing to destroy and devour. The carriage was in no hurry to arrive at its destination. The horses seemed to trot in slow motion. It all looked so surreal. Carl closed his eyes and began to pray. *Please, God. Please forgive me for being here. Please don't let this happen. Please save us, God.* He continued to pray with his eyes shut until the chanting ceased.

He opened his eyes to see an exotic young woman stepping out of the carriage. Men in red-hooded robes flanked both sides of her tiny figure. The men helped The Vessel to the altar. She was absolutely stunning. Her Middle Eastern features were evident in her beautiful eyes. Her olive skin glowed as the torchlight kissed her face. Once she removed her robe, it was clear that she was nine months pregnant. Carl adjusted his glasses, making sure the center was pointed directly towards the altar.

The chanting resumed, but this time they were saying, "Let her drink." One of the men handed the woman a crystal goblet. His face was hidden behind the shadow of his hood, making his appearance ghoulish. The Vessel nodded her head in a gesture of thanks before closing her eyes. As she drank, the chanting continued, "Let her drink," then—only silence.

*****

Keith should have felt exhausted, but his mind was too active to sleep. Jacinda and Jill were still sitting on the couch, chatting away. Since he was sleeping on the couch, he had to wait for them to clear out before sleep was even an option. Jacinda turned from Jill to look at Keith. "You never told me about Rob Livingston. How is he involved?"

Keith sighed. "I guess he used to be part of The Brotherhood. I don't know, maybe he just went to the grove once, and was never really a member. I haven't really figured it all out. But he's the reason your story didn't air. He sneaked into George's office and stole the tape. He replaced it with a fake one."

"How do you know that?" Jacinda asked.

"I know because I saw the security camera footage after my phone was returned."

Jacinda looked confused, but Keith continued. "That's not important; it's a long story. But the short version is that he's the one who gave me the safe phone and told me he believed Kyler and Lyla were in Oklahoma City."

"No, how do you know he switched the tape?"

"He told me."

"Okay, how did he know they were in Oklahoma City?" Jacinda questioned.

"I don't know. He said something about there being video of her boarding a bus. Anyway, he's the one who gave me the five thousand dollars cash, along with the station's camera."

Jacinda absentmindedly bit her lip. "So, he's one of the good guys? Who would have guessed?"

"I know, right?" Keith responded. "Anyway, he's the one who called Carl. I guess The Resistance is everywhere. It's a network similar to The Brotherhood, except they're not evil. Plus their purpose is to derail The Brotherhood's plans. Okay, it's not similar to The Brotherhood at all. Forget I said that," he rambled. "Livingston told me to document everything. He said proof would be our life insurance. I've never given life insurance much thought, but it's kind of a priority now, if you know what I'm sayin'."

Jill interrupted, "I hate to be the one to point out the obvious, but we can't stay in this house forever. We need a plan. We need to actually be doing something. It's not that the house isn't lovely; it is. But I'd kind of like to go home at some point."

"She's right," Jacinda agreed. "We can't stay here forever. We came to expose The Brotherhood, and we need to get a move on it. The only plan we've had so far was getting here to see what Jill found on Gregory's computer. We've done that. It's time for another plan."

Jill's face lit up. "To expose people, we have to know who those people are, right?"

"Right." Jacinda replied, hoping Jill would get to the point.

"Well, I have the email address and name of every person who's ever had any contact with Gregory regarding BARAchip. We're lucky he's been using the same laptop for four years!"

Jacinda's eyes darted to Jill. "He has an older one."

"An older one? Like, how old?" Jill asked.

"I don't know, but it still works. He's never been much of a gadget guy. He usually just uses things until they stop working. He would have continued using that one, but switched to this one when he received it for Christmas."

Keith looked skeptical. "How do you know? He's been using this laptop since before he met you. How would you know he got it for Christmas?"

"He told me. My laptop's motherboard died, and he told me he had an old laptop that still worked. He said it was in the office closet. I figured the thing was a dinosaur, so I bought a new one, but who knows how long he used the old laptop. Lord only knows what Jill could find on that computer."

Keith's eyes looked like those of a crazed man with a brilliant idea. He focused on Jill. "You can recover information, but do you know how to actually *post* information without it being linked back to you? I mean, is there a way to…"

Jill cut him off, "Post the members' names? Yes! I can make it look like the information came from any server in the world. I didn't even think of that!"

Jacinda began to rock her body back and forth as she soothed her toddler to sleep. "So, what if you post all of their names? Who's going to believe you?" Jacinda asked. "What do you plan on doing? Are you going to start a website with the sole purpose of exposing members of an ancient, evil society?"

"Yes," Keith stated matter-of-factly. "That's exactly what we're going to do, but not until we get more proof."

Jill clapped her hands together once, before saying, "So, first order of business: retrieve Gregory's old computer. Any takers?"

*****

Within minutes of drinking from the goblet, The Vessel's body lay motionless on the altar. Blackness settled over the grove, leaving only torches to illuminate The Vessel's body. Carl feared such poor lighting conditions would distort any video the tiny camera in his glasses would be capable of capturing.

Three hooded figures stood behind the altar. They

were chanting, but Carl couldn't make out what they were saying. It sounded Latin again. For a moment, all was quiet, until one of the hooded figures screamed, "Let him be born!"

Within seconds, everyone began chanting in unison. "Let him be born!" Carl watched as the hooded figure in the middle used both hands to raise a dagger into the air. The dagger was aimed at The Vessel's heart. Carl closed his eyes tightly, and tried in vain to drown out the sounds of cheers echoing around him.

He looked up to see a man place the bloody dagger on a cloth. Another hooded figure held a scalpel to The Vessel's pregnant belly. The cuts to The Vessel's abdomen were precise and deliberate, leading Carl to believe the man must be a surgeon. Within seconds, he ripped the baby from the womb and held it up like a trophy. He laid the baby on a cloth, and used a device to suck mucus out of the baby's mouth. Instantly, the baby's cry rang throughout camp. Everyone stood to their feet and began cheering. Men hugged, chanted, and were excited beyond measure.

The excitement dwindled as the bloody Vessel was lifted from the altar and placed in the glass hearse. As the men made their way to the hearse's path, the mood grew solemn. The men lined up, as if they were members of a wedding party waiting to greet their guests. One by one, the men began to bow as the old glass hearse passed before them. The old-fashioned hearse creaked with each stride of the horse that pulled it. Inside was the sacrifice—a bloodied, murdered woman they simply referred to as *The Vessel*.

Carl fought back the urge to vomit. He desperately wanted to leave, but felt paralyzed by fear. He wanted nothing more than to flee this wicked place and return to the safety of his own home. But he had to stay the night. He knew he couldn't miss tomorrow morning's banking conference. Not only did he not want to be suspiciously absent, but his presence was extremely important to The Resistance. He needed to attend so that he could relay The Brotherhood's plans. It was his duty. He realized he had to pull himself together. Tomorrow, after the meeting, he would be able to excuse himself, go home, and fall apart. Until then, it was mandatory that he put on a brave face and move forward. He glanced back at the altar, where the baby was still lying. The infant was no longer crying. A medical team gathered around the newborn, checking his vital signs. When it came to the health of the anti-Christ, The Brotherhood would leave nothing to chance.

*****

Jacinda turned to Keith. "Are you ready for us to leave so you can have your couch back?"

"No," Keith said, yawning and stretching his arms. "I'm tired. I haven't slept in forever, but I don't think I can sleep."

"We haven't watched the news for a while," Jacinda said, "but after Gregory and Chandra, I'm scared to even turn on the television."

"I know what you mean," Keith replied. "Trust me."

Jill leaned towards the coffee table to retrieve the remote control. "Well, we can't avoid current events forever. Knowledge is power, dear heart," she said, before flipping the television to a news station.

Keith instantly saw the fear in Jacinda's eyes. He turned to face the television. Gregory Kilmeade had been released from jail on $40,000 bail.

"He's out," Jacinda said. She spoke through her hand, which was covering her mouth. "He's out of jail."

The news showed Gregory walking from the jailhouse to a waiting car on a constant loop. He looked broken. His eyes looked dead. His usually perfect posture was slouched, and it was clear he hadn't slept. The Kilmeade smile that had made him famous was absent. He looked like a shell of the man he used to be.

"No," Jacinda said. "They wouldn't. Would they?"

"Wouldn't what, hon?" Jill asked.

"They found him with the kidnapped child. They wouldn't let him out of jail. How is that even possible?"

Keith didn't wait for Jill to answer. "He was just let out on bail, Jacinda. He will still have a trial, and my guess is he'll serve some time, but they weren't going to hold a senator in county jail forever. Plus, he's not much of a flight risk."

"Not a flight risk?" Jacinda protested. "He has a ton of money. His mother just committed suicide. His wife is missing!"

Jacinda fought back nausea. She felt dizzy, and the room around her seemed to spin. Jill touched her arm. "Jacinda, honey, are you okay?"

Jacinda didn't answer. She simply stared at the television as the color drained from her face.

"Jacinda, look at me. I need you to look at me," Jill

begged. Jill's voice sounded distant. It sounded as if she were in a tunnel.

Jacinda stared at the television, seeing a man who looked destroyed. *No!* She thought. *I will not feel sorry for him. He did this. He knew where Kyler was the entire time. He lied to me. He used me. I will not feel sorry for what he's done to himself—to Kyler—to me!* Despite willful resistance, compassion touched her heart. The man on television wasn't the charismatic senator she had fallen in love with. He wasn't even the same man who had lied to her and used her for The Brotherhood's purposes. The man she saw on the screen was a different man altogether. Gregory was a man so annihilated that he was virtually unrecognizable.

Jacinda moved toward the television. "I have to know," she said, never taking her eyes off the screen.

"Know what?" Jill asked in a voice that indicated she knew she wasn't going to like Jacinda's answer.

"Why," Jacinda said. "I have to know why he did it. I need to know how he could pretend to love me. How he could watch me suffer, and why he kidnapped that child."

"No," Jill responded defiantly. "Absolutely not.

No."

"I have to, Jill."

"You have to do no such thing! That man lied to you. He manipulated you. He watched you suffer. He was going to let your son be murdered."

"But why? Why did he leave before I woke up? Why didn't his parents know where he was? Why did he abduct that child?"

"Who cares why?" asked Jill. "What difference does it make *why* he did it? The fact remains, he did it!"

Jacinda turned to Keith. "He knows more than we do right now. What if he's willing to talk?"

Before Keith had a chance to respond, Jill grabbed Jacinda's arms and pulled her around to look her in the eyes, "You're not really thinking about talking to him, are you? Oh, no, Jacinda. You aren't thinking of… I mean. You don't want go back to him, do you?"

Jacinda looked horrified. "Go back? You mean, make small talk and share a bed with the man who helped them steal my baby? Are you insane? How weak do you think I am?" Her anger made Jill nervous. It was a side of Jacinda she'd never witnessed. She'd seen Jacinda angry, but that anger had never been directed at her.

"No, I just mean that you seem to be sympathizing with him," Jill clarified.

"I'm not sympathetic, Jill. I'm curious! His mother is dead. According to Lyla, she was more than likely murdered by the very organization he'd aligned himself with. Nobody has heard from Nicholas. Gregory's political career is as good as dead. What if he's ready to talk? What if he has answers?"

Keith turned off the television and took the seat next to Jacinda. "I'm probably going to regret saying this, since you're clearly angry."

Jacinda glared at him, "I'm not angry, Keith, I'm…"

"Acting a little crazy?" As soon as the words escaped Keith's lips, he knew he should have kept his mouth shut. "I don't mean crazy. I mean that you aren't thinking straight. You're tired. We all are. Nobody can make rational decisions after what we've been through. Not to mention how sleep deprived we've all been."

"He's right," Jill agreed. "Why don't we go to sleep, and we'll talk about this in the morning."

Jacinda looked at her watch. "It is morning," she

said. "It's morning. Kyler will wake up soon, and I'll need to feed him breakfast."

"Lyla will feed him breakfast," Jill assured her.

"You mean like she's done for the past two years? I'm his mother, Jill. Me! I should be the one feeding him breakfast!"

Last week, when Keith had met Jacinda Kilmeade in the newsroom of *Your Nation Now,* he never would have believed he would witness her emotional breakdown. It was amazing how much could change in a matter of days.

"Jill's right, Jacinda," Keith agreed. "If you want to be any good for yourself, your son, or revealing the monsters who stole your son, you need sleep. Once you wake up, we can regroup and decide what needs to be done. Until then, you need rest. We all do."

CHAPTER 6

Gravel crunched under Carl's feet as he walked down a trail to the conference. He knew those trees had been there long before he was born, and would remain long after he was gone. Acknowledging life was short renewed a sense of responsibility to expose The Brotherhood. He felt it his duty to educate the world about the New World Order. Alone, he could accomplish nothing, but with the growing network of The Resistance, he felt hopeful he'd stand a chance.

Carl hadn't always been so righteous. Like many others, ambition led him to The Brotherhood. Initially, he'd been enchanted by the wealth and privilege membership provided. Eventually, his conscience had gotten the best of him. He now had a healthy fear of The Brotherhood, but felt convicted to derail their wicked plans.

He entered the rustic lodge, taking a seat alongside the others. The turnout was higher this year than last, but he expected attendance to be high. Even men who rarely attended retreats wouldn't miss the anti-Christ's birth; everyone would come. This morning's conference was career-specific. The featured speaker would be India's Finance Minister, Aadi Kapoor.

The lodge reeked of coffee and cigar smoke. Carl immediately recognized Mike Gouree. Mike was a legend among bankers. He was the best of the best. He was also rotten to the core. After making eye contact, Carl had no choice but to sit next to him.

"Hi, Mike," Carl said, in a less than friendly tone.

"Carl! I haven't seen you in a while. How have you been, buddy?"

"Busy," Carl replied, hoping to avoid a lengthy discussion.

"So, last night…" Mike said, alluding to the sacrifice.

Carl winced, but didn't have time to respond. The speaker walked onstage, and a hush fell over the crowd. Kapoor gripped the sides of the podium and bellowed a greeting. His voice demanded attention. "It has begun!" he said, with a look of smug satisfaction.

Kapoor spoke with precision. His English was impeccable, but he was unable to mask his thick accent. "We have a great responsibility as world leaders," he said, making eye contact with several men in the front row. "For we must lead the world!" This got a chuckle from the audience.

Lead the world straight to hell, Carl thought.

Kapoor continued, "I am both honored and humbled by my brothers choosing my homeland to launch the cashless system that will soon dominate the world. This year, 1.2 billion of our residents have been given a unique identification number. I am proud to say that India will be the first country to use biometric data for identification purposes on a national scale. The biometric information we have collected includes fingerprints, iris scans, and photographs of faces. Of course, we began this experiment with the poor."

The word *poor* drew laughter from the men in attendance. "Oh, yes," Kapoor continued, "but we did not stop with the poor. We are collecting biometric information of all *little men*. As most of you know, we are currently processing one million people a day. Our citizens have been informed that inclusion is not mandatory. However." He paused and winked. "If they wish to have a bank account, medical care, a driver's license, or government services, the program is required." That comment also made the men snicker.

It's only mandatory if you want a life, Carl thought. *It's only mandatory if you want to provide for your family.* Carl fidgeted in his chair, trying in vain to release nervous energy. He knew India was the testing ground for a cashless society, but didn't expect the program to progress so quickly. He couldn't believe India was already processing one million people a day.

Kapoor weaved his fingers together, and placed his hands on the podium. "This is, of course, for the good of the people." His statement drew even more laughter from the crowd. "Oh, no," he assured them, "they are lining up. You must remember that they are dependent on our government to survive. It is that level of dependence that is crucial to our very survival, my brothers. Without their dependence, we cannot be victorious. They will seek inclusion to provide for their families. They must feed their children, and desperately need medical assistance. They need their government for their very survival. You see, my brothers, this is why government dependency is so crucial as we work towards the New World Order. In order for this to work, they must willingly give us access to all of their biometric data, as well as accept a chip for surveillance. For, without the chip, they will not be able to receive medical care or food. They will want the chip. You must trust me on that, but only if the chip is presented correctly.

"We use the information for identification, tracking, and surveillance. Oh, yes, my brothers. You must always make your people think it is in their best interest. If not, you will have an uprising. Once you convince them enrollment will be to their benefit, they will demand inclusion!"

Carl was lost in thought. He had never given much thought to biometrics. It was happening in America, too. He remembered having to put his thumb on a machine that captured his unique thumbprint when he renewed his driver's license.

Kapoor lit a cigar, lazily blowing the smoke towards the ceiling. "Nobody wants their identity stolen. It is a huge problem, isn't it, America?" He winked at the United States Secretary of the Treasury.

"It is, indeed," replied the short, balding American. The Secretary of the Treasury mistook Kapoor's rhetorical question as an invitation to speak.

"Identity theft has become such a problem that people are scared to use their…"

Kapoor cut the Secretary of the Treasury off mid-sentence.

"They are scared? Are you saying Americans are fearful?" The Secretary of the Treasury smiled and nodded. "Perfect," said Kapoor. "Perhaps America is ready to remedy this fear, wouldn't you say?"

A sense of dread washed over Carl. A cashless society, biometric data, and complete control meant it was only a matter of time before the New World Order was in full effect.

*****

George woke up, unable to feel his arm. The weight of his body had cut off circulation to his arm. How long had he been asleep? He struggled to sit up, but found the task difficult having both hands tied behind his back. He put his head against the side of the shack to use as leverage, and inched his way to a sitting position. The bag still covered his head, shrouding him in darkness.

"Tony," he whispered. There was no response, so he spoke louder.

"Tony. Hey, Tony, are you okay?" There was still no answer. "Tony!" he screamed. His voice bordered on panic. He didn't know why Tony was mute, but felt fearful beyond words. "Tony, say something!"

George was answered with the deafening hum of silence. George pushed off the ground with his feet before falling to his knees. The weight of his body made his knees dig against the hard floor. Scooting toward the other end of the shack, he continued shouting for Tony. It took less than fifteen seconds for George to make it from one side of the shack to the other. Tony never responded, and George felt certain he would have run into him while scooting across the shack.

"Tony!" he screamed one last time, before realizing he was alone.

*****

Keith was asleep when Carl entered the house. The clunk of Carl's keys being thrown on the counter woke him instantly. Keith sat up and rubbed the sleep from his eyes.

"So," Keith said. "Did he have cloven hooves?"

"What?" Carl asked.

"The anti-Christ. Was he born with a tail?"

Carl stared at him, "Are you serious?"

Keith shrugged. "Only if it isn't a stupid question."

Carl dismissed him. "It is."

Keith wasn't offended. "I'm sorry. I've never witnessed the birth of the anti-Christ. I guess I just don't know what he looks like. I've always kind of pictured him with a tail. No tail, huh? How about horns?"

"Enough," Carl said, his agitation obvious.

"What?" Keith asked, failing to understand Carl's irritation.

"I just got back from a conference about a cashless society, but not before watching a woman be murdered, then having her bloody body rolled through camp in a glass hearse. I guess I'm just a little irritable."

"Irritable enough to tell the story on camera?"

Carl considered Keith's question.

"No, not on camera, but off camera. I'll tell you what I saw, but you can't show my face. Once I've been exposed, I'll be useless, not to mention dead. But I joined The Resistance to shed light on the truth. So, yes, I'll tell you everything, but not on video. Just audio."

Keith was in no position to argue. He was dying to hear about the retreat, and was curious about everything Carl had witnessed.

"All right," Keith said. "Just sit down. I'll leave the lens on the camera, and you can tell me everything."

"What about my voice? I don't want anyone to recognize my voice."

Keith waved his hand. "All that can be fixed in post production. I'll distort your voice; nobody will know it's you."

Carl nodded his head. He removed the glasses from his pocket and handed them to Keith.

"Here's the video. If you remove the left lens, you'll see a tiny USB port." Carl picked a cord up from the kitchen counter and handed it to Keith. "You can use that cord to charge and upload. Use that video in your story."

*****

George felt the sensation of a thousand tiny needles piercing his arm. The sensation was painful, but he was relieved to have had any feeling at all. He rolled his shoulder in an effort to increase circulation until he felt satisfied the damage wasn't permanent. He wasn't sure what had happened to Tony, but he was certain he was now alone in the shack. Anything could have happened to the music executive. He could have been freed or killed. George had no clue. The only thing George knew for sure was that he was alone.

He didn't like being alone. It gave him too much time to think. Could Tony's stories about demon possession be true? Could the music industry be that wicked? BARAchip was one thing, but letting teenagers sell their souls? Was there really a Twenty-Seven Club? Were demons summoned into music tracks? Could any of what Tony had said be real, or had he just been scared and talking crazy?

George heard the shack door creak open before he registered sunlight through the burlap sack. Two men gripped his arms—one gripped his right, and the other grabbed his left. Without saying a word, the men lifted George to his feet.

The men marched George down a long path. George panicked and wondered if he was being led to his death. He was relieved to feel cool air touch his skin as the men led him indoors. Without freeing his hands, one of the men pushed George into a chair before removing the burlap sack from his head. Sweat poured from George's forehead. His face was beet red. He didn't know if he should feel relieved or scared. He looked at his captors, recognizing them both. They were two members of the council. He'd known them for years. Both men had worked closely with George to craft the BARAchip story.

"You failed us, George," said Richard Sutton.

Sutton was the man who'd originally told George about the BARAchip story. George tried to speak, but only stuttered.

"Silence!" demanded the man to Sutton's right. George recognized the man next to Sutton as Tyler Wilkes, Public Affairs Councilman. Tyler continued, "We took a chance on you, and you made us look like fools!"

This time, George found his voice. "It won't happen again. I promise."

Tyler looked disgusted. "It can't happen again, because there won't be another chance to introduce The Mark as ancient prophecy predicted. You've failed us."

George knew they were right. His impatience to get to the retreat had not only cost him his job, but quite possibly his life.

"I wasn't worthy of such a critical task." George said, casting his eyes towards the ground.

"You're right," Tyler agreed. "You weren't. But now it's time to clean up the mess you've made.

You must still introduce the BARAchip before
Jarrod Kabbul wins the presidency in November.
By the time Kabbul enters the White House with his
beautiful wife, and brand new, bouncing baby boy,
every parent will demand BARAchip implants to
protect their children. In forty-eight hours, Kabbul
was supposed to be all over the news, gushing about
his newborn son. He was supposed to say how
thankful he was that BARAchip technology existed.
Of course, thanks to you, nobody has heard of
BARAchip."

Richard Sutton looked at George. "Thanks to your
incompetence, nobody will know what Kabbul is
talking about. You have twenty-four hours to
inform the public of the life-saving implant, and the
clock starts now."

George moved his beady eyes from one man to the
other. "That's it? You're giving me another
chance?"

Richard Sutton leaned into George, leaving only an
inch of space between their noses. "Yes, you could
say that. Only the next time you fail, you won't live
to regret it. There will be no shack, and no second
chances. Did I make myself clear?"

George nodded like a maniac. "Clear. Crystal clear.
I'll leave now. I won't let you down. How fast can
I get back to D.C.?"

Sutton checked his watch. "Your private jet leaves in one hour." He stepped back, turned his head, and yelled, "Driver!"

A tall man entered the cabin. Sutton nodded at the man in greeting. "Driver, I believe Mr. Dittmeir is ready to be transported to the jet."

With one swift nod of his head, the driver said, "As you wish."

Richard walked to a desk, opened a drawer, and removed a pair of scissors. He walked slowly towards George without ever breaking eye contact. He stepped behind George and cut the rope that tied his hands together.

George immediately pulled his wrists in front of him, and began moving them in tiny circles. "Thank you," George said. "I won't let you down."

Angela Caldwell

CHAPTER 7

Jacinda made her way from the bedroom to the living room. She saw Keith interviewing Carl, and immediately apologized for the interruption.

"It's fine," Carl assured her. "We were just wrapping things up."

"Are you sure?"

"Positive," Carl said. "Can I get you something? Would you like some coffee?"

"I don't want you to go through any trouble," Jacinda responded.

"It's no trouble," Carl assured her as he walked towards the kitchen.

Keith put the camera back in its case, while continuing to process everything Carl had said

104

about a cashless society. Everything Mitch had predicted in his book was happening. This both terrified and excited him. He looked over at Jacinda. She still looked exhausted.

"What time is it?" she asked. "Where are Lyla and Kyler?"

"It's 3:30," Carl answered. "I saw Lyla and Kyler in the backyard. Lyla said Kyler loves playing outdoors."

Jacinda leaned forward. "Do you think it's safe?"

"Of course," Carl assured her. "Nobody knows you're here, and it will do the kiddo good to get some fresh air."

Jacinda walked to the window and peeked through the shutters. Kyler was playing with one of his many new toys. Jacinda's face lit up. The sight of her son always put a smile on her face. He was having so much fun while Lyla sat by and watched him adoringly.

Jacinda was absolutely certain Lyla would protect Kyler with her life.

"Turn on the television," Jacinda demanded.

Keith cringed. He knew they were about to revisit the conversation about Gregory. Keith turned on the television at the exact moment Lyla and Kyler walked through the back door.

"I hungy," Kyler said, smiling at Jacinda.

"You are, are you?" Jacinda cooed, focusing all of her attention on her baby boy. "What would you like to eat?" Jacinda asked the love of her life.

"Skeddi!" Kyler replied.

"Come here," Jacinda said, beaming from ear to ear. She couldn't wait to get her precious son in her arms.

She glanced at the television just in time to see a picture of Jarrod Kabbul flash across the screen. A pretty, blonde news anchor said, "Presidential candidate Jarrod Kabbul's wife just gave birth to a healthy baby boy early this morning."

Her co-anchor, a man in his late forties, smiled and said, "Could this be the next First Baby?"

"It could, indeed," replied the blonde. "Kabbul is dominating in the polls, and his popularity doesn't seem to be waning. His wife, Ellie, gave birth in California. She was accompanying her husband on his campaign tour. The presidential candidate released a statement saying both mother and baby are doing well, and that the excited couple couldn't wait to take their little bundle of joy home."

"That's not her baby," Lyla said.

"What?" asked Jacinda.

"It's not her baby," Lyla repeated. "It's him, the anti-Christ. The child born from The Vessel."

"How do you know?" Keith inquired.

"Lucio. I overheard a lot, being Maidservant. I mean, Kyler's keeper. This was planned from the beginning. Kabbul and his wife, Ellie, will raise Lord Maitreya, the anti-Christ, as their own, until he is sixteen. At that time, he will take the throne."

Keith eyed her suspiciously. "The throne?"

"Sixteen?" Jacinda asked skeptically.

Lyla sat on the couch, and began absentmindedly twisting her hair around her finger. "He's not a normal child. He brought with him the wisdom and evil that he will use to rule the world once it becomes a one-world government."

"At sixteen? Nobody will ever let that happen," said Keith.

"Oh, you'll be surprised at what people will let happen," Lyla assured them. "You also might not think anyone would let a president remain for four terms, but it will happen, wait and see. It's all been prophesied. Kabbul will enchant the world. He'll convince everyone he's their only hope, and they'll believe his deception."

"But the Constitution," Keith offered in defense.

"Before long, they'll convince the American public that the Constitution is just an outdated document of primitive ideas," Lyla said confidently.

"Sixteen?" Keith repeated. "I'll believe that when I see it."

Lyla seemed unfazed. "Suit yourself."

Jacinda wasn't finished engaging Lyla in conversation. "So, what happened to Ellie Kabbul's baby? I mean, if she's raising the anti-Christ or whatever."

"What baby?" Lyla asked.

"She was pregnant," Keith said.

Lyla shook her head. "Oh, no, she was never pregnant. She was made to look pregnant using a prosthetic belly, but she never was. The Vessel carried the child. In fact, The Vessel is Kabbul's sister on his father's side. They have different mothers. Jarrod's mother is American."

"What?" Keith's expression twisted in confusion.

"Kabbul and Ellie will raise the child." Lyla continued, "It's almost silly to call him their child; after all, they, along with the rest of The Brotherhood, worship him. I was told he would be our great savior. Of course, I now know that's a lie. My eyes were opened, thanks to Marlene. The only thing that will save us is Jesus, not the anti-Christ."

"Sixteen?" Keith repeated in shock.

"It will be a different world then, you'll see," Lyla said.

"In sixteen years?" Keith asked. "It will be a different world in sixteen years?"

Carl interrupted, "She might not be too far off. The things I heard and witnessed at the World Banking Seminar indicate there will be a cashless society in just a matter of years. Things are happening quickly. Too quickly."

Jacinda turned to Lyla. "But who's to say Kabbul will even be elected?"

Carl took the conversation from there. "Jacinda, I'm afraid there is a lot you don't know about The Brotherhood. They control everything from banks to the government, and also law enforcement— everyone is in their pockets. Do you know how you watch your television on Election Night, and the states turn red or blue?"

"Of course," replied Jacinda.

"Well, have you ever counted those ballots? Do you know anyone who has counted those ballots, or do you just have faith in the government to protect our democracy and do the right thing? Do you just assume that if a state turns red that a Republican is leading?"

Jacinda looked defeated. "Does that mean our elections are rigged? That our votes don't count?"

"What do you know about the ancient bloodline?" Keith asked Jacinda.

"Not a lot, I guess. I mean, nothing really. What is it?"

Keith tried to sound like an expert on the subject, but in reality, he knew very little. Lyla was aware of his ignorance, and decided to speak on his behalf.

"The Pharaohs began the bloodline, which is now referred to as the ancient bloodline. King Tut ruled at a very young age. He became a Pharaoh at the age of ten. His bloodline continued, as members of his family migrated to Europe, where they established themselves as Royalty. While the Pharaohs seemed to disappear, they simply migrated to different continents. That bloodline continued to interbreed, keeping both the power and the money within the family. Over time, the bloodline was spread among thirteen families. The families now control just about everything. They've waited thousands of years to once again control the entire world, and ancient texts reveal the time is coming. A child was to be born and raised in an environment where he could take his throne at the age of sixteen."

"His throne?" Keith repeated, still sounding unconvinced.

"Hush," chided Jacinda. "You already said that."

Keith ignored her. "You can't even run for President until you're thirty-four."

"Thirty-five," Jacinda corrected him.

"I told you," Lyla said, "a lot of things are about to change."

"I don't doubt they'll change," Keith told her, "but I seriously don't see a sixteen-year-old boy taking a throne or anything else. That's a little too out there. I mean, this has all been crazy, but that's a whole different level of insanity."

Carl looked at Lyla. "You know so much; are *you* part of the ancient bloodline?"

Lyla shook her head. "No, I'm not. But Lucio is, and my father was his assistant and confidant. I've heard a lot. Kabbul is also part of the bloodline, and so is his wife."

"His wife?" asked Keith. "Then why didn't she give birth to the anti-Christ?"

Lyla shrugged. "Perhaps she had no desire to be sacrificed."

"Fair enough," Keith agreed.

CHAPTER 8

Rob Livingston's personal cell phone rang. He didn't recognize the number, but answered regardless. "Rob Livingston."

"Rob, it's Richard Sutton." Livingston knew all too well who Richard Sutton was. He was brotherhood council member. He made and enforced plans when the public needed to be influenced. Rob met him at the grove, but wondered why he would call on his personal cell.

Of course, Sutton had no reason to believe Rob was now part of The Resistance, so maybe it wasn't *that* strange for him to be calling. However, Sutton usually went straight to the man in charge--George Dittmeir.

"Hi," Livingston said, trying to sound as casual as possible. "How can I help you?"

"First of all, Rob, my condolences. I heard you lost a member of your family." Livingston had used a family emergency as an excuse to avoid the retreat, but never believed it would work. However, he'd never said a family member was dead.

Not wanting to fall into a trap, he simply said, "Is there something I can help you with, friend?" The word *friend* burned his tongue. This man was a lot of things, but he was not anyone's friend, especially not Livingston's.

"Well, Rob, I'm calling to inform you that George Dittmeir is on a private jet en route to Washington D.C. By now, I'm sure you've heard he mishandled the BARAchip story, and, while we can't turn back time and make it right, we are giving him twenty-four hours to introduce the chip to the world. I've been told that our original reporter, Mrs. Kilmeade, is missing, so I don't suppose we can count on her for the story. I'm calling to inform you that The Brotherhood needs you to step forward and right the wrongs of your boss. I feel you're more competent than Mr. Dittmeir. Your Brotherhood needs you to work closely and quickly with Mr. Dittmeir. BARAchip *must* be introduced before Jarrod Kabbul gives his first interview as a new father."

"Of course," Livingston assured him. "You can count on me. I'm headed to the station now. Once

George arrives, we'll get started."

"Wonderful," purred Richard Sutton. "I knew we could count on you. You've always been one of my favorites, you know. You're dedicated enough to The Brotherhood to do your job without always feeling the need to participate in the festivities. You are truly devoted, and don't think I haven't noticed. Your boss, on the other hand, he's in this for one thing, and one thing only--the privileges of membership."

With that, the phone went dead. Livingston was wrong. He wasn't suspected as a traitor. In fact, they admired him for *not* indulging in the finer things that came with membership. They must have viewed him as a sort of purist. Maybe he wasn't a dead man, after all. Maybe he could continue to help The Resistance. The prophecy had already been wrong. Jacinda, the woman of God, and mother of *the sacrifice*, had not introduced BARAchip to the world. In fact, the child had never been sacrificed. So much of what had been prophesized hadn't played out the way The Brotherhood had hoped.

Livingston felt rejuvenated. He felt a whole new sense of purpose. He could continue to monitor the direction of the news from inside the nation's most powerful newsroom. He was back in the game, and it felt great.

*****

Gregory Kilmeade sat on his couch inside of his D.C. Condominium. Jacinda's absence made the condo feel not only lonely, but it also felt cruel. He sensed that the emptiness mocked him. His father, Nicholas, had sent someone down to post his bail, but his father was the last person he wanted to speak to right now. Gregory had been ignoring Nicholas' calls since he'd been released. The only person he wanted to hear from was Jacinda.

How has my life come to this? he wondered. He was sure Jacinda knew he had been found with an abducted child, but he had done it for her. "I did it for love. I did it to save her son. I did it so we could be a family. Won't she be able to see how much I've sacrificed? I did this for her!" He was mumbling to himself. He was becoming more and more unhinged.

His mother was dead, but he felt little grief. Chandra had never liked Jacinda, and she'd made that fact painfully clear. Gregory had always pretended not to notice. He'd hoped that, in time, his mother would come to love his wife as much as he did. Now, she would never have that chance. His mother had deprived herself of loving the most perfect human being on the face of the planet.

It was her loss, he thought. *Maybe she deserved to die the way she did.* "She probably hung herself out of jealousy," he said to no one in particular.

He couldn't let thoughts of his mother distract him from his mission—finding his wife. He called everyone he could think of in The Brotherhood, but none of them were willing to speak to him. He called *Your Nation Now* to discover that nobody had heard from Jacinda. He wouldn't lose her. He couldn't. She was the only thing that mattered to him in the world.

His father had pushed him to become involved with BARAchip. Nicholas had orchestrated everything, including the interview with Jacinda. At the time, it hadn't seemed hard. How difficult could it be? He'd simply had to swoop in and play knight in shining armor to a beautiful, grieving woman from Texas. He could charm anyone. It was his gift. He knew he could make her fall madly in love with him, but he'd never expected to fall hopelessly in love with her.

He would do anything to get her back—anything. After all, she loved him. *I will just have to make her see that I took the child to save Kyler. She will understand that, right? She will understand that a child had to take Kyler's place as the sacrifice. She will forgive me. The three of us can live happily ever after somewhere far away from Washington D.C. Where does George's daughter live? Thailand? Maybe we could live in Thailand. Somewhere far away where nobody will ever find us.* His mind was reeling. He was plotting—grasping. He stood to pace the condo, walking from his room to the office, then back to the couch. Nervous energy propelled him from room to room. He simply could not sit still.

*****

Rob Livingston was already sitting at his desk when George rushed past him. With shaky hands, George unlocked the door to his office. Bertha approached him, but Livingston saw him wave her off. George appeared shaken—scared. No, he looked terrified. George closed the blinds to his office, which was something he rarely did. Livingston strolled over, not bothering to knock before opening the door to George's office. It looked as if George was ransacking his own desk. He pulled each drawer out, recklessly throwing all of the drawer's contents on the desk. It wasn't until Livingston closed the door behind him that George realized he had company.

"I'm busy," George said, not bothering to look up.

"I can see that," Livingston responded.

"Now isn't a good time," George announced, as he continued to rummage through the piles of paper on his desk. Beads of sweat trickled down his forehead, and he was clearly terrified. Livingston calmly took a seat in the wobbly chair that faced George's desk.

"Is there something you want to talk to me about, George?"

"No, I have nothing to say. I'm busy. You'll have to come back later, I'm…"

"Scared?" Livingston asked, finishing his sentence. George buckled in his chair and buried his face in his hands. He began to mumble. Livingston strained to hear what George was saying. "I can't hear you, George."

George looked up and met Rob Livingston's eyes. "They're going to kill me, Rob. If I don't introduce the BARAchip, they are going to kill me."

Livingston shrugged his shoulders, leaned forward, and said, "They'll kill you regardless."

George knew Livingston was right. He collapsed his head into his own arms, which were crossed on his desk, and began to sob, "I deserve to die. I *deserve* to be killed."

"Why is that, George?" Livinston asked. "Is it because you failed? Do you deserve to die because

119

the BARAchip story didn't air?"

George looked at him through crazed eyes. "I'm glad it didn't air! They don't just want to rule the world; they want to send us all straight to hell!"

Livingston didn't seem shaken. "You didn't know that? I was fairly certain you knew that."

George looked hopeless. "I knew about The New World Order. I knew about the political agenda. I was aware a savior would be born, but I didn't know about bargains with the devil, and I didn't know they would eat their own!"

"Eat their own?" Livingston asked, not entirely sure what he'd missed at the grove.

"Yes. One slip up, and BOOM—you're dead! Just like that! You aren't thanked for your service. You aren't given a gold watch. You're killed. That's how they thank you. I was sent back to finish the BARAchip story, but I'm as good as dead whether I finish it or not."

Once again, George made eye contact with Livingston, "Get out, Rob."

Livingston stood to leave. "No!" George shouted. "Get out of The Brotherhood. They'll kill you, too!" Livingston slowly returned to his seat.

"No offense, George, but you're acting a little crazy."

"I'm acting crazy? Oh, you think I'm acting crazy? I'll tell you why I'm acting crazy. I just spent God only knows how long in the sweat shack with a burlap sack over my head. I was sure I was going to die in there. Do you know why I was spared, Rob? I was spared because I have a job to finish. I was spared because I have yet to serve my purpose."

George noticed that Livingston appeared entirely too collected, given the situation.

"George, what would you say that purpose is?" asked Livingston.

"Isn't it obvious? It's to shape the news. It's to craft public opinion. We say it, so it must be true. Right? Wrong! Do you know who was in the sweat shack with me? Tony Randall."

Livingston tilted his head. "Louden Records, Tony Randall? I remember seeing him at the grove."

"Yeah, well, you probably won't be seeing him again."

"Why? What happened?"

George looked even more maniacal than ever. "I

don't know! He was in the sweat shack with me, and then he just disappeared. He couldn't wait to send his musicians to hell; he expected to go there himself."

Livingston leaned forward. "So, what was he doing in the shack?"

"He fell in love."

"They put him in the shack for falling in love?"

"No, they put him in the shack for not wanting the woman he loved to sell her soul to the devil for a music career."

Livingston looked confused. "I thought you said he wasn't worried about hell, for himself or his musicians."

"He wasn't. But he didn't want her to leave this earth before he did."

Livingston stared blankly at George.

George threw his hands in the air. "The Twenty-Seven Club! She's twenty-one. He didn't want to take the chance of losing her in six years."

Livingston leaned back in the wobbly chair, trying to find his center of gravity. "Slow down, George. The Twenty-Seven Club?"

George waved his hand. "It's not important. None of that is important. Don't you see? We're all going to die!" It was clear to Livingston that George was having a psychotic breakdown. Livingston was curious to know what George had endured in the shack, and wondered if he'd ever come to his senses.

"Why are you telling me this, George? You know I'm one of them. What's to stop me from calling them right now and telling them you're spilling secrets?" Of course, Livingston would never do such a thing. He was part of The Resistance, but George didn't know that.

"Well," George said, still shaking, "I suppose they'd kill me. Oh, wait," George paused for dramatic effect, "they're already going to kill me." Rob took George's psychotic episode as an opportunity to collect ammunition for The Resistance.

"Are you mad, George?"

"Of course I'm mad! I'm not just mad; I'm disgusted! Demons, knowingly sending young kids to hell—they're wicked, Rob. Wicked! And I'll tell you something else. I don't care if I die. I'd rather die than continue to live as a puppet of The Brotherhood."

Rob stared at him for a long moment, then said, "Do you really mean that, George?"

George was so mad, spittle flew out of his mouth when he spoke. "I've never meant anything more in my life."

"Are you serious about this?"

"Of course I'm serious! Call them. Tell them I'm serious. Tell them to come kill me. I don't care anymore." George was still raging like a madman. Livingston stood and walked towards George.

"I'm not going to call them, George, but I am going to call someone. How mad are you? Are you mad enough to tell me everything you know on camera?"

"On camera, on live television—I don't care. I'm a dead man. I'm a dead man, and I don't care who knows what they're planning."

Livingston simply nodded, "That makes me very happy, George. Follow me."

CHAPTER 9

Jill stood and looked at Carl. "We need to get Gregory's old laptop. What do you suggest? How do you think we should get it?" Carl took a seat on the barstool.

"With all due respect, I'm a banker. I don't mastermind missions. Until Livingston called me, I simply let The Resistance know what was going on in the world of banking. I'm out of my element."

Jill acknowledged Carl's words and nodded. "I don't think you give yourself enough credit, hon."

"How so, ma'am?"

"Well, I think you understand more than just numbers. You've managed to stay undercover in

The Brotherhood without being suspected of collecting information for The Resistance. You managed to rescue me, even though my house was more than likely under surveillance. You pulled all of this together, and have kept us safely hidden away. You may think of yourself simply as a banker, but I'd say you can offer a lot more to The Resistance than tracking financial trends."

Carl had never really given his position in The Resistance much thought. Once he'd recognized the evils of The Brotherhood, he'd wanted no part of it. It was Livingston who'd talked him into keeping up appearances for the good of humanity. Maybe Jill was right. Maybe he was far more valuable than he gave himself credit for. Maybe he could help craft a plan.

"We need leverage," Carl said. "We need to hold them accountable, so if anything happens to any one of you, they risk being exposed."

Jacinda looked towards Gregory's laptop. "Everyone who is involved with BARAchip is listed in recovered emails. Jill, make a list."

Jill looked at Jacinda.

"You want me to name them all?"

"You said you could post a website and make it

look like it's coming from any server in the world. Let's create a site. You have the email addresses of everyone involved with BARAchip. Email all of them. Make it look like the email is coming from overseas. Tell them we have evidence of a conspiracy."

"Like what? Nothing discussed in those emails leads to a smoking gun, Jacinda."

"Bluff. They don't know what we do and don't know. The fact that you know who they are in the first place will startle them. Tell them that if anything happens to us, you'll post all of the evidence on the worldwide web for everyone to see. Play their game."

Jill looked nervous. "Why? What are you planning? If I specifically tell them that no harm is to come to us, they'll know we're all involved."

Jacinda swatted away Jill's concern with her hand.

"They already know we're involved. They got me involved two years ago, remember? Lyla got involved the minute she rescued Kyler. You and Keith have been involved since that night at my condo."

"Yes, but they'll know we're fighting back, hon. It will take it to a whole other level."

"Good!" Jacinda said defiantly.

"I just don't want your anger to get us killed, Jacinda." Jill said.

"It won't because you're going to keep us safe. You doing what you do best will ensure nobody touches us. I'm willing to risk it. I need to go to my condo and get my hands on that old laptop. I won't be able to get within two miles of my condo without being spotted. Some kind of order needs to go out that I'm not to be harmed. For all they know, I'm going home. I'm going home, and I'm going back to work."

Carl stood from the stool and walked around the counter. "I'll make coffee."

"That's it?" Jill asked. "That's all you have to say? You'll make coffee?"

Carl shrugged. "I think her plan might work. The last thing The Brotherhood wants is exposure. They will weigh the pros and cons of hurting you guys. I think Jacinda would be our best bet at recovering the computer. Killing her doesn't further their purposes, especially since they don't realize how much she knows. She's been off the radar. They probably suspect she knows something, but can't possibly be sure of the extent of her knowledge. Plus, their egos won't let them believe Jacinda could do any harm. They think they're brilliant and untouchable. The Brotherhood won't see Jacinda as a threat. I think they'll let her go home, especially if she lays low and doesn't act like a madwoman with a secret to expose."

Jacinda looked at Jill. "He's right, Jill. They know I know about being chosen, and they know I know they were responsible for taking Kyler, but they have no idea there is a resistance. They'll probably think I'm tucking my tail between my legs and returning to my life because I have no other choice."

Jill shook her head. "I don't like it."

"It's all we've got. Please, just email everyone involved with BARAchip. Bluff. Tell them if any harm comes to us, their names and proof of a conspiracy will light up the internet."

"They'll know it's me, Jacinda. They heard us talking in your condo. They know I recovered all of his emails. They'll know I'm the one who is threatening them."

Jacinda walked to Jill and took her friend's hands in her own. "Please. I'm so sorry you're involved. I know what I'm asking of you, but I think I can find a way to keep all of us safe. Right now, even if you don't send that email, they'll kill you. You'll have to hide out forever, because they know you know. If you go along with my plan, I think I can figure something out that will let us all be able to reclaim our lives."

Keith looked at Lyla. Her face was drained of all color. "What?" Keith asked. "What's wrong, are you okay?"

"What about Kyler?" Lyla asked. She was on the verge of tears. "You can't parade him in front of The Brotherhood, you just can't!"

Jacinda looked at her son. He was completely self-occupied, sitting on the floor, playing with his new toys. She walked over and sat down beside him. Pulling him into her lap, she hugged him against her and rocked back and forth. Taking his little hands in her own, she kissed them, as tears filled her eyes. "I won't take him with me. It's going to kill me, but I'll have to go without him. I don't want them to know I've found him. I won't put him in that kind of danger."

Carl walked around the counter holding a coffee filter. "They can stay here. I'll keep them safe. Jill, too. Nobody knows they're here."

Keith's eyes darted around the room. "What about me?"

"You'll go back to D.C. a few days after Jacinda. Go back to work. Your absence might have been suspicious, but you can't be connected to anything. They know you suspected where Kyler was, but for all they know, you never found him. Jill can put you on the list of people not to harm.

"What about exposing them? We've come too far to just try to get our lives back. What about the story?"

Carl recognized the ambition behind Keith's question. "Don't worry. You'll still have a story. You'll just have to craft it slowly."

Jacinda turned to Keith. "You already have quite a bit. Edit that. You'll have to keep the video somewhere other than your apartment."

"What about the safe house? I can probably keep it at Andy's." Keith said.

"Who is Andy?" Jacinda asked.

"He's who I was going to see when I realized Livingston was on our side. They were having a meeting there. I can keep all of the footage there." He looked over at Lyla. "Or maybe it would be better if I stayed here." He couldn't believe the thought of leaving Lyla was so painful. Never in his wildest dreams would he think he'd volunteer to

131

stay holed away in some safe house instead of returning to the D.C. hustle and bustle.

"No," Carl said. "You'll be more useful there. I can keep Lyla, Jill, and Kyler safe. Nobody will ever think to look for them here."

Jacinda stood before placing Kyler on her hip. She sat next to Lyla on the couch, and let Kyler crawl from her lap to Lyla's.

"I trust you, Lyla. I know you'll keep him safe. He loves you. It won't be for long. I'm going to go back to D.C. to collect as much information as I can. I'll come back in a week or two with the computer in hand. By the time I return, I hope to have enough information to expose them all. Until then, can you stay with Kyler?"

Tears streamed down Lyla's face. "Of course. Of course I'll take care of him. I feel so blessed to be able to spend more time with him, but I feel so guilty that you two have to be apart again."

Jacinda smiled at Lyla and hugged her close. "It won't be for long. I'll go do what I need to do *for* our safety. By the time I'm done, we'll be able to lead normal lives."

"What about me? Keith asked.

Carl knew exactly how to answer Keith's question.

"Keith, once you expose the story of a lifetime, your life will never be normal again." That statement would have terrified most people, but not Keith. Every nerve in Keith's body buzzed with excitement.

*****

Livingston and George sat alone in the meeting room. Livingston placed a microphone on George's collar, before aiming a camera at the man who was coming unhinged in front of his eyes. George was experiencing a fear that couldn't be faked, and Livingston knew that would show on camera. Never had he imagined he would be getting testimony against The Brotherhood from George Dittmeir, but it couldn't have come at a better time.

"George, I need you to keep your eyes on me. Don't look directly into the camera. I want you to look at me, and tell me everything," Livingston instructed.

Sweat dripped from George's face, and his eyes were still darting around like a maniac.

"George, I need you to look at me. Look into my eyes and start from the beginning. Tell me about BARAchip. Tell me about how you crafted the story to shape pubic perception. Then, I want you to tell me about the grove and the sweat shack. I

133

want you to name names. Tell me about Tony and what he told you in the shack. We have all day, George. That door is locked and nobody is coming in here. It's just you and me. I need you to tell me everything."

Livingston hoped he could keep George from falling apart until he had everything he needed on camera. It was a balancing act. He needed George's fear to be evident, but not so consuming that he would appear crazy. He needed the public to believe George, and for that to happen, George needed to appear sane.

"Look at me, George," Livingston repeated. "Nobody is going to hurt you. You're safe here. It's just you and me. You're safe. Just take a deep breath and start from the beginning."

"Why are you doing this? Are you going to send this to them?"

"I'm not sending this to anyone, George. I was called and tasked with being the reporter who introduces BARAchip. I have less than twenty-four hours to put the package together. Look, George, I've worked for you for a long time now. I care about what happens to you. I want to ensure the success of The Brotherhood's plans, but I also want to ensure your safety. What The Brotherhood doesn't know won't hurt them. You already said you're a dead man, so what could your testimony hurt?"

George's panic seemed to wane. "So you're going to do it? You're going to introduce the chip? You don't know what kind of people they really are, Rob. You've only seen their good side. I promise you, you'll mess up eventually, and then you'll be dead, too." Livingston never lost his cool. He knew George was unstable, and couldn't risk him finding out there was a resistance. He couldn't risk George knowing his allegiance wasn't to The Brotherhood, but the truth-seekers. In the battle of good versus evil, Livingston would die a million painful deaths before submitting to evil, but George couldn't know that. He wasn't stable enough to keep such a secret. If Livingston's cover was ever blown, he would be useless to The Resistance.

"So, you're going to help me?" George asked. His eyes finally stopped darting around the room. He looked confused but comforted.

"Yes, George. I'm going to help you, because you're my friend. I'm going to help you stay alive, but you can't let anyone know."

"Who am I going to tell? Even if the BARAchip story runs, I'll be killed. Nothing will save me."

"That's not true. They won't have the opportunity

to kill you, because you'll never leave this office."

"Are you suggesting I *live* here forever?"

"Do you feel safe going home?"

"I don't feel safe anywhere."

Livingston desperately wanted to get him to a safe house, but couldn't risk exposing The Resistance. George simply wasn't stable enough to trust. For now, this would have to be his safe house. As long as he was in the studio, they wouldn't kill him. It couldn't last forever, but it might keep him safe until Livingston could craft a better plan.

*****

Nicholas Kilmeade entered Lucio's office inside the Luciferian temple. Lucio sat at his desk studying ancient scrolls. He looked older. Tired. Without lifting his head, his wicked eyes looked up to meet Nicholas'.

"What is it that you want from me, Nicholas?"

"You killed her, didn't you? You killed my wife."

"I told you that your entire family would be killed," he said nonchalantly, and continued pouring over the scrolls.

"I understand," said Nicholas. "You did what you

had to do, but please don't turn your back on me. Take Gregory, and Lyla too, if you must. But let me be by your side. Let me help prepare this world for our savior."

Lucio looked up from the scrolls. "Your son betrayed us, Nicholas. Not only did he fail us, any legislation he had been working on will be flushed down the toilet when he is officially removed from the Senate. I expect his resignation any day now. He set us back."
"I know," said Nicholas, "and for that he deserves death."

Lucio stood and pushed his chair back with his legs. The chair banged loudly into the wall, causing Nicholas to jump. His nerves were already standing on end, but the loud noise brought him to his knees. There, on his knees, in front of Lucio, he begged.

"Please don't turn your back on me. My son failed you. My daughter failed you, but I will not fail you. I will help our savior reign. I will do whatever it takes."

"Whatever it takes?" Lucio asked, eyeing him suspiciously.

"Yes, Worshipful Master. Whatever it takes."

"Would you sacrifice your only son?"

"Gregory? Would I sacrifice Gregory?"

"That's what I'm asking you. Would you sacrifice Gregory?"

Nicholas looked down, "Of course."

The corners of Lucio's lips curved up in a wicked smile. "But would *you* sacrifice him with your own hands? Here in the temple?"

Nicholas never looked up. "I would. Of course."

"You may stand," Lucio said as he returned to his chair.

Lucio glared at Nicholas. "You will sacrifice your own son to our savior, here, at this temple. The sacrifice shall be done at the time of my choosing. I need to study to see when the sacrifice would be most powerful."

"Yes, Sir." Nicholas responded. "I will wait for your orders."

"Have you spoken to Gregory?"

"No, Sir. I've tried, but he won't accept my calls."

Lucio was silent. He began tracing the scrolls with his finger. Nicholas wondered if he should excuse himself or continue standing. Moments later, Lucio looked at Nicholas and said, "Maybe it's best if you leave him alone. We will let him think all is forgiven. I will tell the brothers to extend their support. He shall think we understand his reasons, and we appreciate his efforts. You, Nicholas, must stay away from him until the night of the sacrifice."

"You can count on me, Worshipful Master."

"If you fail, I will kill your daughter. Then it will be your turn to die."

"I understand, Worshipful Master," Nicholas said in a relieved tone.

"Now, be gone. I have work to do."

"Of course." Nicholas pivoted on his heel and exited the temple.

CHAPTER 10

Jacinda's flight from California to Washington D.C. was unnerving. Jacinda half expected an assassin to be waiting for her when she stepped off the plane. She was even suspicious of the cab driver, although he did nothing to warrant her suspicion. Jacinda stepped out of the cab and prepared herself for the very real possibility of Gregory being home. She ran though every possible scenario a million times on the plane. She decided she'd play naïve. She'd see how much he knew, and make a plan based on that.

It would take everything she had not to rip into him with her fists. It would take every bit of self-control not to scream at him, and ask him why. But she couldn't let her emotions betray her. She had to get inside, get the computer, and gauge his state of mind. Since the arrest, he'd been off the radar. There was chatter of his resignation, but nobody had heard from him. She didn't know if he was at the condo, or staying at the Kilmeade estate. Perhaps Nicholas and Gregory needed each other's support after Chandra's suicide. Of course, she doubted it had been suicide. She suspected it had been a hit, but would Gregory suspect The Brotherhood?

She prayed Jill's email made it to the proper channels so that she would be safe. She only needed to be protected long enough to recover a little more information. *What if Jill's email didn't work?* she worried. *What if someone is waiting on the other side of that door?* She couldn't let fear consume her. Fear would only distract her, and she needed to focus if she planned on staying alive and collecting information.

As her hand touched the warm doorknob, she closed her eyes to collect herself. After taking a cleansing breath, she put the key in the lock and turned the knob. Not knowing what she'd find on the other side of the door, she slowly pushed it open.

Fearing the worst, Gregory sprung to his feet. Once he saw it was Jacinda, he began to weep.

"Baby, I didn't know if you were…. I mean, I

hadn't heard from you, and was so scared that you…" Gregory trailed off, never finishing his sentence. "Look at you. You're safe!" He closed the gap between them, taking Jacinda into his arms. The very scent of his cologne made vomit rise in her throat. Never had she felt so betrayed by anyone.

Gregory couldn't possibly think she hadn't figured out his role in Kyler's disappearance or her late husband's death. He couldn't really think she came home hoping to find him there. She couldn't get emotional. She had to keep her anger at bay. If she was going to collect his computer, and get back to California alive, she had to play it cool. She had to play a part—a character. Her survival depended on how well she could manipulate Gregory into feeling unthreatened. He had to think his beloved wife was home to stay.

She looked at the face she'd once found so beautiful, but now she only saw evil.

She couldn't look him in the eyes. Instead, she headed towards the couch. She placed her purse on the coffee table.

"Of course I'm safe. I haven't been doing much at the station, and you were gone, so I figured I'd go home for a little while. I've been missing Texas." Gregory studied her face. He was searching his wife's features for emotion, but she never let her expression reveal her feelings. Gregory was still in tears.

"I have horrible news, Love. Mom is dead."

"She's what?" Jacinda asked in mock horror. "When? How?"

"A few days ago. They think it was suicide."

Jacinda reached deep to find her inner actress. She walked over to the husband she now found so repulsive, wrapped her arms around him, and asked, "Are you okay?" The weight of Gregory's body was crushing. It was all she could do not to fall backwards onto the couch. She struggled to remain balanced, and continued to hug him.

"I don't know if I'm okay or not," Gregory admitted.

"What about your dad? How is he?"

"I haven't been able to get a hold of him," Gregory lied. "Jacinda, I have so much I need to tell you." Gregory walked away from Jacinda, and sat on the opposite end of the couch. He placed his head in his hands, and fixed his eyes on the carpet. "I've been lying to you, Jacinda. Everything has been a lie."

Is this it? she wondered. *Is he confessing? Could he be?* A confession was the last thing she expected to hear from him, and she was completely unprepared for his honesty. Suddenly, she remembered their condo was bugged with listening devices.

"I know," said Jacinda.

"You do?" asked Gregory. He looked surprised. Jacinda walked to the kitchen drawer and pulled out a pen and piece of paper.

"Yes, I know all about her." As she spoke, she scribbled a note, and walked towards Gregory. "I know you still talk to your ex. I've seen the phone records." Before Gregory could protest, she shoved the note in front of him. It simply read: **They can hear us-- listening devices.**

*****

Lyla and Kyler were playing with toys on the living room floor when Carl arrived home from work.

"Where's the van?" asked Carl.

"Jill took Keith to the airport, but she's not coming back."

"What do you mean she's not coming back?" asked Carl.

"She decided the email she sent would ensure her safety. She said if anything happens to her, Keith, or Jacinda, the link to all the evidence would be sent to every news outlet, blog, forum, and email in the country. I think she's feeling too confident. She has no idea what they're capable of."
Carl looked at Lyla, certain he misunderstood. "So she just went home?"

"That's what she said. She told me we would be able to pick up the van. She left it at the airport, and took a cab to the bakery to get her car."

"So, how do we get the computer to her once Jacinda returns?" Carl asked.

"She has a plan for that, too. She said to just pretend like you're mowing the lawn. When you go to the door to collect the payment, you can slip her the laptop with the clipboard."

"She really thinks she has it all figured out, doesn't she?" Carl asked.

"I couldn't talk her out of it. Believe me, I tried."

Carl placed the grocery bags on the counter. "Well then, I guess I probably bought too much food."

Lyla smiled. "It will get eaten. With Kyler around, there is no such thing as too much food. What would you like me to cook?" she asked, knowing she had no idea how to cook. Carl looked at her like she'd just asked a ridiculous question.

"What do I want you to cook? Nothing. No ma'am, I'm cooking dinner."

Lyla grinned. "You can cook?"

"As a matter of fact, I can. What, do you think that just because I'm a man I can't cook?"

Lyla looked embarrassed. "I didn't mean…"

Carl let her off the hook. "I'm just giving you a hard time. Most people assume I can't cook, but I've been single for a while; I've learned a thing or two."

Lyla's embarrassment eased. "Single for a while? Were you married?"

"I was."

"Did something happen to her?"

"Yes."

"I'm so sorry," Lyla said, regretting asking the question.

"Nothing serious. She just went crazy."

"Crazy?" Lyla repeated, looking concerned.

"She fell in love with her boss. You've never met

her boss. If you had, you'd know her going crazy is really the only explanation." Lyla giggled, and immediately apologized.

"Why do you always apologize?" Carl asked.

"The way you said it was funny, but I know it must also be hurtful, so I shouldn't have laughed." Carl looked at her a long moment before smiling.

"It was a long time ago, Lyla. I'm over it. In fact, she's the one who helped me rescue Jill. She's Maggie of Maggie's bakery." Carl smiled at her. "You're very concerned about people's feelings."

"Everyone should be concerned about other people's feelings, shouldn't they?"

Carl nodded. "I suppose, but you're *really* concerned. Concerned to the point that you are afraid to say anything."

Lyla pushed her shoulders back. "I'm not afraid. I mean, not really. I wouldn't say I was afraid." She was babbling, and Carl found it adorable.

"Do you like steak and potatoes?" Carl asked. He began pulling groceries out of the bag.

"I love steak!" Lyla said, before looking at the toddler. "I don't know if Kyler will eat steak though; he's a pretty picky eater." Carl just smiled and lifted a jar of spaghetti sauce and a package of noodles out of the bag.

"How did you know?"

"I listen," Carl said. "I heard he's on a spaghetti kick." Lyla smiled. "Is there anything I can do to help?"

"Sure, why don't you boil some water for the spaghetti, and I'll go fire up the grill for our steaks."

Lyla looked over at Kyler playing with his toys on the floor. He seemed so happy—so content. She too felt happy, and, even more amazing, she felt safe.

"You know what?" Carl said. "Let's feed Kyler, and then we'll all go outside while I grill the steaks. It's a beautiful evening, and I bet the little tyke could use some fresh air."

"I have an even better idea," Lyla said. "We have leftover spaghetti in the fridge. I'll warm it up in the microwave, and he can eat his dinner outside now. That way, we can enjoy every last moment of sunlight."

Carl looked at Kyler, then back at Lyla. "That sounds perfect."

*****

Livingston sat alone in the editing room, crafting his masterpiece. It was his job to introduce BARAchip to the country via *Your Nation Now.* He only had one shot. He had to show the American public the chip was not in their best interest, but a way for the government to gain complete control. He needed to convey the chip had absolutely nothing to do with child recovery, and everything to do with world domination.

America wasn't ready to learn about the New World Order. All of that would have to wait. For now, he simply had to plant a seed of doubt in the minds of the viewers. He uploaded videos he'd found on the internet that warned against the chip. He carefully put the warnings together in a format that was very similar to a news package. Tonight, the world wouldn't learn all about BARAchip, but they would learn far more about it than The Brotherhood intended. The Brotherhood would go into crisis mode once the video aired, and that brought Livingston joy.

He'd decided he couldn't keep George in the newsroom forever. He already had a friend secure a hotel room in his friend's name, and drop the key off at the station. Before the video even aired, George and Livingston would be on their way to the hotel. There, they would devise a plan to move forward. Ordinarily, Livingston would stay with Andy, but he couldn't risk exposing Andy. He didn't trust George, or his state of mind, so he had to keep George as far away from The Resistance as possible.

Once the American public knew about the dangers of BARAchip, they needed to know that evil dominated the music industry. If everything George had said was true, Americans needed to know their minds were being poisoned, and their children were being desensitized. *Could they really conjure demons into the music? How much of what George said was true?* Livingston's curiosity was at an all time high.

Livingston put the final touches on his BARAchip story before taking the tape to the control room. Bertha yanked the tape out of Livingston's hand.

"It airs in forty seconds. I didn't think you were going to have it finished," she said.

"It's all cued up and ready to go," Livingston assured her, before turning to leave.

"I'll just have to trust you on that," said Bertha as she disappeared back into the control room.

Livingston stopped by the conference room, stuck

his head in, and said, "George, let's go."

George was slouched over in his chair. Livingston's heart skipped a beat. *They couldn't have gotten to him already.* George snored loudly. *Thank God,* Livingston thought. *He's just sleeping.* Livingston raised his voice. "George, lets go. Now!"

George opened his eyes and looked around the room. It was clear he was a little disoriented. He opened his mouth to ask Livingston a question, but Livingston put up a finger to silence him. "Now, George, if you want to live, you have twenty seconds to get out of that chair and into my car." Livingston double-checked his briefcase to make sure he had the tape of George's testimony before both men headed to the car.

*****

Lucio sat speechless as the anti-BARAchip story aired live across the nation. His expression turned from confusion to twisted rage. The veins in his forehead visibly throbbed, and his face was a furious shade of crimson.

"Call Jarrod Kabbul. Tell him he must not mention BARAchip! It can no longer be introduced as a child protective device. If he so much as mentions it, nobody will trust him. Kill George Dittmeir and

Rob Livingston, but not before you bring them to me. I want to watch them suffer before they die. They will both regret the day they crossed us.

Lucio's staff stood on pins and needles, awaiting their next order. He stood and crashed his fists down on his desk, "Now! Do it now!"

*****

Lyla and Carl sat at the picnic table in Carl's backyard. The grill was heating up, and Kyler was inhaling the spaghetti that sat on the plate in front of him. "You look like a spaghetti monster," Lyla said to the beautiful toddler.

Kyler giggled and held up his spaghetti-stained hands. "Grrrr," he said between fits of laughter. Something flashed behind his eyes, and it was clear he had an idea. "Ticko monner," Kyler said, hoping Lyla would play the game.

"No way, angel boy. I'm not coming near you until we've cleaned you up!"

Carl stood up. "I forgot the best part!" He walked towards his back gate and returned, pushing a small jeep.

"What is it?" Lyla asked.

"It's a motorized jeep. It's for the little tyke. He

loves playing outside, but doesn't have any proper outdoor toys. Besides, he's what? Two? It's time he learns how to drive." As soon as Kyler saw the candy-apple red jeep, his spaghetti was forgotten. Lyla had never seen him move so quickly.

"Dar!" Kyler said, excitedly clapping his hands.

"Not just a car," Carl assured him. "It's a Jeep. A man's vehicle!"

"Deep," Kyler repeated.

"Yup, Jeep, and it's all yours. Go on, get in; I'll show you how to drive." Lyla stood to join them.

"Are you sure it's safe?"

"Of course it's safe. He can't go very fast." Lyla looked unconvinced. "Get on in, buddy. You just take that foot and push that pedal." Before Carl could finish, Kyler was halfway across the yard. Squeals of excitement filled the backyard.

"No, honey, the fence!" Lyla warned, but she was too late. Kyler plowed the Jeep into the fence. Lyla ran to Kyler, praying he was okay. By the time she caught up to him, he had a grin that stretched from ear to ear.

"Gin, Gin!" Kyler insisted. Lyla relaxed and let herself smile.

"Again? You want to drive again?"

"Gin!" Kyler repeated, as he turned the steering wheel from side to side. Carl walked over and lifted up the Jeep, not bothering to remove Kyler beforehand.

He turned the toy around and said, "There you go, buddy. It's all you."

It didn't take Kyler long to learn how to avoid hitting the fences. He became a master at steering. Lyla and Carl ate their steaks without taking their eyes off of Kyler, who was having the time of his life.

"He really loves it," Lyla said. "I don't think I've ever seen him have this much fun."

Carl smiled. "He's just finally able to be a kid. It's good for him." Lyla didn't know how to respond. It was true, Kyler had never really gotten to do the things other children did. He had been so protected that even the swings had been prohibited. When they had gone to the park, it was to watch other children play. Kyler had been a spectator, and, looking back, Lyla realized how cruel it truly was.

She had just wanted Kyler to get fresh air, and thought it was important for him to get out of the apartment. She had thought playing in the sandbox with the other children was enough, but he must have been longing to swing on the swings and slide down the slides. Without realizing it, tears formed in her eyes.

"What? What is it?" Carl asked, concern evident in his voice.

"I've deprived him of so much," Lyla said through tears.

"You didn't deprive him of anything, Lyla. You protected him. If it wasn't for your bravery and love, he'd be dead right now." Carl realized he'd chosen the wrong words when he saw her body tense at the word *dead*. She began crying even harder.

"He's fine, Lyla. Look at him. He's having the time of his life. He hasn't stopped smiling since he got in that Jeep. He's a natural. He only hit the fence once. You saved him, Lyla. Now he's free to be whatever he wants to be. By the skills he's exhibited this evening, I'd say he might grow up to be a NASCAR driver."

Lyla wiped her eyes and giggled. "Stop," she said, still giggling.

"No, I mean it," Carl continued. "Look at those skills. He's barely two-and-a-half, and he's operating that Jeep like he's at least five. He's years ahead of where he should be. Look at him. He's a natural!" With that, the Jeep hummed loudly and crawled to a stop.

"Go!" Kyler ordered, but the Jeep remained motionless.

Carl stood and walked towards the toddler. He bent down on his knee and pressed the pedal with his hand. "You wore it out, buddy! We have to recharge the battery."

"Baddy?" Kyler repeated, making it sound like a question.

"Yes, battery. Do you want to help me charge it?" Carl didn't wait for a response. He pushed the Jeep to the back porch, and retrieved a cord from his car. Walking back through the gate, he held up the cord. "This will recharge the battery, and you'll be zipping around here by morning."

"Now," Kyler said, before jumping back into the driver's seat.

"Sorry, little guy, it's got to charge." Carl said.

"So do you," Lyla said, as she plucked Kyler out of the Jeep. "You need a bath and sleep. You look exhausted."

"Dive," Kyler said, as he arched his body and tried to wiggle out of Lyla's arms.

"You can drive until your little heart is content tomorrow. Tonight, you need to sleep." Lyla looked at Carl. "Thank you so much for everything. The steak, the Jeep—just everything. You didn't have to do all of this. You probably won't believe me, but this is the most fun I've ever had in my entire life."

Carl smiled. "You're right, I don't believe you."

"Well, it is. I can't thank you enough."

Carl waved off her praise. "You don't have to thank me. I should be thanking you. I haven't had this much fun in a long time. Why don't you go put him in the bathtub, and I'll clean up."

"No, you don't have to do that. Let me put him to bed and I'll clean up."

"Don't be ridiculous," Carl said. "Put him down and once he's asleep, you can finally just relax."

CHAPTER 11

Livingston and George sat in the backseat of a taxi, heading towards the hotel. Livingston decided driving his own car was too risky. Neither man said a word. Livingston was deep in thought about the ramifications of his story, and that such a betrayal would mean certain death. George seemed to be in shock, still shaken from his experience at the grove. George's cell phone rang, bringing them both back to the present. George answered.

"Hello." He was silent for a moment before saying, "Brenda, you can't contact me for a while. I can't explain."

Livingston grabbed his cell phone and threw it out the window. "I didn't even think about your phone. It would have led them right to us." George sat in silence. "George," Livingston said, trying to get his attention. "George." George slowly turned his head, and his terror-filled eyes locked with Livingston's.

"Brenda. Will they hurt my girlfriend? What about my daughter, Susie?"

*****

Keith was exhausted, and while he'd never considered his tiny apartment home, it was the next best thing. He never thought the tiny bed would feel so comfortable, but after sleeping on Carl's couch, the bed felt luxurious. He had been told to return to his internship at *Your Nation Now*. Bertha sent him an email, scolding him for taking a vacation. She'd attached a picture of him on a beach. *I know you were in Cancun*, she'd written in the email. **I should fire you, but the internship is almost over. Sending you home would cause more trouble than it's worth, but don't expect any more favors.**

Of course, Keith hadn't been to Cancun. He'd never been on a beach like the one in the picture. He could tell the picture had been altered. Someone had him a lifeline. Better that Bertha think he had sneaked away to Cancun than know he was on a mission to expose The Brotherhood. It was all so unbelievable.

Before returning to his apartment, he'd had the taxi take him straight to Andy's. He'd left the edited footage to keep it safe. If The Brotherhood ransacked Keith's apartment, they'd find nothing suspicious. His tracks were covered. With the Cancun ruse, he felt even more confident about his safety. *Bertha thinks I went to Cancun. That's awesome!* he thought, impressed by The Resistance and their methods.

As he folded his laptop to place it on the nightstand, his safe cell rang. For a moment, Keith considered not even answering it. He was exhausted, and figured whatever it was could wait until the morning. However, his sleepiness would never beat out his curiosity. "Hello," Keith said, answering on the third ring.

"Keith, it's Andy. Listen to me. Don't say anything. There is a very good chance your apartment is bugged. I want you to simply listen. Your response should sound like you're talking to your mom. Sound casual."

"Hey, Mom. Listen, I know I haven't called in a while. I've just been busy."

"That's good," Andy said. "Keep it up. I just got off the phone with Livingston. The BARAchip propaganda has been squashed. But it's a tiny victory. There's so much more that needs to be exposed."

Keith was just about to ask how the story had been squashed, when he remembered he was supposed to be talking to his mother. "Like what?"

"How would you like an internship at Louden Records in New York City?"

"What?"

"If it's the story of a lifetime you want, you'll get it at Louden. We have an insider there. He's a PR executive for the company. Livingston talked to a mutual friend and got his number. He's on board with taking you on as an intern. We're hoping you can use your talent as a reporter to piece together a story."

"Mom, that sounds great, but my internship is here in D.C. I'm interning at *Your Nation Now* until August. I can't possibly fly all the way home for a birthday party."

Andy chuckled. "You're not very good at improvisation, are you? Birthday party? I've got it all set up. Your plane leaves tomorrow morning at 8 A.M. You're taking Transcon Airlines from Dulles to JFK. A man named Eric Fisher will be by the baggage claim to pick you up. I've described you to him. He'll be wearing a suit and fedora so you can spot him in case he misses you. He'll fill you in on the rest."

Keith sat up in bed and placed his feet on the floor. "Mom, you can't be serious."

"As serious as a heart attack. Once he explains everything to you, you'll thank me."

"Mom, I can't leave. What about my internship here?"

"It's all been taken care of."

"Are you sure?" Keith asked.

"Everything is under control. Mr. Fisher will explain things once you arrive."

"All right. I guess I'll see you soon." Keith paused and then said, "I love you too, Mom," before hanging up the phone.

*****

Jacinda and Gregory strolled hand in hand down the streets of D.C. Touching him sickened her, but she was sure they were being watched. She had to appear as if everything was normal in case they were under surveillance. It was crucial she played the role of a devoted wife. "Gregory, they're watching us. You know that, right?"

"I know," Gregory responded. "How much do you know?"

"Enough," Jacinda replied.

"I've known where Kyler was since the day I met you."

Jacinda wasn't ready for that kind of confession. She stopped in her tracks and faced him. She remembered they were being watched, and continued her stride. "You what?" she asked.

"I knew. I've always known. I lied to you the entire time."

"But why?"

"Because I'm evil."

"You're what?"

"I'm evil. Wicked. Horrible. I did it for BARAchip."
Jacinda continued to walk, refusing to look at Gregory.

"Why are you telling me this?"

"Because I've lied long enough. I regret hurting you. I know I can't take back what I did, but I need you to know why I did it." Forgetting there was a good chance they were being spied on, she turned to

Gregory in anger.

"That's it? You're going to confess everything, and you think that makes it okay?"

Gregory began sobbing. "No, I don't think it will make it okay. I just want you to know what I've done. I want you to know how sorry I am. I want you to know why I did it."

"Okay, Gregory. Why? Why did you do it?"

"I did it for my father. My entire life, I've been groomed to be a senator. I was raised to believe love was a lie, and that love was impossible until our savior was born."

"Your savior?"

"Yes, Lord Maitreya."

"Your father seems to love you. You love your father. What do you mean love was impossible?"

"Our relationship was one of convenience. I obeyed him because he was helping to bring in the age of Lord Maitreya. Only then would true love be possible. The way we act in front of you, and in front of everyone else, is completely different than the way I grew up. It's an act, Jacinda. I've spent my entire life acting."

"Why are you telling me this, Gregory?"

"Because it was a lie."

"How do you know that?"

"Because I fell in love with you, so it had to be a lie. Everything I was taught was a lie. I've used people my entire life. I've been used my entire life, but the love I feel for you is so pure, that I'm sure everything I was told was a lie."

"Who told you love couldn't exist until your savior was born?"

"My father."

"And you believed him?"

"Of course. I had no reason not to. Not until I fell in love with you."

"Gregory, why did you kidnap that child? What were you doing?"

"I was going to trade him for Kyler. I was going to bring Kyler home to you so we could be a family."

"You were taking another child to the slaughter? What about *his* parents, Gregory? Did you ever think about how *his* parents would suffer?"

"No," Gregory admitted, sounding full of shame.

"All I could think about was ending your suffering."

Jacinda looked at him. "He was born, you know. Your savior."

Gregory gripped her hand tightly. Through gritted teeth, he said, "He's *not* my savior. It was all a lie, Jacinda. It had to be."

"But you do know the anti-Christ was born."

"Yes, I figured."

"Then you must know that your buddy Jarrod Kabbul is going to raise him as his own son."

"Yes," Gregory admitted. "I know that, too."

"How do you know Jarrod anyway? You said you were old friends, but you never told me how you met him."

"We grew up together. He was considered royalty in the…"

"Say it, Gregory," Jacinda pressed. "Finish your sentence. He was considered royalty where?"

"In The Brotherhood. Unlike most of The Brotherhood, Jarrod is Illuminati by blood. It's stuff you wouldn't know anything about."

Jacinda couldn't believe Gregory was being so

honest. She expected him to continue his charade, but it was clear he was broken. He truly was a shell of the man he used to be. He seemed desperate. His once charming demeanor was now one of despair. It was obvious he didn't know what to believe. All he knew was that his entire life had been a lie.

"How do I know you're being honest with me, Gregory? How do I know you aren't lying to me right now?"

"Ask me anything. I have nothing left to lose. The only thing I care about in this entire world is you. I don't expect you to love me after what I've done, but I promise you, I will get your son back."

Jacinda didn't dare reveal that she had already found Kyler. She hadn't had time to process Gregory's betrayal of The Brotherhood, or his brutal honesty.

"You're going to prison, Gregory. You know that, right?"

"I do."

"How do you expect to bring me my son while you're in prison?" Gregory began to cry again.

"I don't know. I haven't figured it out. I just know that I will find him. I will play the game. I will earn

The Brotherhood's trust again. I'll find him, Jacinda. I promise you, I'll find him."

In that moment, Jacinda felt an emotion she didn't anticipate—empathy. *After everything he's done to me, I can't feel sorry for him,* she scolded herself, but she did feel sorry for him. She felt sorry for this destroyed man standing beside her. She didn't feel the love she'd once felt. Those feelings were gone, but she felt compassion. They walked past a food market, and she pulled him inside. "I need to use the restroom, I'll be right back."

Her mind was dizzy. It was reeling--spinning in circles. She hadn't prepared for this, and she couldn't handle it on her own. She walked into a bathroom stall, locked the door, and fell to her knees. The stench of urine burned her nose, but she didn't let it distract her. Silently, she prayed. *God, I need guidance. I wasn't counting on this, and I don't know what to do. I know forgiveness is the right thing to do, but I don't know that I'm ready. I don't even know if I should trust him. What do I do, God? What do you want me to do?*

Her mind was overflowing with questions, but it was there, on her knees, on the filthy restroom floor, that she received her answer. She didn't know how she knew, but she knew The Brotherhood would kill him before the week was over. She also knew where he'd be safe—the Mission she'd volunteered at so many times as a child. It was located in Mexico, just across the Texas border. He would be protected there. She may never be able to love him in the same way as before, but at least she could set him on a spiritual path that could quite possibly save his soul.

*****

Lyla sat on the couch and pulled her hair into a ponytail. "Kyler was exhausted," she said to Carl. "He fell asleep before I even finished reading his book."

"What about you?" Carl asked. "Are you ready for bed?"

"No, not yet. It's just been such a wonderful night that I don't want it to end."

Carl smiled, which was something he had done a lot of today. "I know what you mean."

"I hope you don't mind me asking," he said, "but I find your life intriguing. What was it like growing up the way you did?"

Lyla pulled her knees to her chest. "I don't mind you asking."

"I just don't know anything about you. I don't even

know your last name," Carl said.

"It's Rockefeller."

Carl's eyes grew wide. "So you *are* part of the bloodline?"

"No," Lyla assured him. "My mother had her name legally changed to Rockefeller so people would think she was, but she wasn't. She was a liar."

Carl immediately regretted asking the question. "I'm sorry, maybe we should talk about something else."

"No, it's okay. I'm not part of the bloodline, but I've grown up around the Illuminati my entire life. I've seen a lot."

Carl nodded. "I can only imagine."

"Oh, you couldn't possibly," Lyla assured him.

"I'm sorry. You're probably right."

"Please don't be sorry. It's just that most people wouldn't believe me if I told them about my childhood, that's all."

Carl looked into her eyes. "I believe you. I will believe anything you tell me."

Lyla felt warmth spread throughout her body.

Where were these kind people while she was growing up? She had no idea such kindness existed.

"I want to know about you, too," Lyla said. "I mean, if you don't mind sharing."

Carl smiled a warmly. "What do you want to know?"

"Everything. But first, I want to know how you got involved with The Brotherhood."

Carl put his hand on his neck, and leaned his head from side to side in an effort to relieve the tension in his muscles. It was obvious the topic made him uncomfortable.

"I was ambitious," Carl admitted. "I was in the business that happens to be the backbone of the Illuminati. I'm a banker. Without money, the Illuminati would cease to exist. You wouldn't believe the things that go on in the financial world. You couldn't imagine how corrupt it really is." Carl seemed to relax a little, leaning back into the couch. "I had a boss who drove an expensive sports car. He wore expensive Italian suits and lived in a mansion. I knew he couldn't live that kind of lifestyle on his salary or even his commissions. I wanted to be him so badly. I wanted to live that life.

"One day, after work, I went to happy hour with him. He ended up drinking a little too much. We both did. Anyway, I asked him how he could afford everything, and he told me. He saw my hunger—my ambition. The next thing I knew, I was invited to Rhapsody Grove. I was blinded by the lifestyle. I didn't have a care in the world. I continued working for the bank, but I moonlighted as a banker for the financial institution that funds the Illuminati. It's overseas, but has pull with almost every bank here in the States. I was promoted to Vice-President, although I was far too young and inexperienced. I was being paid so well by the Illuminati that my first instinct was to rush out and get the car of my dreams. That's when I was told I wasn't to flaunt the money because people would get suspicious."

Lyla tilted her head. "What about your boss? Didn't he flaunt his money?"

"Yes, but I later found out that his family had been part of The Brotherhood for generations. He came from a very wealthy family. His father had died years earlier, and everyone just assumed he inherited his fortune."

"So then you had to be discreet?" Lyla asked.

"That was the exact word he used, yes," Carl answered.

"My parents used that word a lot, too."

"Livingston tells me that your father is Nicholas Kilmeade. That makes your brother Gregory Kilmeade. Didn't Gregory just win some magazine's contest for most charismatic man of the year?"

"Yes. Never trust charisma. It's deceptive. Lucifer couldn't have accomplished half of what he has without charisma. Think about it, every wicked man you've known in the high ranks of The Brotherhood has probably been charismatic."

Carl thought for a moment, "Now that you mention it." He then looked confused. "Of course, many Christians believe that charisma is a gift that comes from being filled by the Holy Spirit."

"Yes, Lucifer would want you to believe that, wouldn't he? He's deceitful. Lucifer has always been known for his beauty and charisma."

"So are you suggesting that anyone who is charismatic has received that gift from Lucifer and not God?"

"I'm not saying that. I honestly don't know much about it. I haven't gotten that far in my studies of the Bible. It's just an observation. I look at my father and Gregory. I see they've been gifted with charisma, but I can assure you they didn't get that gift from God."

Carl nodded, acknowledging her statement. "I noticed that you call Nicholas your father, but you've never called Gregory your brother."

"I guess that's because I've never met him," Lyla said.

"Is that weird? Is it strange knowing you have a brother you've never met?"

Lyla smiled. "It's actually probably the most normal thing about me."

"So then, you must know a lot about the Illuminati?"

"I know enough to know they're wicked. I also know they rule the world. You're a banker; surely you know they even designed our money."

"Most people don't know that," Carl said. "Not only did they design it, but their plans are all over it."

Lyla tilted her head. "What?"

"Take the twenty-dollar bill, for instance. If you fold it just so, you'll see the twin towers in flames."

"No way."

"It's true; grab that laptop, and put it in the search engine." Lyla leaned over to pick the laptop off of the coffee table.

"Even better," Carl said, as he took a twenty-dollar bill out of his pocket. "I'll show you." Carl folded the bill as he spoke. "Even the fact that it's on the twenty is significant. 9 plus 11, or 9/11, equals twenty." Lyla looked intrigued. When Carl finished folding the bill, he held it up. "Those are the two World Trade Center towers in flames." Lyla leaned forward.

"It is, isn't it?" Carl flipped the bill around.

"Do you recognize that?" Lyla's gaze indicated she didn't recognize what she was looking at. "That's the Pentagon in flames," Carl said.

CHAPTER 12

Keith instantly spotted the man in the suit and fedora as he arrived at baggage claim. He was short, and appeared to be in his mid-fifties. He looked exactly like Keith had imagined someone who worked in the music business would look--flashy. Of course, he didn't expect a public relations executive to dress like a record executive, which threw him for a loop. His fedora was gray, but had a red, paisley tip, which matched his tie. He wore a thick gold chain. Rings adorned his fingers. His eyes were beady, and his face had deep wrinkles. His fedora covered what Keith imagined was a bald head. Keith hesitantly approached the man.

"Are you Mr. Fisher? "

"I am. You must be Keith."

"Yes, sir," Keith replied.

"Keith. I can call you Keith, right?"

"Of course," Keith said, still unsure as to why he was even there.

"I hear you're a reporter."

"A student actually, but, yes, I want to be a reporter."

"Have you ever thought about PR?"

"Not really, but a professor once told me I should consider it as a career."

"You'll see the two career fields aren't all that different. We shape public perception."

"I wouldn't have agreed with that statement until recently," Keith said.

Keith spotted his luggage on the carousel. "That one is mine. I just have the one." Keith pulled it off the conveyer belt, and lifted the handle so he could roll it out of the airport.

"Ever been to the Big Apple, Keith?" Eric asked.

"No, sir."

"Oh, enough with the sir nonsense. Call me Eric. Of course, in front of anyone at Louden, you'll call me Mr. Fisher. You know what, let's just start that now. I don't want you to slip."

"Okay, Mr. Fisher. I was hoping you could explain why I'm here."

"In due time, Keith. By the way, your name is now Keith Smith."

"Why?"

"You're officially in hiding. Are you hungry? Want to grab some lunch? What do you want? Choose anything. New York City has it all, but if you don't mind me making a recommendation, there's this little hole in the wall pizza joint that is to die for. It's magnifico! They have every topping you can imagine: sardines, pineapple, olives, pepperoni, eggplant—you name it."

"Eggplant?" Keith asked. He crinkled his nose in disgust.

"Don't knock it till you've tried it, kiddo."

Kiddo? Keith thought. *Did he seriously just call me kiddo?*

"Sure," Keith said. "Pizza sounds fine."

"I was hoping you'd say that. We can talk more there. I know the owner. Nice guy, but he doesn't speak a lick of English. He stays in the kitchen, so it's private."

"I'm surprised anywhere in New York City is private."

"You can find privacy anywhere with enough money. I slip him a hunny, and he lets me eat in the private room."

"A hunny?" Keith asked.

"Sure, kid, you know, a hundred dollar bill."

"Of course," Keith said before thinking, *I'm really going to hate this place.*

*****

Jacinda dropped her prepaid cell phone into her purse before she entered the news station. Paula Strong was the first person to greet her when she walked through the door.

"Well, she returns," Paula said in a tone that could either be construed as friendly or condescending. Jacinda didn't know how to read her, and frankly, she didn't care. She was there for one reason, and one reason only—to stay in the public eye.

She had to appear as if everything were normal. She feared being alone, and knew it would be harder for The Brotherhood to kill her if she stuck to a very public routine.

"Hi, Paula," Jacinda said. "I love your jacket." Jacinda was not usually one to pay empty compliments, but she didn't have anything else to say to the seasoned reporter. Paula smirked.

"I saw the BARAchip story. It was a joke, right? Surely it was a prank. If you don't get fired over that one, I'll know for sure you're only here because you're Senator Kilmeade's wife."

"Wait, what did you say?" Jacinda asked.

"About what?" replied Paula.

"The BARAchip story--it aired?"

"Well, sure. It's all anyone's been talking about."

Jacinda looked around the newsroom. "Is Jerry here?"

"Jerry? Who is Jerry?"

"Jack. Is Jack here?"

"You mean the editor?" Jacinda was losing patience.

"Yes, the editor. Is he here?"

"I don't know. I haven't seen him. If he's here, he's

probably in an editing bay."

"Thanks, Paula," Jacinda said as she rushed past her.

Jacinda walked as fast as she could without actually running. She knocked three times on the editing room door,before hearing Jerry say, "Come on in." Jacinda opened the door. "Well, look who it is. Mrs. Kilmeade. To what do I owe this honor?"

"Hi, Jerry," Jacinda said, trying to appear collected. She decided she'd skip polite conversation and got right to the point. "Everything is digital, right? Do you have access to last night's show?"

"Sure, man. I can pull it up, why do you ask?"

"I need to see the BARAchip story. Remember, the story you were putting together for Paula Strong?"

"Sure," Jerry said. "But they never ran that story."

"Did you see the broadcast last night?"

"Can't say I did, but you know me, man, they've always got me tucked away in this little cage." Jerry replied.

"Can you please pull it up? I want to see it."

Jacinda entered the dimly lit editing room and

closed the door. She took a seat next to Jerry, as he pounded away at the keyboard. She saw the opening of the news broadcast. Jerry turned the knob, fast-forwarding through the opening credits.

"There!" Jacinda said. "Rewind it a little. It's right there." Jerry and Jacinda sat in silence while they watched video of a needle inserting a chip into a hand. The text above the hand read **BARAchip**. The video was a series of Illuminati symbols: an owl, a pyramid, and the all-seeing eye. The symbols began flashing too fast to process. An image of the chip was once again on the screen. The text above the chip simply read: **mark of the beast.**

Jacinda and Jerry sat in silence, both trying to process what they had just witnessed.

"Well, ain't that something?" Jerry said, finally breaking the silence. "If that story didn't call a spade a spade, man. That was awesome."

Jacinda looked at Jerry. "So then, you didn't edit it?"

"I wish I could take credit for it, man, but no. I didn't have anything to do with it. It's gottta be a joke, right?"

Jacinda nodded. "I'm sure it was."

"Someone's gunna get fired over that one, man.

That was some heavy stuff."

"Thanks, Jerry. I'll see you in a little bit," Jacinda said before exiting the editing room. She stood in the hall and wondered who was responsible for airing the story.

She hadn't had time to watch the broadcast the night before. She'd been too busy putting Gregory on a private jet to Mexico. Father Garcia had agreed to let Gregory seek refuge at the mission. It hadn't been a hard sell. Father Garcia didn't keep up with American politics, and was far too busy to keep up with American current events. She felt guilty she didn't tell him the whole story, but felt God would understand. She didn't fear for Father Garcia or anyone else at the mission. Gregory wasn't a threat to anyone in his current state of mind. Nobody could fake that kind of remorse. He was broken, and she knew the mission welcomed broken people. After all, only Jesus could make the broken whole again.

She only hoped the cash she'd given him would buy off the Mexican authorities. The pilot of the private jet had no problem pocketing the money, and she hoped the Mexican authorities would be just as corrupt. Growing up, she'd heard about the corruption of Mexican custom agents. She felt ashamed, praying for corruption, but knew it was the only chance Gregory had for survival.

*****

Keith and Eric Fisher sat in what was perhaps the shadiest private room Keith had ever seen. The tiny dining room looked more like a closet with a table and four chairs. Tape adhered an unframed poster to a concrete wall.

"Mobsters own this place, right?" Keith asked.

"Mobsters?" repeated Mr. Fisher.

"Never mind," Keith replied. He scolded himself for voicing his every thought.

Keith looked up and saw a beautiful Italian girl in her late teens enter the private dining area. She wasn't wearing a server's uniform. She was dressed casually in jeans and a t-shirt. She turned the pad of paper to a blank page, and placed the tip of her pen on the paper.

"Are you ready to order?" the waitress asked.

It was clear Mr. Fisher was familiar with the girl. "Theresa! Where have you been? I've eaten here for the past month and haven't seen you once," he said in his best faux-Italian accent.

"I've been busy with my studies, Mr. Fisher."

"Well, that's good. Study hard. You tell your dad that we have a first-timer here, and he needs to cook to impress."

"Doesn't he always?" Theresa sassed.

"That he does. That he does. Listen, load my pizza up: ham, sausage, bacon, pepperoni, and sardines. You know what, if it ever walked or swam, I want it on my pizza."

Keith was repulsed by Mr. Fisher's order. He wasn't going to voice his opinion this time, but it was disgusting.

"This is my friend, Keith. He's an intern. Hook him up with the best you've got!"

Theresa looked at Keith. "What toppings would you like?"

"Cheese," Keith replied, before turning his eyes to Mr. Fisher for approval. Fisher chuckled.

"I bring him to the pizza joint with the best toppings in town, and the kid just wants cheese! Whatcha gunna do?"

Theresa smiled at Keith. "Are you sure you don't want anything that walked or swam?"

Keith winced. "No, I'm good. It's possible I might

never eat anything that walked or swam ever again. I think I just became a vegetarian." Mr. Fisher let out a belly laugh.

"I like this kid! You like this kid, Theresa? He's a card!" Theresa promised to be back shortly with their order and turned on her heel to leave.

"All right, kid. I know you're probably wondering why you're here."

Keith nodded. "Yes, sir, that question has crossed my mind."

"What do you know about Tony Randall?"

"To be honest, I don't know anything about him. I've never heard of him."

"He's a legend around here. He's a record executive at Louden Records. He's missing. I know he's up to his fedora in The Brotherhood, but he never came back from the grove, and nobody has heard from him."

"Does everyone in this town wear a fedora?" Keith asked. Mr. Fisher stared blankly at Keith.

"What?" Fisher asked.

"Nothing. Okay, so Tony Randall is part of The Brotherhood, and he hasn't returned. Maybe he stopped off at Disneyland. It's only been a day or two."

"Not possible. He's been courting a band for months. He's been dying to sign them. They were supposed to have a *make it or break it* meeting yesterday, but Tony didn't show."

"Has anyone tried to contact him?" Keith asked.

"Of course. What most people don't know is that inside intelligence said he was punished at the grove. The man who witnessed the punishment said he just disappeared. My guess is they whacked him." *This guy is in the mob,* thought Keith. *I can't believe Andy sent me to work with the mob. This is fantastic. What? Was Iraq too safe this time of year?*

"He knew things, Keith. He knew how things were run. What do you know about the music business?"

"Not a lot, sir." Keith admitted.

"Well, I'll educate you. Music is used as a vehicle for the Illuminati."

Keith's ears perked up. *Now we're getting somewhere*, he thought excitedly.

"The Illuminati totally controls the music industry. They use music to a cast a spell over the listener.

Music desensitizes our youth, and most musicians know exactly whose message they're spreading." Keith nodded.

"What do you know about symbols?" asked Mr. Fisher.

"Illuminati symbols?" Keith asked.

"Yeah, Illuminati symbols. Take, for instance, the all-seeing eye. What do you know about that?" Before Keith had a chance to answer, Mr. Fisher continued. "Watch music videos. Look at magazines and award shows. Notice how many musicians cover one eye. They're mocking God. It's a tribute to the sun god, Lucifer. When you get to your apartment, break out your computer and type in *music industry and covered eye.* That's as good a place as any to start. Click on the images. Your computer will be flooded with them."

Keith looked intrigued. "Anything else? Are there any other symbols I should look for?"

"Absolutely. Pyramids. It's not enough to have pyramids in their photo shoots or on their clothes. They actually make the sign of the pyramid with their hands. Type that in your search engine. You'll be surprised."

"Okay, but aside from the symbols, do they pose

any real threat?"

Mr. Fisher looked around the room before leaning towards Keith. "You have no idea how much of a threat they pose."

*****

Livingston sat with George inside their tiny hotel room. His original plan had been to go back to Andy's after he dropped George off at the hotel, but he didn't feel right leaving George alone. George remained pensive. He'd barely said two words since they had arrived at the hotel last night. He'd cried for a while, but then something changed. Maybe he was in a state of shock. He looked void of emotion.

Livingston switched on the television. He was curious to see how the public received his BARAchip story. He watched the national news for thirty minutes with no mention of his story. The news anchor said, "We're going to take you to a live feed of Jarrod Kabbul leaving a California hospital with his wife, Ellie." Livingston watched as a nurse wheeled Ellie Kabbul out of the hospital. Ellie was holding her little bundle of wickedness. Jarrod smiled and waved to the media. The news anchors spoke over the live footage, "That could quite possibly be the new First Baby. Kabbul is leading in the polls, and shows no sign of losing momentum. He's still the frontrunner."

Livingston watched Ellie, knowing she hadn't given birth to the wicked baby she now held in her arms. He wondered how many people in the hospital knew of the charade. The doctor who'd supposedly delivered the baby had to be part of The Brotherhood. The nurse had to be in on it, too.

As the live coverage continued, he heard the anchor say, "Is it possible we're going to get our first glance of baby Kabbul? Yes, it looks like...." Livingston tuned the news anchor out completely, and focused his attention on the video. Ellie Kabbul pulled the blanket off the baby, revealing the anti-Christ. He was stunning.

The male news anchor continued, "We've just been told the happy couple named their son Raider. Raider Maylot Kabbul."

The female's voice chimed in, "Raider Maylot, that's an interesting name." The video showed the family being transferred to a car. "We don't seem to be getting audio, but I was just told that Maylot is actually Ellie's maiden name."

"Well, there you have it," the female reporter continued. "Jarrod Kabbul's baby has been born, and he's absolutely beautiful. Congratulations to the happy family."

CHAPTER 13

Jacinda stepped out of the news station to call Livingston. She walked down the street, trying to keep her distance from everyone. After dialing his number, the phone rang three times. "Pick up, Rob. Come on, pick up!" Livingston answered on the fourth ring. "Rob, hey, it's Jacinda. I just saw the BARAchip story. I couldn't believe it. Did Keith pull that off?"

"No," Livingson responded. "I did."

"You? Rob, you won't be able to show your face again. They'll kill you."

"They'll have to find me first."

"Okay, the BARAchip story was crushed. We won, right? That's all we had to do. We had to stop BARAchip from being introduced."

"Actually, it was introduced."

Jacinda rolled her eyes. "You know what I mean; it was cast in a negative light. We're not going to have a line of people wanting it implanted in their children. But I think most people thought it was a joke--a prank."

"Better they think it's a joke than an innocent device that will locate their children in case of abduction."

"True," Jacinda agreed. "We're done, right?"

"Done? You do realize BARAchip was just the beginning. Once Kabbul enters the White House, it will be the beginning of the New World Order. Not only that, but he's literally raising the anti-Christ. The anti-Christ will be in the White House. Our fight has just begun. We won a battle with the BARAchip story, but there's an entire war to be fought."

"So, what now?" Jacinda asked. "Do we try to stop the people from electing Kabbul?" Jacinda asked, temporarily forgetting that the people's votes had never mattered.

"It's not that simple, Jacinda. Kabbul is going to be our next president whether the people elect him or not. We have to accept that as a given. But what we can do is expose the Illuminati and The Brotherhood. Not all at once, of course. Nobody is ready to have that kind of truth revealed all at once. It won't be believable. We'll be labeled nuts and conspiracy theorists. No, we have to expose them a little bit at a time."

"But you can't expose anyone, Rob. You can't even show your face."

"That's not true. I'm in the process of starting an online news site that will move servers every couple of days. Nobody will know where I'm broadcasting from or how to find me. You, on the other hand, can still walk around freely. You can be an insider in the news business. I'm afraid those days are over for me."

Jacinda sighed. "I'm not staying here, Rob. I'm going back to my son. I've already been away from him for too long. I can't stand it. I miss him more than you could possibly imagine. I needed to ensure it was going to be safe for me to announce I found him. I want to live a normal life. I don't want to have to keep my son stashed away forever."

"Jacinda, from the day The Illuminati chose you, your chance at a normal life was destroyed. You have to accept that. You life became public the day you married Senator Kilmeade." Rob paused. "Speaking of Kilmeade, he's missing." Jacinda remained silent. Livingston repeated himself. "Did you hear me? He's missing."

"How do you know that?" she asked.

"He had a court hearing today. He didn't show up."

Jacinda wanted to tell him that she'd sent him to safety, but he'd never understand. In Livingston's eyes, Gregory was evil personified. Livingston didn't see the broken man who had been waiting at the condo when she'd returned from California. He wouldn't believe that Gregory was remorseful. He'd simply think he was manipulating her. Jacinda's decision to send Gregory to the Mexican mission was something she wasn't ready to divulge.

*****

Mr. Fisher led Keith down the hallway of a high-rise apartment building.

"This will be home for a while, kiddo." He stopped in front of a door and fished a key out of his pocket. "Before we go inside, I want to warn you, someone's in there."

"Someone?" Keith asked nervously.

"Just a musician. She's a former Louden artist who wants to tell you what she's experienced. She just wants to give you an idea of what you're walking into. Remember, you're free to leave at any time, but I'm offering you access. I'm letting you see what goes on inside the music industry so that you can tell a story. I'm just exposing you to the truth. I pray you use that information to shed light on the darkness that shrouds the music industry, but I'm not forcing you to do anything. We're clear, right?"

Keith never removed his eyes from the door. He couldn't wait to see who was waiting on the other side. "Yes, sir. We're clear. I'm ready."

Mr. Fisher opened the door. Inside sat a small-framed girl in her mid twenties, whom Keith recognized as a Tula. Tula had dominated the charts as recently as five years ago. She had been one of his favorite musicians in high school. She'd been on top of the world before virtually disappearing into obscurity. Keith felt star-struck. He was standing in front of Tula. Part of him wanted to scream like a twelve-year-old girl and ask her for an autograph. That wasn't entirely true. All of him wanted to scream like a twelve-year-old girl and beg for her autograph.

Tula stood to greet him. She looked much shorter in real life than on television and in pictures.

"Hi, I'm Tyla." She said. "It's nice to meet you." Keith puffed out his chest in a ridiculous display of machismo.

"I'm a huge fan. It's an honor," he said. He was grateful he didn't trip over his tongue. "You just introduced yourself as Tyla, but I thought your name was Tula," Keith said, clearly confused.

"I'll get to that," Tyla explained.

"Sit down, kiddo," Mr. Fisher said, as he pointed toward a chair. "I wanted to introduce you to a musician who was a part of the Illuminati machine, but later turned her back on the organization. Tyla is a product of the modern music industry. Pay close attention to Tyla's story, because you're going to see firsthand how artists like Tyla are created."

Again with the Tula/Tyla confusion, Keith thought. Mr. Fisher continued, "Tyla is taking a huge risk by speaking to you and revealing her secrets. I hope you realize and respect that."

"I do, sir." Keith replied.

"Good," said Fisher. "Tell her why she can trust you. Tell her why you're here."

Keith looked at Mr. Fisher. "With all due respect, I don't really know why I'm here. I was told to get on a plane, and that I had a new internship, but the details have been pretty vague."

Mr. Fisher smiled. "Is that all they told you? I heard

you wanted to blow the story of The Brotherhood wide open. I was told you were a reporter who was working on the story of a lifetime. Here's the thing—you can't tell the story of The Brotherhood or the Illuminati without understanding how they control America through the music industry. This is ground zero for their message. The entertainment industry is the training ground for Illuminati puppets, and at the end of the day, that's all entertainers really are—puppets. They're puppets or slaves. Sometimes both. You have people much higher in the echelons pulling the strings.

"Sitting before you is a former puppet. She has agreed to tell you her story. After hearing her story, you'll be given access to Louden Records as my intern. If anybody asks, you are a handler from the West Coast. Tell 'em you're exploring your options, capiche?"

Keith nodded, "Capiche. I mean, yes. I understand." Keith's eyes kept making their way back to Tyla or Tula—he was so confused. She looked different in person, almost elflike. She wasn't all made up, and looked very much like a normal girl. That surprised him. She was still beautiful, but not the larger-than-life pop star he was used to seeing in pictures and on television.

Tyla reclaimed her spot on the couch. "First of all.

Do you even know who I am?" Tyla asked Keith.

Keith struggled to hide his excitement. *Of course I know who you are,* he thought. *Are you kidding me? You're Tula! Everyone knows who you are!* Keith decided against his internal ranting and simply said, "Yes." Keith felt proud of his use of restraint. "I've followed your career."

"Oh, so then you noticed my career went from super-hot to sub-zero in less than a month?"

"I did notice that you kind of disappeared," he admitted.

Tyla smiled. "I didn't disappear, I reappeared. Myself, I mean. The real me reappeared. The spell was broken."

"The spell?"

"Yes. Like an actual spell; I know it sounds crazy. I came from nothin', Keith. My name is Tyla, not Tula. Tula was my stage name—my alter ego or familiar. One day nobody had ever heard of Tula, and the next it was a household name. It all happened pretty quickly. Since I was a little girl, I always wanted to be like Whitney Houston or Madonna. I always pretended that my hairbrush was a microphone. I sang in front of my mirror for hours. I'd always wanted to be famous. I would have done anything to be famous—anything.

"I worked as a waitress, and spent every penny I made recording demo tapes. I was only sixteen, and the producers couldn't believe how ambitious I was. I mean, there I was, a little girl, using her own money to record demos. Anyway, one day I walked in for a recording session, really excited about a song I'd just written. I couldn't wait to lay down my vocals. It's all I could think about all week. Sorry, I'm getting off track. So, I walked into the studio, and you'll never believe who I saw: Tony Randall. *The* Tony Randall.

"He was sittin' there in a power suit with all his jewelry. I couldn't believe I was in the same room as Tony Randall. All I could think about was how I'd get his attention. I wondered who he was there to check out. I hoped against hope that I could at least slip him a demo. I was digging in my purse, looking for a demo tape, when I noticed he was still watchin' me.

"He stood up and said, 'You must be Tyla.' I nearly fainted, I'm not even lyin'. I nearly keeled over and died. I straightened my back, stuck out my hand, and said, 'Yes, sir, I'm Tyla January; it's nice to meet you.' He let my name roll off his tongue a few times. 'Tyla,' he said a few different ways before saying, 'Yes, I like it. I heard you can sing.'

Angela Caldwell

I leaned back against the wall, because I didn't trust myself not to collapse. I would have, I promise. I literally pinched myself to make sure it was real. It hurt, so I knew I wasn't dreamin'.

"First, he asked if me and my parents wanted to go to dinner. I told him that both of my parents worked two jobs, three sometimes if there were openings. I let him know that I didn't need my parents' permission, and we could go to dinner alone if he wanted. Tony said he understood, that his mom worked three jobs too, and how would I like it if my parents could both quit their jobs? I told him I'd love it, who wouldn't? He told me he could make my dreams come true, but I had to want it. He told me I had to really want it, and I did. I wanted it more than anything.

"Things moved really quickly after that. Within a week, me and my parents were in Tony Randall's office. I was signin' a recording contract. He offered me a $200,000 advance, and my parents couldn't have been more excited. He said that $200,000 would be chump change once my album debuted. Then, he turned to my parents and wrote them a check for $300,000, and told them to stop workin' so hard. Half a million dollars total: do you have any idea how much half a million dollars was to my family at the time?

"After that, I don't know who was more excited, me or my parents. Tony told my parents he would make sure I was paired up with the best writers, managers, and publicists. He told them that, because I was so young, I would be assigned a handler. My handler, Lori, drove me to interviews, helped set up appointments, and was just supposed to help look after me.

"She introduced me to my producer and everything. I'm sorry. It's so hard to tell this story, because I don't remember everything. Lori gave me a pill. She told me it would help me relax. I took it and didn't think another thing about it.

"The producer put me in front of the microphone, told me to lift my arms and invite the creative spirit in, and let the spirit sing through me. I didn't know if he meant my creative spirit or what. I just did what he told me. That's when things got really foggy. I was aware of everything around me, and I was singing, but it wasn't really me who was singing. I mean, it was me, but it wasn't me. I know that probably makes no sense.

"I never said anything to my parents. It never really bothered me. I heard the song we recorded, and it was beyond anything I could ever imagine coming out of my mouth. I sounded like a superstar. Before I knew it, I had a stylist, money, and fans. I had fans! Everybody knew who I was. I mean, they knew me as Tula, but they still knew me."

Tyla finally paused. Keith looked over at Mr. Fisher, and back to Tyla.

"I mean, that's a great story, but aside from your handler giving you drugs, I don't really get how this is connected to The Brotherhood." Tyla gave him a knowing look. "That's because I haven't gotten to the good part."

Keith's ears perked up, "The good part?"

"Well, actually, I guess I should have said the bad part."

"I'm listening," Keith said.

"I didn't tell you about the programming facility. I didn't really remember this part until after I escaped the business, but once I got out, my memories started returning. This is going to sound crazy, but I was sent away to a programming facility for about four months before I recorded that amazing track that I told you about. I didn't remember it being a training facility, but that's only because they wiped away my memories of the place."

"But you remember it now?" Keith asked.

"I remember more than I'd like to remember. I

don't want to go into detail, because it's embarrassing, but I was tortured. I was tortured in ways that I don't even feel comfortable repeating."

"Why?" Keith asked her. "Why would they torture you?"

"They had to break me down before they built me into a superstar. I had to completely lose touch with reality before my alter egos could share my body— before Tula could share my body."

*****

Jacinda entered her condo and took a cautious look around. She knew there were listening devices scattered throughout, and used that to her advantage. After all, The Brotherhood didn't know she was aware of them, so she was able to put on a show.

Pulling her new, prepaid phone out of her purse, she dialed Jill's number. Jill had also recently purchased a few prepaid phones. Jill answered on the first ring, but sounded a little distracted. "Are you okay?" Jill immediately asked Jacinda.

"Peachy, how about you?" she asked, sounding as casual as possible. Jacinda could hear voices in the background. "Where are you?"

"I'm at the supermarket, so I'm free to chitchat.

Lucky timing. Well, unless they have listening devices behind the soup cans. I wouldn't put it past them."

"Work went well," Jacinda offered without being asked. She wanted whoever was listening to her conversation to think she was settling back into her normal life. "So, weirdest thing—Gregory was here yesterday when I got home."

"Gregory? Jacinda, tell me you're kidding."

"No. As you know, he's being charged with kidnapping, but I'm sure he'll beat the charges."

"Jacinda, say something whimsical to let me know you're okay."

"Whimsical," Jacinda said.

"Are they listening?"

"Yes," Jacinda replied. She kept her tone casual.

"Oh, I see. Well, then I'll talk. For now, I think I'm safe. Every six hours, each person on that email list gets an email from a different country. For all they know, if anything happens to me, there are people all over the world who will expose them with the push of a button. I'm sure they're watching, and I'm sure they're listening, but I'm not giving them anything to write home about. I'm keeping things pretty low key. Were you able to get Gregory's computer?"

"Yes, and I found the cutest matching hat," Jacinda said, hoping Jill would follow. "I just knew you would have to have it. I can't wait to send it to you. I was kind of thinking of waiting till your birthday, but the entire outfit will probably be completely out of style by then."

"Wow, you're pretty good at this," Jill said.

"Yes, you know how crazy I am about shopping. We have the cutest boutiques here. There's stuff you simply can't get in your hopelessly fashion-backward part of the world. I'll send you all of your new goodies tomorrow."

"Great! Did I tell you I'm having my house swept for cameras and listening devices tomorrow? The guy is phenomenal. He calls himself The Exterminator. Get it, because of the bugs?"

Jacinda rolled her eyes, "I got it. Wait, so you went home? Are you sure that's a good idea?"

"Look, Jacinda, they know I know. They also know that if I die, that list, along with the other proof, will be blasted all over the internet. I'm installing my own cameras. I'll email them the feed from different servers every day. I'll let them think that I have people all over the world watching. They won't dare touch me."

"I hope you're right," Jacinda said, before adding, "If it rains, the entire party will be ruined. I hope you have a backup plan, like a tent or moving the party indoors."

"Was that code, Jacinda? Or are you still doing that nonsensical, fake conversation so they have no idea what we're talking about?"

"Both."

CHAPTER 14

Carl walked in the door from work to find Lyla cutting lettuce.

"I hope you don't mind," she said. "I'm just making a salad to go with the leftover steaks from last night."

"Leftover steaks," Carl said, before crinkling his nose.

"We can do something else; I just figured that would be easiest."

"I have stuff to make hamburgers. Let's just put those on the grill."

"Do you grill everything?" she asked.

"It's just a nice evening, and the little tyke had so much fun speeding around in his Jeep yesterday."

"Ah, yes," Lyla said. "It's all he's wanted to do all day. I haven't been able to get him out of it. Even when I plugged it in to charge, he insisted on sitting in the driver's seat and making vroom, vroom noises." Carl found the story amusing.

"Where is he, anyway?"

As if on cue, Kyler peeked around the corner of the counter and said, "Boo!"

"There he is," Carl said. Carl walked over and hoisted Kyler above his head. Kyler giggled uncontrollably.

As soon as Carl put him down, Kyler raised his little arms and said, "Gin!"

"Again, huh? You want to fly?"

"Bly!" Carl raised him above his head and walked around the house making airplane noises. As soon as Carl put him down, Kyler lifted his arms, smiled charmingly, and said, "Bly!"

Carl ruffled the hair on Kyler's head. "Maybe a little later, buddy. First, I've got to get out of this suit."

Lyla finished cutting the lettuce and walked towards the refrigerator. "What do you want, angel? I doubt you'll eat a hamburger. Do you want peanut butter and jelly?"

"Sketti," Kyler said as he ran to assist Lyla in opening the refrigerator door.

"I don't know why I even asked," she said, as she leaned over to kiss his soft, little head. "You know, you can't eat spaghetti forever. We're going to have to broaden your horizons a bit."

"Sketti," Kyler replied, refusing to be dissuaded.

Carl walked into the living room wearing athletic shorts and a t-shirt. "Are you hungry now? Do you want me to light the grill?" he asked.

"Oh, I can eat whenever," Lyla said, passive as usual. "Have you heard anything from Jacinda? What about Jill? I hope they're both okay," Lyla said.

"Actually, things have been pretty quiet, which I'm going to take as a good sign. If anything bad happened, we would have heard about it." Lyla decided his answer made sense.

Carl grabbed the ground beef and buns before heading out the back door. "Can you grab a few plates? These won't take long to cook."

"Sure," Lyla said. "I'll bring the salad, too."

"Deep!" Kyler said as he squeezed past Carl's legs to get to the backyard.

"Hold on, buddy. I need to unplug it." Kyler was in the driver's seat before Carl could finish his sentence.

Once Kyler was happily zipping around the backyard, Carl lit the grill. He looked over at Lyla, who looked lost in thought. "What's wrong?" Carl asked. He hoped he hadn't done anything to upset her.

"It's just that I feel like such a burden. I know you're ready to get rid of me, but I honestly don't even know where I'm supposed to go. The plan was to go with Jacinda and Keith, but now they're back in D.C., and I have no idea where I fit in."

Carl smiled. "Ready to get rid of you? Hardly. Do you have any idea how nice it's been to come home to something other than my couch? I can't even remember the last time I ate dinner outside. This has been great." Lyla smiled, but still looked distracted. "Look," he continued. "It won't be like this forever. Right now, we're working with the best in the business to get you a new identity. You'll get a whole new start in life. You'll get a new birth certificate, social security card, name—you'll be all set."

"A new life?"

"Yup, a whole new start."

"A start to do what? Where do I start? I've never really had a job. Who would hire me?"

"You won't have to worry about money."

"What do you mean? Why not?"

Carl focused his attention on the grill.

"You just won't. You'll be taken care of."

"By whom? I mean, Jacinda left me money, but it won't last forever. Besides, I would feel guilty keeping it."

Carl turned to grab the hamburger patties and put the meat on the grill. Without looking at her, he said, "You'll have a trust fund."

"A trust fund?"

"Yes, once you get a new identity, I'll set up your trust fund." Carl realized he had said too much.

"You? You'll set it up? How?" Lyla asked.

"Those details aren't really important; just know you'll be okay."

"I would argue that those details are very

important." Lyla cut herself off, fearing she was being too aggressive. "I'm sorry. I've just lived so much of my life at the mercy of others, and I feel like I've finally taken control. But I haven't. Have I? For all intents and purposes, I'm still at the mercy of others, because I don't have the resources to survive on my own."

Carl turned to face her. "Remember how I told you that I was paid a fortune by the Illuminati?"

"Yes, the money you weren't allowed to flaunt?"

"Yeah, that money. I didn't flaunt it. I moved most of it to offshore accounts. After breaking with The Brotherhood and becoming part of The Resistance, ethically I couldn't let myself touch the money. I mean, I still work for them, but it's only to gather information. Every penny they paid me has sat untouched. I've been looking for the perfect way to spend their money against them."

Lyla saw where Carl was going and shook her head in protest.

"No, Carl. I can't. I won't accept your money."

"It's not my money. Since I joined The Resistance, I've viewed it as blood money. I told myself I would only use it for good. I would only use it against them. But not everything has to be done against them. Sometimes, retributions need to be made for the lives they've destroyed. Lives like yours."

"But you could do other things with that money," Lyla protested.

Carl locked eyes with Lyla. "With the money I have in those accounts, I can make sure you are financially set for the rest of your life, and I'll still have plenty of money left over."

*****

Andy Barlow lit a cigar and studied his list of contacts. Now that Keith was safely out of D.C., he needed to find a safe house for Livingston. Livingston had bravely derailed BARAchip, but The Brotherhood would find a new way to present the chip. It was just a matter of time. Once Jarrod Kabbul became President of The United States, everyone would be required to accept the chip to so much as buy a candy bar. Livingston's betrayal of The Brotherhood had delayed the acceptance of BARAchip, but it also marked him for death.

Since leaving the CIA, Andy had devoted his life to revealing the U.S. government's role in helping to craft the New World Order. His job as a CIA agent exposed him to organized corruption around the world. The Brotherhood's plans reached far beyond

North America. Once the New World Order was in place, it would rock the entire world. He knew some wars were created for profit, while others were waged as a show of strength. A United States President had once said, "You are either with us, or you're against us." Andy knew he hadn't been referring to America, but The Brotherhood. He knew it was a common tactic to create chaos as a distraction to push political agendas. He had witnessed smoke and mirror politics for years before leaving the CIA.

He knew all the buzzwords that struck fear or patriotism in Americans: terrorists, terror, and freedom, to name a few. Americans would move mountains to protect their freedom, but very few realized their freedom was slowly being stolen. He knew that if The Brotherhood got their way, everyone would soon be enslaved by the government in one way or another. Of course, The Brotherhood always convinced American citizens that their agenda was for the good of the country, but those in the know were able to see through their rhetoric.

Andy glanced at the newspaper and spotted another story about a mass shooting. He sadly shook his head. Andy was certain The Brotherhood was behind the tragedy. For years, he'd witnessed MK-Ultra, trauma-based mind control. He knew all too well that every assassination in recent history had been perpetrated by an MK-Ultra mind control slave. MK-Ultra had been developed in the fifties by the CIA. Its goal had been to use mind-controlling drugs against the Soviets. The CIA had poured millions of dollars into research to create the perfect truth serum. It was their hope that prisoners of war would sing like canaries if given the right drugs.

However, the CIA hadn't just been looking to make their prisoners talk, but had hoped to control the prisoners' minds so that they could transform them into weapons against their own countries. They had soon realized that pills weren't enough. The mind control slave had to first be exposed to some kind of trauma, be it physical, psychological, or sexual torture. Through trauma-based mind control, the prisoners of war would then return to their countries and create chaos. The glory of the program was that the mind-control slaves had no recollection of the crimes they had committed. It hadn't taken the CIA long to realize that hypnosis was also a valuable tool when prepping an MK-Ultra slave. While the program had eventually been shut down, proof remained. Documents had been found in the seventies, revealing that US citizens had been experimented on. The government had used its citizens like guinea pigs. The MK-Ultra program was officially abandoned. Unofficially, however, it's used to this day.

Andy flipped on the television to watch coverage of the latest shooting. He recognized the dazed look in the gunman's mug shot all too well. Andy had no doubt the gunman was a slave. He would recognize the crazed, empty eyes of an MK-Ultra slave anywhere. He knew the man wouldn't remember his crime, but he would pay the price regardless. Andy knew the gunman was a sacrificial lamb for the gun control agenda, and it sickened him that he had to sit helplessly by and watch The Brotherhood destroy even more lives. *How can people not see the similarities in the shooters?*

Andy thought of all the childhood actors and actresses who were now described as crazy. It seemed like they all lost their minds during the transition from child star to adult. Most of those actresses came from a single television network that was geared towards children. He wondered how everyone could just accept that they all went crazy. They were constantly in the tabloids for their antics, whether for shaving their heads or talking to people who didn't exist. How was it that this television network turned out so many child stars that became adult schizophrenics? Andy knew it wasn't a coincidence. Those children were traumatized, drugged, and used as puppets of The Brotherhood.

Once the entertainers had broken free of their captives, they began acting out. The public assumed they were just being bratty, but without the drugs and the hypnosis, their minds really had gone haywire. He knew that being swept away to rehab wasn't for substance abuse as the media claimed—it was for reprogramming.

Andy knew about Hollywood, and hoped Keith would realize the same was also true in the music industry. Keith would have been killed, had he stayed in D.C. Andy had to hide him until the BARAchip sabotage died down. He would be told to use a fake name so The Brotherhood wouldn't make the connection. For all intents and purposes, Keith Ludwig had just disappeared off the face of the Earth. Andy wondered if Mr. Fisher had told him that he would be using a fake name for the duration of his internship. Andy would have told Keith himself, but didn't want Keith backing out due to fear. The truth had to be revealed slowly.

CHAPTER 15

Once Kyler was fast asleep, Lyla joined Carl in the living room. As usual, Lyla was exhausted from keeping up with Kyler all day. He was the light of her life, but tending to him was a full-time job. Lyla pulled her knees to her chest and covered herself with a throw blanket that was draped over the back of the couch.

"Are you cold?" Carl asked.

"A little, but this is fine," Lyla replied.

"Are you sure? I can adjust the AC."

"Don't be silly. I'm fine." Lyla was still in awe of Carl's kindness and attentiveness to her needs. He noticed she was cold, and was trying to make her comfortable. She felt sad that it had taken her so long to meet people like Marlene, Keith, Jacinda, and Carl. She'd had no idea such kindness existed.

She began twisting her hair around her finger. Carl immediately recognized she was about to discuss something that made her uncomfortable.

"It's okay," Carl said. "Just say whatever is on your mind."

"How do you know that I…"

"You're playing with your hair; that means you're nervous."

Lyla smiled. "I guess you've got me figured out, huh?"

"Not completely, but I'm learning," Carl said with a smile. Lyla looked down to avoid eye contact.

"It's just that things seem so perfect right now, but I know it won't last."

"What do you mean?" asked Carl.

"It's just that I still have Kyler, and now you, but soon it will all be taken away, and I'll be alone." A tear streamed down Lyla's face. Carl moved beside her and pulled her into his arms. She rested her head on his shoulder and fought back the sobs that were welling up inside of her.

"Don't be upset," Carl said. "I'm sure you'll

always be a part of Kyler's life, and someday you'll have your own children. You're going to make such a wonderful mother."

Lyla didn't pull away from Carl. Instead, she let the weight of her body lean against him. "Do you really think I'll make a good mother?" she asked.

"I know you will. Look how well you've done with Kyler. He adores you."

"Not as much as I adore him," Lyla said.

"That's debatable," Carl replied.

Lyla straightened her body. "Besides, he's not mine."

"Maybe not," Carl agreed. "But you'll have one of your own. You'll have a child that *is* yours. You'll see."

Lyla let her stiffened body relax into his arms again. "Who's going to want me? Who? I can't very well introduce anyone to my family. I don't even have a family. I can't tell them about my past. I'm damaged beyond repair."

Carl put his hand on her chin and lifted her face. He looked into her eyes. "You may feel too damaged to repair yourself, but I assure you that no damage is too great for God." Carl's simple statement warmed her, and she nuzzled her head against his arm. "Besides," Carl said. "I know about your past, and hearing what you were born into and how far you've come, it makes me like you even more. You're an inspiration."

Lyla's lips formed a crooked smile. "Do you really mean that?"

"Of course I do. You've never been given a shred of love as a child, and watching you shower Kyler with love shows what a beautiful, resilient, amazing woman you are. I don't think you give yourself enough credit." Lyla pulled away from Carl and rested her back against the arm of the couch.

"I'm sorry I turned this into a pity party. I really didn't mean to. You've been so generous and kind." Carl didn't respond immediately; he simply watched her.

"What do you mean, kind?" he finally asked.

"I just mean that you've been so good to Kyler and me. You bought him the Jeep, and the cookouts, and…" Carl smiled in a way that made her cut her sentence short. "What?" she asked.

"That wasn't me being kind, Lyla. I've truly loved every minute you've been here. I've loved every minute of Kyler zipping around the backyard. I can't wait to get off work and come home to the two of you. You may interpret it as me being kind, but honestly, I'm just having the time of my life. I know this sounds cliché, but I finally feel alive again."

Lyla smiled. "Do you really mean that?"

"Of course I do. I feel like I have a family. I know I don't, but if this is what a family feels like, I want one. Soon. I've never been happier."

Lyla didn't know how to respond. There were simply no words that would do her feelings justice, so she decided to remain silent. She shifted her weight from the arm of the couch back onto Carl as he hugged her tightly. It was true that she felt safe with Marlene. In fact, she didn't think she could ever feel safer, but that was before Carl had held her in his arms. This was what safety felt like, and it felt more wonderful than anything she could have imagined.

CHAPTER 16

Jacinda walked to the office closet to retrieve Gregory's old computer. As she opened the closet door, she felt a rush of relief when she saw the old laptop was still there. She had seen it earlier, but worried The Brotherhood had somehow heard of her plan and had retrieved it. She grabbed an old suit coat hanging in the closet and wrapped it around the computer. Once the computer was hidden, she made her way to her own closet. Stepping inside her closet still took her breath away. It was so large and luxurious. None of that mattered now. It was impressive, but she was more than willing to walk away from all of it to have a normal life with her son.

She opened a dresser drawer and pulled out a large, paper bag from a local boutique. She was horrible about throwing bags away. It was in her nature to avoid waste. She never knew when a large bag might come in handy. Feeling grateful she had saved it, she tucked the jacket and computer inside. Jacinda checked her face in the mirror before stepping out of her closet. She noticed she looked too thin and a bit sickly. She was pale and had dark circles under her eyes. In the past, this would have made her feel self-conscious, but not today. She couldn't care less that she looked like a zombie. She simply had to complete her mission. She had to mail Gregory's computer to Jill. Jacinda hoped to make it look like she was mailing her an outfit from the pricy boutique. She didn't want to risk The Brotherhood intercepting the computer, but felt certain Jill would remain at home until the computer arrived. Jacinda grabbed one of Gregory's baseball caps and pulled it down over her eyes. She didn't want anyone to recognize her. She put on a pair of oversized sunglasses to complete her disguise.

Jacinda grabbed her purse, left her condo, and locked the door behind her. Stack and Pack was only two blocks away. A bubbly teenage girl behind the desk greeted Jacinda as she walked inside the office.

"Hello, ma'am," said the teenage girl. "Is there something I can help you with?" Jacinda studied her for a moment. She realized the girl didn't recognize her. Jacinda felt a sense of relief wash over her.

"Yes," replied Jacinda. "I need to mail a package, but don't have a box."

The teenage girl smiled. "It's your lucky day; turns out we have lots of them. It's kind of what we do," the teenager said before winking. Jacinda noticed the name-tag on the girl's shirt said *Katie*.

"Katie, is it?" Jacinda asked. The girl looked a little embarrassed.

"Actually, it's Stella. I left my name tag at home, so I borrowed this one from the girl who had the shift before mine."

Jacinda smiled. "Stella, I need to ship this overnight, but it's fragile." Stella smiled and pointed to the bubble wrap.

"No problem, we've got bubble wrap over there. Do you want me to wrap it for you?"

Jacinda walked towards the bubble wrap. "No, I appreciate it, but I'll wrap it myself."

Jacinda opened the package and turned her back to Stella. She took the computer out of the coat before wrapping it and sliding it back inside the bag. She slipped the coat back into the boutique bag, and turned to face Stella. "All set," Jacinda said. "Now

I just need a box."

Stella reached her hand over the counter. "No problem, just hand it to me and I'll box it up for you." Jacinda felt uncertain.

"Are you sure? I can box it up myself."

"Don't be silly, ma'am. It's my job." Stella seemed a bit too bubbly, and for whatever reason, it was beginning to annoy Jacinda. How could anyone be so happy when the world was falling apart? How could someone be so chipper days after the anti-Christ was born? Of course, Jacinda knew that Stella wasn't burdened with such knowledge. *Ignorance really is bliss,* Jacinda thought.

"Ma'am," Stella said, snapping Jacinda back to reality. "Your bag," she said, as she reached over the counter to take the bag from Jacinda.

"Of course," replied Jacinda. "I'm sorry. I'm just scattered today. Stella placed the bag in a box and taped it closed.

"You'll need to fill this out," Stella said. Jacinda's heart sank. She couldn't put her own name or address. Feeling relatively certain the clerk didn't recognize her, Jacinda decided to use the name Isuri Smith. She'd once known a girl named Isuri, and it was the first name that popped into her head. She used the address of her condo, but changed the unit number. She filled out Jill's address, wondering if shipping the computer to Jill was a mistake.

Jacinda slid the paper towards Stella. Stella studied the form for a moment before saying, "Isuri, that's a unique name. It's beautiful." Jacinda smiled, grateful the bubbly clerk still didn't recognize her. Stella began typing the information into the computer and waited as the printer spit out a sticker. Stella slapped the sticker on the box, looked up, and asked, "Will there be anything else?"

"No," Jacinda replied. "That's all." Turning to leave, Jacinda felt relieved to have completed one more task. She could finally focus on getting back to Kyler. Her heart ached to hold him. He was all she'd been able to think about. She was counting the seconds until she could hold him in her arms again.

Jacinda made a mental list of things she needed to pack before returning to California. She still wasn't sure when she would be able to return to California, but hoped The Resistance would help her craft a strategy. She wanted to jump in the car and head west, but knew she needed a better plan.

Walking back to her condo, she noticed a small group of paparazzi gathering in the parking lot of her complex. Stella may not have recognized her, but the paparazzi noticed her immediately.

"Mrs. Kilmeade," one of the photographers said, "how is your husband?"

Jacinda smiled politely, but declined to answer. A security guard arrived and told the photographers they had to stay twenty feet from the building. Jacinda quickened her pace to her condo. As she put the key in the lock, she glanced towards the parking lot to see a news van pull into the complex. She turned the key, but it refused to budge. It wasn't locked. Feeling foolish for leaving the door unlocked, she opened the door. She went inside and dropped her purse on the counter. She headed around the wall that separated her kitchen from her living room, and heard a noise that made her heart skip a beat. Suddenly, she feared she wasn't alone. Had Gregory returned?

Slowly making her way around the corner, she found Agent Asher sitting on the couch. "Hello, Mrs. Kilmeade. Remember me? It's fancy meeting you here." That kind, helpful persona he once exuded was gone. He now looked angry and threatening. Before she could run, he lifted a gun. "I wouldn't even think about running or screaming, Mrs. Kilmeade. I'd hate to get blood all over your beautiful, white couch."

Jacinda took a cleansing breath, trying in vain to

pull herself together. In the most controlled voice she could manage, she asked, "What are you doing here?"

"That's it? You're not even going to offer me a drink? Come on, Mrs. Kilmeade, you're America's sweetheart. I would think you'd be a better hostess."

Jacinda didn't move. Again, she asked, "Why are you here?"

"You know, Mrs. Kilmeade, you sound like a broken record. You already asked me that."

"You never answered."

"Well, since you asked so nicely, I suppose I'll tell you. It appears your husband didn't show up for court. In fact, nobody has been able to contact him. I don't suppose you know where he's scurried off to?"

"No," Jacinda said. "I have no idea."

"Have you seen him?" Agent Asher asked, looking as if he already knew the answer. Jacinda thought about lying, but remembered her apartment was bugged.

"Yes," Jacinda admitted. "I saw him the night I returned home from Texas. I haven't seen him since." Agent Asher smiled and let a moment of silence pass before he responded.

"Texas? Really? That's funny. The only time your name came up on flight records was from California."

Jacinda felt her heart drop to her feet. Improvising, she responded, "You clearly aren't as good at your job as you'd like to think. I did fly out of California when I went to visit my friend, but if you would have investigated further, you would have seen that I was on a flight to Oklahoma. From there, I drove to Texas. I flew from Texas to California before returning home. What's your point?" Jacinda surprised herself with her defiant, confident attitude. Agent Asher didn't seem as surprised as he did angry. He didn't like being disrespected, and that much was clear by the expression on his face.

Jacinda continued, "Why are you here? What do you want with me?"

"Well, Mrs. Kilmeade," Asher responded, "it's not you I want. Your husband is actually the person I'm looking for, but since nobody has been able to locate him, I figured you'd be the best person to lure him out of hiding."

"Me? What would make you think that? Do you not remember him disappearing with nothing more than a note? He didn't care enough about me to tell me where he was going then, what makes you think he'll care enough about me to return now?"

Agent Asher twisted his lips into an evil grin. "Don't toy with me, Mrs. Kilmeade. We all know why he did what he did. He did it because he loves you. He kidnapped that child so he could return yours. Don't play me for a fool. It's a game you can't win." Jacinda's stomach twisted, and she felt as if she were about to vomit. "Mrs. Kilmeade, you're not looking well. Maybe you should sit down. Take a load off."

"What are you going to do with me? Are we just going to wait here, hoping he calls or comes home?"

"Here?" Agent Asher said, gesturing to her living room. "Are you asking if we'll stay here, where everyone knows you live? Do I appear stupid to you, Mrs. Kilmeade?" Jacinda decided not to answer his question; she knew she was in enough trouble. "I asked you a question. Do. I. Appear. Stupid?" Jacinda dug her nails into the palm of her hand and answered.

"No. No, you don't appear stupid." Jacinda remembered the prepaid phone in her purse. She couldn't let Asher find it. It had the phone numbers of Jill, Carl, Livingston, Lyla, and the mission in

Mexico. Raising her hands, Jacinda said, "I'll do whatever you want; I'm just really thirsty. Are you thirsty?"

"I could use a drink," Asher replied.

"All right, are you going to let me go to the kitchen?"

Asher thought a minute. "You're not going to try to bring a knife to a gunfight, are you sweetheart?" Jacinda shook her head.

"I'm not going to do anything stupid. You have a gun. Do you want a drink or not?"

Asher allowed her to move to the kitchen, but she knew it was only a matter of time before he would be right behind her. She quietly reached inside her purse and removed the prepaid phone before sticking it into the garbage disposal. Looking up, she saw Asher entering the kitchen. Lifting a plate from the sink, she said, "He never puts dishes in the dishwasher. It's like living with a child." She studied his expression, eager to see if he bought her ruse. He didn't look suspicious, so she moved to the cabinet. "What would you like?" Jacinda asked. "I think we only have soda and water."

"Water is fine. Give me your phone."

Jacinda felt as if an icy hand had clutched her heart.

"My what?"

"Your phone. Where is it? Is it in your purse?"

Relief washed over Jacinda. "Yes, it's in my purse. Why do you want my phone?"

"New rule. I ask the questions. You answer them," Asher said, as he dug through her purse. He found a cell phone and placed it in his pocket. It was her personal cell phone. The only numbers of interest he would find would be Gregory's and Jill's. Jill had ditched her persona phone after buying a prepaid one. Jacinda had made Gregory throw his phone into a dumpster before going to the airport.

Jacinda handed Asher a bottle of water. He drank the entire bottle in three gulps and plopped the empty bottle on the counter. "All right, let's go," he said.

"Go where?"

"Don't worry your pretty little face about that, Mrs. Kilmeade. I'm the one who asks the questions, remember?" He placed the gun inside his jacket. "If you make any sudden movements, or draw any attention to us, I won't hesitate to shoot you. The official story will be that I shot you in self-defense. You are, after all, wanted for questioning in the disappearance of your husband."

*****

Keith arrived at the building that housed Louden Records. As Keith opened the door to the opulent structure, he was awestruck. Louden Records consumed the first five stories of a gorgeous high-rise building. Keith made his way to an attractive girl behind the front desk.

"I'm interning under Mr. Eric Fisher—public relations. Can you tell me where to find his office?" The receptionist smiled, picked up her phone, and punched in two numbers.

"Mr. Fisher, a…" she cupped the phone with her hand before asking Keith's name. Keith couldn't remember the phony last name he was told to use, but didn't panic. "Keith," he responded, bypassing the last name altogether. "He'll know me."

"I'm sorry, Mr. Fisher," the woman continued. "A man named Keith is here to see you. He says you know him." She looked up at Keith and gave him a saccharine, sweet smile. "Yes, sir, I'll send him up now."

Keith rode the elevator two floors to Mr. Fisher's office. He stepped off the elevator and immediately spotted his destination. Before he opened the door, he pulled the glasses Carl had given him out of his pocket, and switched the tiny lever to the record position. He stepped into the office, and smiled at the beautiful woman sitting behind the front desk. *Apparently being attractive is a prerequisite to getting a job answering phones around here*, he thought to himself.

The woman smiled. "Hello, may I help you, sir?" Keith's face flushed as it often did around beautiful women.

"Um, yeah," Keith said, stumbling on his words. "Mr. Fisher is expecting me."

The woman stood to lead Keith into Mr. Fisher's office. "Follow me," she said, as she led Keith six steps to Mr. Fisher's door. Knocking twice before entering, she opened the door. "Mr. Fisher, Keith is here."

"Ah, yes, Cindy. Thank you. Please send him in." Keith was struck by how professional Mr. Fisher sounded. Yesterday, he'd sounded like a mobster. Today, he sounded very much like an executive.

Keith walked into Fisher's office. He couldn't help but feel impressed by the pictures hanging on the walls. Keith recognized most of the celebrities that graced his wall of fame. Most of them were very successful recording artists.

Fisher saw the awe on Keith's face and said, "You

like what you see, kiddo?" There it was. This was
the Mr. Fisher Keith had met yesterday. The
pretentious executive-speak ended the moment the
receptionist closed the door. This was the Mr.
Fisher Keith knew—the one that called him *kiddo*.

"Sit down. Make yourself comfortable," Fisher said,
motioning to a chair in front of his desk. "You're
here just in time. I expect Chyanne to be here any
minute. Chyanne is, or was, Tony Randall's
girlfriend. She's on the fast track, if you catch my
drift. She's coming to me because it's time to
change her image. It's my job to sanitize her for the
public and make her seem far more interesting than
she really is. You know the drill. She wants to go
to the next level, and Louden policy states, that
anyone we pour money into has to visit a vocal
coach in Florida," Fisher said with a wink.

"Florida? You mean, like the place they'll program
her? The place they sent Tyla? Are you kidding
me?"

"I wish I was, pal, but I'm not. I can't stop it. All I
can do is play the game until these monsters are
exposed."

Keith looked around nervously.

In a hushed tone he said, "How do you know they
aren't listening?"

Mr. Fisher laughed.

"I have my office swept for listening devices every two days. So far it's been bug-free. They have no reason to suspect me. Plus, they don't want any proof of what they think goes on in my office. I'm one of the bad guys, remember?" He winked again. The winking was beginning to creep Keith out. It was starting to look like Fisher had a facial tic.

"So, Keith, my main man, I've got a new job for you."

"You mean other than just an internship?"

"That's what I mean, kiddo. I have papers here that say you've been trained as a handler. Of course, here at Louden, outside handlers must be trained by the Louden staff. So basically, they think you know what goes on at these training facilities. You'll just be interning under Lori Wallace. Lori has worked at Louden for years. She was Tyla's handler. I just need you to see for yourself what goes on in that den of evil. You want the story of a lifetime, kiddo? Here's your chance."

Mr. Fisher slid a watch across his desk. This isn't a regular watch, kid. It's a camera and recording device. I want you to record everything you can." Mr. Fisher then slid a driver's license across the desk. "This is your new driver's license. You'll

notice you're a California resident. You'll need that
to board the plane."

Keith studied the picture. "Where did you get this
picture? It's the same one as my student ID."

"Are you kidding me, kid? It's your student ID
picture. Where do you think I got it?"

"I know, but how did you get it?"

Mr. Fisher laughed. "You've got a lot to learn,
kiddo. By the way, my document guy messed up
your last name. It's Richards now." Keith studied
the phony driver's license.

"Keith Richards? My name is Keith Richards?"

Fisher laughed, "Those document guys got a nutty
sense of humor, don't they, kiddo?"

Mr. Fisher's expression turned serious. "I need to
warn you, kid, you'll be exposed to all kinds of evil.
It's a Monarch training facility. It's not just
showbiz types that are being programed, it's also
people The Brotherhood plans on using as assassins,
slaves, and terrorists."

"Terrorists?" Keith said. "You mean to send to
other countries?"

"Maybe, but a lot of them are used to create terror

right here in the good ol' U.S. of A. I need to know that you can handle what you are about to be exposed to."

Keith swallowed hard. "Exposed? They won't try to program me, will they?"

"No, but you'll get a glimpse of pure evil. I need to know you can handle it."

Keith rolled his shoulders back. "I can handle it. When do I leave?"

"You're a little too eager, kiddo. I'm sending you to the first level of hell, not Disney World."

"Is it that bad?" Keith asked.

"That's what I hear. Anyway, Chyanne and Lori will be here any minute. I'll introduce you. Lori will be your new boss. I'm sending you to observe and document. You're supposed to be an experienced handler, so I need you to go home and educate yourself on Monarch Programming. I have to warn you, it's graphic."

There was a knock at the door as Mr. Fisher finished his last sentence. The receptionist stuck her head in. "Mr. Fisher, Lori and Chyanne are here for their nine o'clock."

*****

Livingston woke up and checked the clock. It was nine-thirty. How could he have slept so late? Sitting up, he looked at the bed next to him. It was empty. "George?" Livingston called out, hoping he was in the bathroom. "George, are you here?" Livingston rubbed the sleep from his eyes and stepped out of bed. Walking towards the bathroom, he saw a note lying on George's bed. It simply read: **Went to Thailand. I have to protect my daughter, Susie. George**

With George gone, Livingston had no reason to stay at the hotel. He picked up his safe cell and called Andy while packing his belongings. Andy answered on the third ring. "Hi, Andy, It's Livingston. George is gone."

"Where did he go?" asked Andy.

"Thailand."

"Thailand?"

"Yes, his daughter is there. He's probably scared they'll hurt her. I just found his note."

Andy sighed and waited a moment before responding. "If his daughter is in Thailand, it's more likely they'll go after his girlfriend. She lives here."

"I know," Livingston said. An edge of sadness

framed his voice. Livingston continued, "I guess you know I can't show my face after sabotaging the BARAchip story, but I think I can make myself useful in other ways. I want to start a website. Surely you have people who can hide my IP address as well as the server, right?"

"I do," Andy assured him. "What kind of website?"

"I want to start a website that will expose The Brotherhood. I want to further prove that The Brotherhood works directly for the Illuminati, even if they aren't aware of that fact." Again, Andy paused before speaking.

"Rob, you know that there are hundreds of websites and even YouTube videos that focus on exposing the Illuminati. How will yours be any different?"

"Mine will be different because I was an insider. Not only was I an insider, I have an entire group of insiders willing to shed light on the truth. I want to open the eyes of Americans. I want to be involved in some aspect of the news, and since I have officially blackballed myself from the conventional media, I'd like to start a type of alternative media— a source of truth, not just propaganda."

Livingston packed his laptop inside his briefcase, and headed towards the door. "I need to call a cab. Is it okay if I come to your house? You're a former

CIA agent, and I'd love to pick your brain for my first story. I remember you mentioning something about political parties, and how they were created to ensure the failure of the American political system. Is that something you'd be willing to discuss?"

Andy let out an audible sigh. "Rob, I have enough stories to fill a hundred books. I'm getting old, you know. I don't want my knowledge to die with me. I think your idea sounds great. Come over. We'll talk about whatever you want to talk about and then some. It's high time I got some of this off my chest. But there's just one condition."

"Name it."

"All of this information has to be released slowly. You can't just put everything out there at once and expect the American people to be able to process it. If you do that, you risk losing credibility. They'll write you off as a right-wing wacko. This has to be done with finesse."

"Of course," Livingston agreed. "You know I've been in the news business for a long time. I'll make sure all the information is timely, and I'll be sure to use plenty of examples."

"Livingston, you know I've always trusted your judgment."

"I appreciate that, Andy. I'll see you in about an hour."

CHAPTER 17

Standing by the front door in Jacinda's condo, Agent Asher placed his hand over the gun inside his jacket. He pulled a smaller gun from his pocket before grabbing Jacinda's wrist and forcing her hand around the weapon. Once her fingerprints were on the gun, he slipped it back in his pocket.

"Don't do anything stupid, Mrs. Kilmeade. I won't think twice about shooting you in self-defense," Asher said in a tone so cold, Jacinda knew he wouldn't hesitate to kill her. She didn't need Asher to explain his plan. She knew her fingerprints were now all over the weapon in his pocket. She knew she should be fearful, but all she could think about was Kyler. Surely God wouldn't bring her this far to let her die. He wouldn't let her find her son, only to be killed days later. Her mind flooded with memories of Kyler covered in spaghetti. She recalled how his little eyes lit up when he would say, "ticko monner." No, she couldn't let Agent Asher take her. She knew that, once she got in his car, she was as good as dead. She wondered if she'd ever see her son again. At that moment, she would have given anything to be in California with Kyler safely in her arms.

As Asher opened the front door, he led Jacinda outside by her arm. He leaned in, and let his mouth touch her ear before saying, "Don't do anything stupid, Mrs. Kilmeade."

"I understood you the first time," Jacinda said, before realizing she needed to keep her anger in check. As they walked around the corner of the complex, they both saw what could only be described as a media circus. News vans lined the small parking lot. Reporters, cameramen, and photographers gathered on the manicured lawn around the condominiums. As the crowd spotted Jacinda, they all made their way towards her with their microphones outstretched.

This is it, Jacinda thought. Relief eased the panic she'd felt just ten seconds ago. *He can't frame me for murder in front of all these cameras.* Everything was happening so fast.

As she jerked her arm away from Asher, he leaned in and whispered, "We have Kyler."

The panic that had dissipated just seconds ago returned with a vengeance. *Is he lying? Do they have Kyler?* She didn't have time to ask questions, and she certainly wasn't going to risk her son's life. Asher had her, and he knew it. Her own safety, she would risk, but she would never do anything to jeopardize the safety of her son.

The reporters were all asking questions at once. It was nothing more than noise to Jacinda. She tuned out everyone and everything except one camera. Looking into the camera, she said, "Agent Asher said they found my son. I'm going with him."

Asher dug his fingers into her arm and said, "She has no comment. Please, clear the path."

The reporters were persistent. One woman asked, "Where did they find your son, Mrs. Kilmeade?" while another asked, "Where is Senator Kilmeade? Have you heard from your husband?" As Asher pushed Jacinda through the crowd, the last question she heard was, "Will you be attending your mother-in-law's memorial service today?"

That question rang in her ears. It rang and reverberated, making her head buzz. *Chandra,* Jacinda thought. *How could I have forgotten about her memorial service?*

Asher opened the passenger door of his car and helped Jacinda into the front seat. He waved at the cameras as he made his way to the driver's side. Pulling out of the parking space, they were both very aware of the cameras. Neither said a word until they were out of the parking lot.

Turning onto the road, Asher gripped the steering wheel tightly with both hands. "I told you not to do anything stupid," he said. "That was stupid."

Jacinda could tell he hadn't expected the media to show up in droves. She knew he wasn't prepared for the exposure, and he certainly wasn't prepared for her statement. If she turned up missing, everyone would know she was last seen with Agent Asher. Not only that, but everyone in America would hear Jacinda say the words, "Agent Asher said they found my son."

As Jacinda placed her hopes of survival on the unexpected media frenzy, Asher pulled a small bottle and cloth from the center console. Dousing the cloth with liquid from the bottle, he used his right hand to hold the cloth over Jacinda's face. She struggled against him before everything faded to black.

*****

Keith sat on the couch of the luxury high-rise

apartment he'd been loaned over the course of his internship. Looking out at the New York skyline excited Keith. *Someday I'll own an apartment like this,* he told himself. *Someday I'll have this view every night.* The skyline impressed Keith. It was the most beautiful view he could have imagined. He gazed out of the floor-to-ceiling windows, wondering if the sight would ever get old. *It really is the city that never sleeps*, he thought. Cabs buzzed around crowded streets, much like they did during the day. The only difference was, the city was now lit by beautiful, artificial light. It might have been a crowded, dirty city, but from this far up, it looked calm and pristine.

Keith wanted to explore. He wanted to join the pedestrians and enjoy the time he had left in the Big Apple. Keith found himself seduced by the bright lights and skyscrapers. He thought D.C. was impressive, but New York was magnificent. He could gaze out of the window all night, but he knew morning would come early. He had a job to do.

He pulled out his laptop and connected to the building's free wifi. He typed **MK-Ultra Monarch Training** into the search engine, and clicked on the first hit. The website was titled *Monarch Training,* and had been authored by the group: Vigilant Citizen. Keith kicked off his shoes, put his feet on the coffee table, and began to read:

Monarch Programming is a method of mind control used by numerous organizations for covert purposes. It is a continuation of project MK-ULTRA, a mind-control program developed by the CIA, and tested on the military and civilians. The methods are astonishingly sadistic. The purpose of programming is to traumatize the victim. The expected results are horrifying: the creation of a mind-controlled slave that can be triggered at will to perform any action required by the handler. While mass media ignores this issue, over 2 million Americans have gone through the horrors of this program.

Monarch programming is a mind-control technique comprised of elements of satanic ritual abuse and Multiple Personality Disorder. It utilizes a combination of psychology, neuroscience, and occult rituals to create altered personas within the slaves that can be triggered by the programmers. Monarch slaves are used by several organizations, which include the government and the entertainment industry.

Although there has never been any official recognition of the existence of Monarch programming, prominent researchers have documented the systematic use of trauma on subjects for mind-control purposes. Some survivors, with the help of dedicated therapists,

**were able to deprogram themselves. They
eventually went on record and disclosed their
horrifying experiences.**

**Monarch slaves are mainly used by
organizations to carry out operations using
slaves trained to perform specific tasks. These
slaves, or puppets, do not question orders. They
do not remember their actions, and if discovered,
some are programmed to automatically self-
destruct through suicide. They are the perfect
scapegoats for high-profile assassinations. They
have also been very successful in the
entertainment industry.**

Keith never expected the subject to be so riveting.
He hungered for more information and was unable
to read the material fast enough. The webpage
continued:

**Monarch programmers cause intense trauma to
subjects through the use of electroshock, torture,
abuse, and mind games in order to force them to
dissociate from reality. Disassociation is a
natural response in some people when they are
faced with unbearable pain. Trauma-based mind
control programming can be defined as
systematic torture that blocks the victim's
capacity for conscious processing. This can be**

achieved through pain, terror, drugs, illusion, sensory deprivation, sensory over-stimulation, oxygen deprivation, etc... The programmers employ suggestion, as well as classical and operant conditioning to implant thoughts, directives, and perceptions in the unconscious mind. The objective of the programming is for the victim to follow directives with no conscious awareness, including execution of acts in clear violation of the victim's moral principles, spiritual convictions, and volition.

What am I getting myself into? Keith wondered. The programming information terrified Keith, but the prospect of going undercover and revealing such an evil facility excited him to the core. Keith lifted his backpack from the floor. He unzipped the front pouch to retrieve both of his spy devices: the glasses and the watch.

Keith knew he wouldn't be able to sleep. His flight to Florida was only hours away. If the website was to be believed, he would be stepping into a world of pure evil. Even with all the information at his fingertips, Keith still had no idea what to expect, which both troubled and excited him.

CHAPTER 18

Lyla walked from the bedroom into the living room with Kyler on her hip. She was still rubbing the sleep from her eyes when she heard Carl say, "Good morning." Kyler wiggled his body off Lyla's hip and walked towards Carl.

"What are you doing home?" Lyla asked.

Carl smiled. "I don't work on Saturdays. That's not entirely true; I do sometimes, but not today."

Lyla threw her hands in the air. "I don't even know what day of the week it is. I guess I just stopped keeping track. Since we escaped, there's really been no need." Lyla knew she sounded ridiculous, but felt the need to explain away her ignorance.

Kyler climbed into Carl's lap. "Wow," Lyla said.

He's certainly taken a liking to you." Carl lifted Kyler above his head, turning him upside down. Kyler giggled joyfully. He loved playing with Carl.

"He only likes me because I buy him Jeeps and fly him through the air. Kids are easy. If only women were that easy to win over," Carl said with a crooked grin.

"I don't know; I bet there are women you can win over with Jeeps."

"Would it have to be a real Jeep, or would a battery-operated one do?" Carl asked.

Lyla laughed. "They'd probably have to be the real thing. Although I highly doubt flying them through the air would win you any points."

"Unless I was flying them to Paris." Carl responded.

"True," Lyla said as she leaned back on the couch.

"Do you want coffee? I made some coffee." Carl didn't give Lyla a chance to respond. He stood up and made his way towards the kitchen. "Sugar and cream, right?"

"That would be wonderful. Thank you," Lyla said with a smile tugging at her lips. She was just thinking how wonderful a cup of coffee would be. How was it that that Carl always anticipated her needs? Not only that, but how was it possible that he was still single? she wondered. Lyla watched as Carl made his way around the kitchen.

"How about you, little buddy?" Carl asked Kyler. "I bet you want some spaghetti."

"No sketti," Kyler protested, twisting his face and crossing his arms.

"What?" Lyla said, cutting her eyes to Carl. "He doesn't want spaghetti. Do you think he's sick?"

"Sick of spaghetti," Carl replied.

"No sketti," Kyler repeated.

Carl laughed, "I heard you the first time, little man. What do you want for breakfast? Do you want eggs?"

"No," Kyler replied, smiling this time.

"Well," Carl continued. "What do you want for breakfast?"

"I bont goffee," Kyler demanded.

Lyla and Carl smiled at each other. "Well, all right then," Carl said. Carl poured milk into a coffee cup and set it on the table. "Come drink your coffee."

"I bont it here," Kyler insisted, as he crawled up next to Lyla.

Lyla stood. "How about we both have our coffee at the kitchen table? Would that be okay?" Lyla asked Kyler, clearly smitten by the toddler.

"Otay," Kyler agreed, happily following her to the table.

Carl joined Lyla and Kyler at the breakfast table. All three drank out of their coffee mugs. Lyla looked nervous as Kyler fumbled with the heavy mug. "It's just M-I-L-K," Carl said. "It's not a big deal if he spills it. Relax. Enjoy your coffee." Lyla leaned back in her chair and smiled.

"Side!" Kyler said, pointing towards the back door. Carl looked at Lyla. "You heard him. He wants to drink his coffee outside."

"I think that's a fabulous idea," Lyla said.

"I do too," Carl agreed before standing to help

Kyler out of his chair.

Stepping into the beautiful sunshine, Lyla and Carl couldn't help but notice what a gorgeous morning it was. The sun was shining, the birds were chirping, and for the moment, all felt right with the world. "We shouldn't waste this day indoors," Carl said.

"We could cook out for lunch."

"I was thinking more like going to the zoo."

"The zoo?" Lyla repeated, choking on her coffee.

"You don't like the zoo?" asked Carl.

Lyla composed herself. "Sorry. The coffee went down the wrong pipe." Carl found it cute that she always justified her reactions.

"Does the zoo make you nervous?" Carl asked.

"I don't know. I've just never been to a zoo. Besides, shouldn't we stay, you know, hidden?"

"You've never been to a zoo?"

"No, never."

"Then we have to go!" Carl exclaimed.

"Aren't you worried people will see us?"

"Nope. Nobody knows you're here. You can pull your hair into a hat and wear sunglasses. We'll put a little hat and sunglasses on Kyler, too. We'll blend in with the crowd. Come on, it'll be fun!"

Lyla didn't even stop to think. "That would be fun!" she agreed, feeling a rush of excitement.

Lyla turned to Kyler. "Do you want to go to the zoo?"

"Doo!" Kyler squealed.

Carl laughed. "He has absolutely no idea what you're talking about, but he's pumped." Carl focused his attention on Kyler. "We'll see animals."

"Aminals!" Kyler giggled. Carl continued, "We'll see tigers and lions and bears. Grrr."

"Grrrr," Kyler parroted. Kyler clapped his hands with excitement.

"Are you sure this is a good idea?" asked Lyla.

"Honestly?" Carl asked.

"Yes, truthfully."

"I think it might be the best idea I've had in years."

*****

Andy and Livingston sat in Andy's tiny D.C. apartment. Livingston listened to Andy's telephone conversation. Judging by his words, something was terribly wrong. Andy's expression never revealed his emotions. *I bet he's a fierce poker player*, Livingston thought. Livingston wondered if it was his CIA experience that made his emotions so difficult to read.

Andy hung up the phone and faced Livingston. "Turn on the news."

"What?" Livingston replied, as he searched for the remote control. Andy grew impatient.

"Hurry up, turn it on." Livingston found the remote and pushed the power button. "She's gone," Andy said.

"Who's gone?"

"Jacinda Kilmeade."

Livingston opened his mouth to ask a question, but fell silent when he saw the live press conference. Andy sat on the coffee table with his eyes fixed on the screen. He watched as Agent Asher stood with several law enforcement officers in front of a courthouse. A podium filled with microphones from all the major networks stood in front of the men. The Chief of Police approached the podium to read a statement:

"Yesterday afternoon, Jacinda Kilmeade was brought into the station to discuss the disappearance of her husband, Senator Gregory Kilmeade. While she wasn't a suspect, she was definitely a person of interest. During questioning, she had requested permission to go to the restroom. She never returned."

A reporter could be heard shouting, "What about her son? She said her son was found."

Agent Asher stepped up to the podium to speak. "Mrs. Kilmeade told reporters that I said we had found her son. The truth is, I had said no such thing. I have no idea what her motivation was behind that statement, but I can tell you it's absolutely untrue."

Asher stepped aside as the Chief of Police resumed speaking. "Yesterday she was a person of interest in the disappearance of her husband, Senator Kilmeade. Her abrupt departure has led us to believe that she knows more about her husband's whereabouts than she had originally led us to believe. An arrest warrant was issued for Senator Kilmeade when he failed to appear in court on charges of kidnapping. An arrest warrant has also been issued for Jacinda Kilmeade, due to an illegal substance that spilled out of her purse when it was knocked off the table after Mrs. Kilmeade fled the building."

Livingston turned towards Andy before asking, "She left her purse? What woman goes to the restroom without her purse?"

"No woman goes to the restroom without her purse," replied Andy, before adding, "No woman leaves her purse at a police station, either. They've got her."

CHAPTER 19

Keith's flight from New York City to Verra, Florida was anything but dull. The flight was loud, full of turbulence, and he was relatively certain the flight attendant was drunk, but at least it was never dull. Keith sat across the isle from Lori and Chyanne. Both Lori and Chyanne were silent most of the flight, which irritated Keith. He had hoped to get to know both of them a little better before they entered the programming facility.

The airplane began its descent into Florida. Keith's stomach dropped when he realized he'd soon be at the facility. He looked across the aisle, wondering if Chyanne was nervous, but her face remained expressionless. *How is she so calm?* Keith wondered. Once it was safe to unfasten the seat belts, everyone stood to exit the plane. Keith, Lori, and Chyanne kept their conversation to a minimum on the way to baggage claim.

Waiting at the luggage carousel, Lori pointed to a large, black case covered in sequins. "Right there, Intern Boy. That's my bag."

Keith knew she was implying it was his job to retrieve her belongings, but stood motionless. Lori pushed past him and collected the luggage herself. She pulled her luggage over to Keith and sat it by his feet. "Let's get something straight, Intern Boy. I am the mentor. You are the intern. I have a feeling you got the wrong memo in terms of intern responsibilities. Since the memo-senders are idiots, I'll brief you right here and now. Your sole job is to be my personal assistant. Got it?"

Lori pushed her long, blonde hair out of her face before she continued. "If I'm thirsty, you ask what I'd like to drink. If I'm hot, you find a fan. If I point at something, it is your responsibility to be able to read my mind and know exactly why I'm pointing at that object. A monkey could do your job. You want to work at Louden?"

"Yes," lied Keith.

"Then you'll do everything I ask. Do you understand?"

Keith nodded and lifted her suitcase before spotting his own. Once Keith saw his luggage on the carousel, he grabbed it with his spare hand. He looked up to see Chyanne standing beside him. Chyanne looked stunning. She wore a simple pair of blue jeans and a plain, white t-shirt. Her hair was cut into a cute bob that was longer in the front than the back. Even with her simple outfit and minimal makeup, she stood out in a crowd. Keith noticed men straining their necks to get a better look at her as they walked past.

Keith waited at the carousel with Chyanne. "I hope you don't want me to grab your luggage. I'm kind of out of hands," he said. While his statement might have sounded rude, it was really just Keith being Keith. He had an awkward way about him.

"No," replied Chyanne. I can get my own luggage. Chyanne glanced back to make sure Lori was too far away to hear their conversation. "So, what do you think of the wicked witch?" Keith knew exactly who she was talking about, but decided to play dumb.

"The wicked witch?" Chyanne let out a fake laugh as if it was the most ridiculous thing Keith could have said. "She's a witch, Keith. It's okay to admit it."

"Is she a real witch, or are you speaking figuratively?"

"Fig-ur-tav what?" she said, pausing after each syllable.

"I mean, does she ride a broom, or is she just mean?"

"I guess you'll find out," Chyanne said, as she reached to pull her luggage off the conveyor belt.

Keith carried both his and Lori's luggage outside, while Chyanne rolled her suitcase behind her. Walking into the glaring sunlight, they spotted a limousine parked next to a man dressed in full chauffeur attire. The man glanced down at a picture he was holding and looked at Chyanne. The Chauffeur waved as he approached Lori, Chyanne, and Keith.

"Chyanne?" The chauffeur asked, looking directly at the beautiful young woman.

"Yes," Chyanne replied.

"I'm Jeeves," the chauffeur replied. Please follow me." Keith cut his eyes over to Chyanne.

"There is no way that is his real name. Are you kidding me?" Chyanne smiled. "No, seriously," Keith continued. "Was he kidding, or does he expect people to believe that he is a limo driver named Jeeves? I mean, was he born into a chauffeur family, and they just named him accordingly?"

Chyanne laughed. Lori gave both Chyanne and Keith the side-eye.

"Enough," Lori said. It was clear she wasn't amused by Keith's comments.

Lori walked ahead of Keith and Chyanne towards the limo. Once Lori was out of earshot, Keith whispered to Chyanne, "Totally the broom type."

Jeeves opened the car door so the three could pile in. He then proceeded to put their luggage in the trunk. Keith had never ridden in a limo. He looked around the luxurious automobile in awe. Two long seats lined the sides with two smaller seats on the ends. Lori chose an end seat, while Keith and Chyanne sat across from one another on the long bench seats. Keith noticed the wall of glass separating the passengers from the driver.

"Can he hear us thought that thing?" Keith asked.

Chyanne shook her head, "No, not unless we push one of these buttons." She pointed at several overhead buttons. Keith followed the direction of her pointed finger with his eyes.   He saw red buttons scattered throughout the limo.

"Convenient," Keith said. It wasn't that he had found the buttons particularly interesting; he just had nothing else to say.

Lori sat with her legs crossed at her ankles. Keith studied her, wondering how long she'd been in the business. He knew she was Tyla's handler, but she didn't look old enough to have been in this business longer than fifteen years. She appeared to be in her early to mid thirties. Her face was bare of makeup, and her facial features were sharp, but pretty. Lori looked distracted. She looked as if she dreaded the days ahead.

"See something you like, Intern?" Lori asked. She could feel him watching her. Keith felt his face grow hot.

"I was just going to ask you about the facility. I've never been to this one."

"Oh, really?" Lori responded. "Which ones have you been to?" Keith panicked. He'd never been to a programming facility, and didn't think to research their names or locations. Luckily, Keith had always been a quick thinker.

"Oh, Lori, you know I can't tell you that. I mean, I could tell you, but then I'd have to kill you." Keith winked at Lori, shifting the dynamic. Lori nodded. Somehow, Keith's arrogant response earned Lori's respect.

"All right, I'll give you that one," Lori replied.

Chyanne absentmindedly leaned forward. "You've been to a facility? What kinds of things go on there? Lori won't tell me much."

Keith looked at Lori, who was shook her head in warning. Keith felt relieved he didn't have to answer Chyanne's question. While he'd read about the torture, he wasn't sure if it was true. What if it was an exaggeration? Lori would know for sure that he was a fraud if he didn't know what he was talking about. Keith smiled at Lori before looking at Chyanne. "I guess you'll find out soon enough."

*****

Jacinda opened her eyes, trying her best to blink away the blurriness. She sat up and immediately regretted that decision. The room felt as if it were swaying. *A boat?* she wondered. Her brain felt foggy as she looked around the room. *Where am I?* She saw cement walls, a toilet, and stairs leading up to a door. Beneath her was a bare, twin-sized mattress.

"Hello?" Jacinda said weakly. "Hello," she said again, this time a little louder. *What happened? Where am I?* she wondered. Her head throbbed wickedly, and nausea gripped her stomach. "I said hello!" she screamed.

Once Jacinda felt certain that nobody would answer her screams, she slowly moved off her mattress. She carefully stood, using her hand to steady herself against the cement wall. Again, she surveyed the room. It appeared the only way out was the door at the top of the stairs. She willed herself to remember what had happened. Her memories were hazy. She recalled mailing the computer, and then walking home. She remembered Agent Asher waiting inside her condo. *Agent Asher,* she thought to herself. *Where is he?* She remembered the cameras and the reporters. *"Kyler!"* she said out loud, before realizing someone might be listening. *Do they really have my baby? How did they find him? What will they do to him?*

It was the thought of Kyler that gave her the

strength to push herself off the cement wall and head toward the stairs. Each wooden step creaked loudly as she made her way to the door. When she got to the top stair, she pulled a string, making a light bulb spring to life. Only then did she realize the door was made of metal. She tried to twist the doorknob, but realized it was pointless. She banged wildly on the door. "Open this door!" she demanded. "Open it now!" She pounded on the door with her fists until it was obvious nobody was coming to her rescue.

"Can you hear me?" she screamed. "If you can hear me, you might want to hear what I have to say. I have information. I have a lot of information. I will tell you everything I know," she lied. She wasn't going to reveal anything, but tried to bait the trap nonetheless. "You can't just leave me here! What good would leaving me here do you?" she yelled, sounding more and more desperate. She wiggled the doorknob, and kicked the door. Her headache worsened, and her mouth was bone dry. She turned, walked down the stairs, and returned to her mattress. Lying down, she used the palm of her hands to massage her eye sockets. *Why?* she wondered. *What do they want?*

*****

Lyla was elated to be at the zoo. She wondered if

Kyler was having half as much fun as she was. She'd never seen a lion or tiger in person, and she viewed them with a youthful enthusiasm that Carl found adorable. Kyler was perched on Carl's shoulders. His snow cone-stained face expressed absolute delight.

"Moneys!" Kyler said, as he tapped on Carl's head. Kyler had a red balloon tied to his wrist. It was his second balloon of the day. His first balloon had been stolen by the wind. Lyla couldn't believe how upset he had been when the balloon had flown out of his hand. His little face had crinkled, and a single tear rolled down his face. It had only taken about thirty seconds for that single tear to be followed by a full-on crying fit.

Carl had wasted no time running back to the souvenir stand to replace it. "Let's tie this one around your wrist," Carl suggested. "If it's tied to your wrist, you won't lose it." Kyler had been perfectly happy to offer his wrist to Carl. That had been over an hour ago. They'd walked at least two miles since then.

"You've got to be getting tired," Lyla said to Carl. "Do you want me to carry him?"

"Me? Tired? No way," Carl responded. "I'm just getting started."

Lyla smiled weakly. Carl placed one arm around her shoulders. "Oh, come on, you aren't tired, are you? I mean, we've only been walking for hours," Carl said sarcastically.

"I just worry about the sun, and Kyler seems to be getting sleepy. He's usually taken a nap by now."

"Lyla, you're wearing long sleeves, a huge floppy hat, sunglasses, and SPF 90. Who knew they even made SPF 90?"

Lyla shrugged. "I burn easily. "

"Does Kyler?"

"I honestly don't know. I've never had him in the sun long enough. When he was in the sun, I've always slathered him in sunscreen."

"Moneys!" Kyler repeated, clearly annoyed that he was ignored the first time.

Carl bounced up and down, making the toddler on his shoulders giggle. "What do you need money for, little guy? What else can you buy? You already have a balloon and stuffed tiger. You've eaten a snow cone and the nastiest hot dog on the entire planet. What more could you possibly want?"

Lyla looked down at the stuffed tiger in her hand. "I was sure he'd pick the bear. He loves bears. And he's not saying money. He wants to go back to the monkeys."

"Are you sure?" Carl asked.

"Positive," replied Lyla.

Carl looked up at Kyler, "Is she right? Do you want to go see the monkeys?"

Kyler began excitedly clapping his hands. "Moneys! See Moneys!"

Carl winked at Lyla. "I guess you're right. I see you speak Kylerese."

Lyla giggled. "You'll get the hang of it."

Carl smiled. "I guess we're going back to the monkeys." He used both hands to lift Kyler from his shoulders and placed him by his feet. Carl pulled a map of the zoo out of his back pocket. As Carl studied the map, Kyler wrapped his arm around Lyla's leg.

"Dygur," Kyler said as he reached for the stuffed animal.

Lyla handed Kyler the tiger. "My dygur," Kyler said, snuggling it against his face.

"Yes, angel. That's your tiger," Lyla agreed. Seeing Kyler so happy made her worry her heart would explode with joy. Each day she thought life couldn't possibly get any better, and each day she'd been proven wrong.

"Monkeys, monkeys, monkeys," Carl said. He slid his finger across the map. "Monkeys are right there." Sliding his finger to the other side of the map, he said, "And we are right here. Oh, good, the monkeys are on the complete opposite side of the zoo."

Lyla picked Kyler up and placed him on her hip. "It's really okay. We can just see whatever animal is close." Carl faced Lyla and did his best to act serious. "Now, Lyla. Maybe you'll be able to sleep tonight if you deprive that sweet child of seeing his beloved monkeys, but I, myself, couldn't rest with that on my conscience."

Lyla laughed harder than she'd ever laughed in her entire life. "How did you…? How did you…?" She was laughing so hard that she could barely speak. "How did you say that with a straight face?"

Carl still looked as serious as ever. "How did I say what with a straight face? Are you referring to the monkey deprivation comment?"

 Lyla grabbed her stomach. "Stop it, Carl," she said between fits of laughter. "Stop it."

"Stop what? Are you laughing at me? I can't believe you're laughing at me." He took Kyler from her hip, "Can you believe she's laughing at me? All I'm trying to do is keep you off a therapist's couch. I don't want to be responsible for you having to go to therapy because you were deprived of monkeys when you were two."

"Moneys!" Kyler said, while doing his best to climb from Carl's arm to his shoulders.

Carl hoisted Kyler to his shoulders and looked towards Lyla. Lyla was still laughing, only now she had tears streaming down her face. "Whatever, Lyla. You can stand here all day and laugh at me if you wish, but Kyler and I have 'Moneys' to go visit. Feel free to join us," he said, never cracking a smile.

Lyla couldn't control her laughter. She bent down and braced herself against her knees.

"Just a minute, I have to catch my breath," she said, still giggling.

Carl looked up at Kyler "You're lucky I came along, little guy. Without me, the monkey depriver might have had her way."

"Stop it," Lyla said, still wiping tears.

Carl felt an overwhelming sense of bliss. Never in

his life had two people made him so happy. He hated zoos. He wasn't even a big fan of animals, but right now, at this very moment, there was no place in the world he'd rather be.

CHAPTER 20

The limo pulled into the parking lot of a very unimpressive building. A small sign outside of the building read Three Ocean Rehabilitation. *Why sugarcoat it?* Keith wondered. *Why not just call it The Torture and Programming Dungeon?* He was curious if girls like Chyanne would ever willingly go to a place with such a name. Although, according to Tyla, they probably would. There wasn't anything they wouldn't do for fame and fortune.

Lori, Keith, and Chyanne walked to the front door. Jeeves walked behind them, pulling their luggage. Keith immediately noticed the diversity between the exterior and interior of the building. The exterior looked somewhat worn down and shabby. By stark contrast, the interior was gorgeous. The marble floor resembled a chessboard with checkered black and white tiles. The entry room walls were made of double-paned glass with water flowing through them like waterfalls. A raven-haired young woman sat behind a modern looking desk. She looked annoyed that customers interrupted her text conversation.

In a very mechanical tone, she asked, "Is there something I can help you with?"

Lori snapped back, "No, go ahead. Keep texting your boyfriend. We don't want to interrupt. We'll just wait here patiently until you're finished."

Lori's sarcastic response did little to rile the receptionist.

"Do you have an appointment?" she asked, without so much as cracking a smile.

Lori grabbed Chyanne by the shoulders. "This is Chyanne. The facility is expecting her. Please tell your boss we're here. Then tell him it would be in his company's best interest to hire a new desk girl."

The receptionist still seemed unfazed by Lori. She picked up the phone, hit a single button, and said, "Hello, Dr. Berg, Chyanne just arrived." She placed the phone back on the receiver and said, "He'll be out shortly."

Within thirty seconds, a man in his early sixties

walked through a pair of swinging doors. His short, pudgy body was draped in a white lab coat. Eyeglasses rested on his round, chubby cheeks. He waddled like a penguin when he walked. His glasses looked entirely too small for his chubby face. Keith, who was still casting characters for the movie of his life, decided this would be exactly the kind of man he would cast to play an evil doctor at a programming facility.

Dr. Berg opened his arms in a welcoming gesture. "Welcome," he said, in a thick German accent, before approaching the group with an outstretched hand. After shaking each hand, he looked at Chyanne. "You must be Chyanne."

"I am," Chyanne nervously responded.

"Well, Chyanne, Alice here will take you to your room," he said, pointing to the beautiful receptionist. "Once you've changed into your gown, your handlers will be able to join you for a short time. Does that sound okay?"

Chyanne looked at Lori.

"That sounds fine," Lori said, realizing Chyanne was too scared to speak on her own behalf.

"Perfect," said Dr. Berg. "Why don't you two follow me to Handler Hall. While Alice shows

Chyanne to her room, I'll show you to yours."

Lori and Keith followed Dr. Berg down a long, windowless hall. The fluorescent lights and white walls hurt Keith's eyes. "I expected the whole facility to look like the front room," Keith said, in an awkward attempt at conversation.

"I'm afraid not," replied Dr. Berg. That would be entirely too comfortable to serve our purposes. This is a programming facility, not a five-star hotel. However, I think you'll be pleased with the handler's quarters." He continued leading Lori and Keith down the hall. Keith heard a rolling sound behind him, and looked around to find a man in white scrubs pulling their luggage. Dr. Berg pointed to a room on the right.

"This shall be your room..." He paused, realizing he never got their names.

"Keith," he said. "My name is Keith. This is Lori."

"Keith. It's nice to meet you. I know Lori. She comes here quite often."

Lori smiled. "I know you didn't put someone else in my room, Dr. Berg," she said. She was flirting with the man, but Keith could tell it was only an act.

"I wouldn't dare," Dr Berg said.

"I knew I could count on you," Lori said with a wink. She headed to the room next to Keith's.

Keith walked into his room and was completely underwhelmed. It looked like a standard hotel room. After seeing the luxury in the front, he had hoped his room would be just as impressive. He turned around to find his suitcase sitting behind him. He lifted his suitcase and placed it on the bed. Keith glanced in the mirror. He felt ridiculous wearing spy glasses. It wasn't that the glasses were particularly hideous; he just wasn't used to wearing anything on his face. He pushed a button on his watch. The watch beeped twice, indicating it had just been turned on. Mr. Fisher had told Keith the watch would save five hundred hours of video. Keith decided to turn it on. He didn't want to miss anything.

Keith heard a knock at his door. Taking one last glance in the mirror, he walked toward the door and opened it to find Dr. Berg standing on the other side. Dr. Berg forced a smile and said, "Are you ready to visit Chyanne's room?" Keith noticed Lori was standing behind the doctor.

"Sure," Keith said, trying his best to exude an air of confidence.

Dr. Berg led Lori and Keith down two large hallways before stopping in front of the last door on the right. "She's in there," Dr. Berg said, pointing to the closed door. "You'll be allowed to spend time with her until it's time for her first session. When the programmer arrives, you must come back to your rooms until you're told to return. Understand?"

Lori smiled at Dr. Berg. "So then you're saying it's the same routine as the last twenty times I was here?"

"Indeed," replied the doctor. "I was explaining for the sake of the young man. I believe this is his first visit to our facility."

"Thank you, Dr. Berg," Lori said, as she opened the door to Chyanne's room. Keith followed Lori, and what he saw stopped him dead in his tracks. He was being dramatic when he thought they should label the place a dungeon, but nothing could have been closer to the truth. The room was a little larger than a typical hospital room. The walls were white, and the floor had the same black and white, checkered design as the entrance.

Unlike a hospital room, the space was filled with what looked like torture devices. Handcuffs hung on the wall above the bed. There were also foot cuffs at the end of the bed. Next to the bed was a second set of hand and foot cuffs. Those, however, were clearly built for someone in a standing position. A device that could only be described as something akin to an electric chair sat in the corner of the room. It had metal cuffs, and was plugged into the wall. Something that looked like a metal helmet sat on a stainless steel cart next to the chair. Next to the chair sat a large machine that reminded Keith of a coffin, although it was larger and made of stainless steel.

"What's that?" Keith asked Lori. He immediately regretted asking the question. After all, if he had been a real handler, as he had claimed, he would probably know the function of such a machine.

Lori sat on the small bed next to Chyanne. "What does it look like?" she asked. Keith decided to let the question go. He was surprised when Lori answered.

"It's a sensory deprivation tank. While inside, Chyanne's senses won't be needed, because there will be no stimulation. It's completely dark. She'll be floating in water the same temperature as her body. She won't be able to see or hear anything. There is nothing to distract her from thinking. In fact, thinking is all she'll be able to do in the chamber. I'm surprised you haven't seen one before."

Keith shrugged. "I've seen sensory deprivation tanks," Keith lied. "This one just looks different than the ones they used back west."

Keith was desperate to turn Lori's attention away from himself. "So, Chyanne, are you pumped about the chamber?" Keith asked, hoping Chyanne would begin rambling. However, Chyanne said nothing. Her head was on her pillow, and her body was motionless. "Chyanne," Keith repeated, "are you okay? "

"She's fine," Lori said. "They've just given her the TRI-1."

"Of course, the TRI-1," Keith repeated, hoping he didn't sound as ignorant as he felt. Keith made sure to look at everything in the room, hoping the camera inside his glasses or watch would capture things just as he saw them.

A woman in a white lab coat entered the room. She looked at a clipboard before speaking. "So, this must be Chyanne."

"Hi, Jenni,"Lori said in a tone that indicated the two were familiar with one another. Jenni looked up. "Lori! How have you been?"

Lori smiled. "I can't complain, how about you?"

Jenni shrugged her tiny shoulders. "I've just been working. It's been non-stop around here."

"Busier than usual?" Lori asked.

"Much busier than usual."

"Entertainers?"

"Some, but mostly sleepers."

"Aw," said Lori. She realized Jenni wouldn't be allowed to talk about anyone the government sent, and decided to change the subject.

"Jenni, I'd like you to meet Chyanne. Chyanne, this is Jenni." Both Jenni and Lori laughed.

"I could be a purple gorilla and she wouldn't notice," Jenni said. "I seriously doubt she'll remember my name."

"Your name?" Lori laughed. "She won't remember her name when she gets out of here."

"Not unless we tell her to," Jenni said, while checking Chyanne's blood pressure and vitals. After Jenni was satisfied Chyanne's vitals were strong enough, she lifted Chyanne's arm by her tiny wrist. She secured her wrist into one of the handcuffs on the wall. She walked around the bed, and clasped Chyanne's other hand into another metal cuff. Jenni walked toward the end of the bed. She placed the leather foot restraints around Chyanne's tiny ankles. Keith noticed how helpless and childlike Chyanne looked in her current state. She was helpless. The chipped paint on Chyanne's toenails inspired ridicule from Lori.

"Do you think we can get her a pedicure before the TRI-1 wears off?"

"I don't know about a pedicure, but I have to get her all hooked up before it wears off." Jenni rolled a stainless steel tray towards the bed. Rolls of wire lay on the tray. Jenni began adhering the wires to Chyanne's petite body. "I've got to hurry if I want to get this finished before she comes out of the TRI-1 daze. Why don't the two of you go back to your rooms, and I'll come get you as soon as I'm finished." Lori did as instructed, and stood to leave the room.

"See you soon," Lori said to Jenni, before motioning for Keith to follow her.

*****

Jacinda awoke to the sound of a latch being slid open. She sat up, and focused her eyes toward the top of the stairs. Two men in suits entered, and closed the door behind them. Jacinda immediately recognized one of the men as Agent Asher. She had never seen the second man before. He was a small man, unlike Agent Asher, although most men would look small next to Asher's muscular frame. Jacinda sat in silence as the men walked down the stairs.

"Hello, Mrs. Kilmeade." said Agent Asher. "This is my associate. His name is…" Asher cut his own sentence short, "I guess you really don't need to know his name, it's not important." Jacinda stared at Asher, refusing to look meek or frightened. "Mrs. Kilmeade. You aren't looking so well," Asher continued. "Let me guess, you have the worst headache of your life and you're dying of thirst. Am I right?" Jacinda didn't respond. "Mrs. Kilmeade, I know the chloroform didn't damage your vocal cords. Is there a reason you aren't responding, or are you just being rude?"

"What do you want?" Jacinda demanded.

"Look at that," he said to his companion. "She can speak."

Agent Asher opened his briefcase and pulled out a bottle of water and some pills. "Take these," he said, throwing her the bottle and pills.

"What are they?"

"They're for the pain."

"How do I know that? They could be cyanide." Asher smiled. His innocent dimples were in stark contrast to the sinister look in his eyes.

"Mrs. Kilmeade, I assure you they aren't cyanide. If I wanted you dead, you'd already be dead," Asher said, before pulling his gun out of its holster. "I know you're a smart lady, Mrs. Kilmeade. I just want to remind you that if you try anything stupid, I won't hesitate to kill you. Only now, I won't have to fill out paperwork because the self-defense story is no longer needed. Nobody knows you're here. I hate the paperwork associated with self-defense killings. I prefer calling a cleanup crew to dump bodies into the ocean."

The man standing next to Asher stepped forward. "I'd drink all that water if I were you, ma'am. You don't want to get dehydrated."

"Are you serious?" Jacinda asked.

"Absolutely," the man said. "But not nearly as serious as dehydration. The average person should drink at least sixty-four ounces of water a day. Our bodies need water to function." Jacinda was not amused.

"Get to the point," she said, before she threw the pills down her throat and chased them with water.

"Feisty, isn't she?" asked the small man.

"Feisty indeed," replied Agent Asher.

"What do you want from me?" Jacinda asked.

"You're not keeping me here for sport. You want something. I can't help you unless I know what it is. Gregory? Do you want Gregory?"

Agent Asher crouched down until his eyes were level with Jacinda's. We don't *want* Gregory, Mrs. Kilmeade. We simply want him to suffer."

"Suffer for what?" She asked. "Suffer for kidnapping?"

"He derailed BARAchip. If it weren't for his stupidity, everything would have happened according to prophecy. He betrayed us. He can't repair the damage he's done, Mrs. Kilmeade. You don't think they'll just let him walk back into the Senate, do you? No. All the expense and effort put into the BARAchip legislation was wasted."

"Then you want to know where he is?" Jacinda asked, wondering if they'd try to pry the information from her. "What about my son? Do you really have my son?"

"Wouldn't you like to know?" Asher said with a grin.

"You said you had my son. Give me proof. Prove to me that you have Kyler."

Asher smirked. "Now, Mrs. Kilmeade. You are in no position to be making demands." Jacinda knew he was right. For the time being, she was helpless.

"Tell me why I'm here!" Jacinda screamed.

"You're here for one reason, and one reason only, Mrs. Kilmeade—to punish Gregory."

*****

Keith followed Lori into Chyanne's room to find Chyanne still chained to the wall. Terror was evident on her tear-stained face. Her body trembled, and she begged Lori to free her from her restraints.

"They hurt so much!" Chyanne said through gritted teeth. "I've never been in this much pain."

Lori laughed. "You think you are in pain now? This is just the beginning, Princess."

"I changed my mind. I don't want to do this anymore."

"They all change their minds at this stage," Lori said. "It hurts, so you want to stop. We won't stop. By the end, you'll be begging for death, but we won't kill you either. This is what you wanted. Remember that."

Keith felt helpless. Should he help free Chyanne, or was he just supposed to watch her be treated in a way that was even against the Geneva Convention? He knew he couldn't save her. Saving her would blow his cover, and ruin any chance he had of collecting proof that such facilities existed. He knew that he had to keep playing a role, even if that role was becoming increasingly uncomfortable.

"Please, Lori. Tell them I've changed my mind. Please tell them!" Chyanne begged.

Lori touched the hem of Chyanne's hospital gown. "You still have this thing on, so I guess they didn't move on to phase two."

Horror filled Chyanne's eyes. "Will I be naked?"

"Not completely. I mean, you'll be wearing some wires," Lori said without much emotion. *She really is sadistic*, Keith thought. *She's enjoying this.* Keith kept his watch aimed towards Chyanne. He hoped the video would be able to capture the panic in her eyes.

Jenni entered the room with two men in tow. Jenni smiled. "Meet Bad and Worse. They'll carry out phase two."

"Bad," Lori said as she nodded a greeting. "Worse," she said as she greeted the second man. "What happened to Frick and Frack?" Lori asked.

Jenni grinned at Lori. "Frick and Frack are down

the hall. They won't be meeting Chyanne until day three."

Jenni retrieved a pair of scissors from a drawer and began cutting Chyanne's gown, causing Chyanne to scream at the top of her lungs, "No! Please. No!" Chyanne begged, but her protests fell on deaf ears.

Keith's heart began to race. He forced his eyes to the ground. He couldn't watch Chyanne get tortured. He felt as if he were doing her a favor by looking away. Chyanne's screams continued to echo throughout the room. While Keith's eyes were fixed on the floor, his watch was aimed towards Chyanne. He tried to preserve as much of her dignity as he could by not watching, but he knew he needed proof that such wicked practices existed.

CHAPTER 21

Livingston sat on Andy's couch with a computer in his lap. "How's the website coming?" Andy asked.

"I'm just designing it right now. I can't upload it until your guy gets here. Are you sure he can get it online without anyone tracing it to the source?"

"Positive," Andy assured him.

"That's what I wanted to hear. I need to get back in the fight, Andy. If I'm able to work in some capacity of the news, I won't feel so worthless."

"Don't be so hard on yourself, Rob. You aren't worthless. You delayed the chip by God only knows how long."

"Delayed being the operative word. The mark of the beast will rear its ugly head eventually."

"Eventually," Andy agreed. "But thanks to you, not

today. Any precious amount of time we can buy is priceless. You know that."

Livingston continued working on the website while Andy anxiously paced around his apartment. "I need a break," Livingston confessed, before moving the computer off his lap. "What's on television?"

"Stuff to poison your brain and distract you from reality," Andy replied.

"I'm amazed you even have a television in your house, as much as you loathe TV."

"I have to have one. People would think I was downright strange if I didn't. Besides, it helps pass the time and occasionally brings us breaking news."

Livingston smiled. "Have you ever thought about where the term *breaking news* came from? I mean, in what way is it breaking?"

"Rob, my dear friend, its time you get some fresh air. I think you're getting cabin fever. You're way overthinking things."

Livingston turned on the television to find a picture of Tony Randall. "Turn it up," Andy said, leaning closer to the screen.

Livingston turned up the volume in time to hear the next story. "Wait, no, go back!" Livingston screamed at the television.

"Has that ever worked for you?" Andy asked.

"Once or twice," Livingston said. "Okay, never," he admitted, before grabbing his computer. After a few clicks on the keyboard, Livingston found what he was looking for. "He's dead. Tony Randall is dead. They're saying he was found in his hotel room in California surrounded by drug paraphernalia."

*****

"I don't think I've ever been this exhausted," said Lyla, as she reclined in the passenger seat of Carl's car.

Carl glanced at Kyler's reflection in the rearview mirror. "He's out cold."

Lyla checked the clock. "We've been driving exactly two minutes. That might be a record. In fact, I know it is. He was exhausted."

"Yeah, but he seemed to have fun." Carl said.

"Seemed to? I assure you he had the time of his life!"

"He deserves it," Carl said. "Poor kid hasn't had much of a childhood."

Lyla looked hurt. "I know. I just wasn't able to expose him to much."

Carl realized that Lyla had taken the comment personally. "No, it's not your fault. You know that. You did what you had to do. You didn't have a childhood, either. None of this is your fault. I hope you know that. You do know that, right? Please tell me you know that."

"I know it's not technically my fault, but it still breaks my heart that I wasn't able to give him a magical childhood."

"Lyla, he's two. I don't think childhood even technically starts until three. In fact, I'm certain it doesn't begin until three."

Lyla smiled. "Where did you get that information?"

"I read it," Carl responded.

Lyla turned in her seat to face Carl. "Where did you read it?" she asked, clearly playing along.

"I can't remember exactly where I read it, but it was somewhere official. That much I'm certain of."

"Official, huh?"

"Yes, official. What's with the interrogation, woman?" Lyla laughed. "Oh, you think interrogating me is funny?" asked Carl.

"I think you're funny," Lyla said. She gazed at him adoringly. Carl pulled up to a stoplight and turned to face Lyla. He looked into her eyes and experienced what could only be described as *a moment*. He'd heard others talk about *moments*, but was never completely convinced they'd existed. Now, Carl Ward was a believer. He'd never looked into someone's eyes and seen so much love staring back. It was breathtaking.

The moment was wrecked by the sound of a car horn behind them. "I guess I should keep my eyes on the road," Carl said, as he redirected his attention to the task of driving. Something fluttered inside his stomach. It felt like the wings of a hundred butterflies were flitting about inside of him. *It's official*, he thought. *I'm in love.*

When he glanced at Lyla again, her face was positively beaming. "What?" Carl asked.

"Nothing."

"It can't be nothing; what are you so happy about?"

"You. That's all. I just find you impossibly charming."

"That's a first," Carl admitted. "Nobody has ever accused me of being charming."

"Well, you are. You're positively charming."

Carl smiled. "I think you're charming, too. In fact, you might be the most charming monkey depriver I've ever met in my life." Those words made her giggle. Carl reached across the center console and took Lyla's small, soft hand into his own. Lyla didn't say a word. She simply squeezed his hand to reciprocate the romantic gesture, letting him know she welcomed his affection. Hand in hand, they drove all the way home in silence. There were no words that would be adequate. No, words would have cheapened the moment. More was said during the precious silence than ten lifetimes of talking ever could have expressed.

*****

Keith sat with Lori in Chyanne's room, still feeling as if he might be sick. "What's wrong, Intern?" Lori asked.

"That part never gets any easier to watch," Keith said, sounding as if it wasn't his first time to witness such brutal abuse. "How long will she be in that thing, anyway?"

"She'll stay in the sensory deprivation chamber until the morning. That will give her plenty of time to think about what just happened."

"She hasn't eaten anything all day," Keith said. "What about dinner?"

"Do they not starve the slaves in the west?" Lori asked. "That settles it. If ever I become a mind control slave, I want to be programmed in the west."

Keith back peddled, "We just don't starve them until day three."

Lori grinned. "Wimps. Here we starve them until day three, at which time they'll be given a live rat in a cage. They usually turn their nose up at the thought of eating the rat, but the rat starts looking pretty appetizing around day eight or nine."

The thought of eating the rat pushed Keith over the edge. He ran out of the room, and found the restroom they passed on their way to Chyanne's room. He barely had time to lock the door before throwing himself in front of the toilet. After vomiting, he scooted backwards on the floor and leaned his back against the wall. Sweat beaded up on his forehead, and his sweat-drenched hands trembled.

The physical abuse was supposed to traumatize the victim, but there were two victims in that room today. Keith knew Chyanne would be far more traumatized than he was, but he also knew witnessing such evil would change him forever. He would never be able to forget her guttural screams in between begging for mercy. Again, Keith lunged towards the toilet. With nothing left in his stomach, he dry heaved until his stomach ached and his head throbbed.

*****

Jacinda's headache was easing. *Why?* she wondered. Why would God take her so far just to let her fall so hard? It seemed cruel that she had been reunited with Kyler, only to have him ripped from her life again. She thought of Lyla, and a sense of peace settled over her. *Maybe he's better off with her, anyway,* she told herself. Jacinda didn't care about her own safety. She would happily give up her life, as long as Kyler was safe and happy. Now that she knew Kyler was in loving, nurturing hands, her soul could rest.

They don't have him, she convinced herself. *If they had him, they would show me proof. They'd want me to suffer. He's still safe. My baby is still safe.* Jacinda was ripped out of her thoughts by the sound of the sliding metal latch. "Who's there?" she yelled. The door still hadn't opened, but she was certain someone was on the other side. She waited for what seemed like an eternity. "Is someone there?" she yelled again, wondering if she'd imagined the noise.

The door slowly opened. A short, unfamiliar man walked through the door. He balanced a tray on his right hand. Unlike Asher and his goon, he wasn't wearing a suit. Dressed in casual attire, he moved slowly. The man never took his eyes off Jacinda. She waited for the man to walk down the stairs, but he never did. Without saying a word, he sat the tray down, and backed out of the door.

Jacinda was starving. She jumped off her mattress and made it two steps before she was overcome by a dizzy sensation. She felt weak and nauseated. *I got up too quickly,* she thought, but never slowed her movement towards the stairs. She used the guardrail to steady her trembling body as she walked up the steps. She had no idea how long she'd been locked inside the room. It could have been days, or weeks—she had no idea. How long had it been since she'd eaten? She barely had the strength to make it up the stairs. When she approached the tray, she was delighted to find a hamburger, French fries, and a drink. Not having the strength or patience to carry it to her mattress, she sat on the top step and devoured the food.

*****

Andy awoke from his nap to find Livingston working on his computer. "Still plugging away, I see," Andy said.

"There's just so much information," Livingston replied.

"Really, you got more?"

"Yes and no. I'm just trying to put all of this information into a timeline that will make sense to the public. There are a million websites about the New World Order and the Illuminati, but ours has to be different. We have to show a timeline of events. We also need to support our claims with examples and video. Our website needs to not only serve as a website, but a news channel. Once Keith arrives with the video, we'll need a way to broadcast it in a way that follows a typical news format. It has to be presented in a way the public is familiar with. If we just lay it all out in front of them, they won't know how to interpret it. They'll just get overwhelmed and tune it out completely."

Andy nodded. "So, did you talk to Fisher?"

"I did," replied Livingston. "He said he sent Keith to a programming facility with Tony Randall's girlfriend, Chyanne."

"Now, that's important," Andy said. He was now sitting directly across from Livingston. "You need to somehow report about George's time spent with Tony in the sweat box. You can say he was killed for encouraging Chyanne not to sell her soul. Then, boom! You have actual footage of Chyanne in the programming facility."

Livingston continued typing. "That's the plan."

"So, I guess you've got this figured out."

"Not completely. No. There's still so much I'm unsure about."

Andy nodded his head in agreement. "There always will be. You just have to report what you do know, and hopefully more truth will rise to the surface as time goes on."

"Still no word from Jacinda?" Livingston asked, in what sounded more like a statement than a question.

"I'm afraid not. Word will come soon. I was in that game long enough to understand psychological warfare. My guess is they're using her to flush Gregory Kilmeade out of hiding."

Livingston stood to stretch his stiff muscles. "I hope she's okay. I expect they'll kill her, but I hope they do it fast. I hope she doesn't suffer." Andy raised an eyebrow. "What makes you think they'll kill her?"

"What other choice do they have?"

"They have a few options. Death seems to be the least likely. No, after Chandra Kilmeade's suicide and Gregory's disappearance, death would look too suspicious. My guess is they'll program her."

"How will they do that?"

"It's easier than you think. It's a process the government has used for years. First, they break you down. Then they build you into whomever they want you to be."

"So, they'll make her a different person?" Livingston asked, sounding unconvinced.

"No, not necessarily. However, with the right mix of pharmaceuticals, hypnotherapy, and torture, they can make her forget anything they don't want her to remember. They can replace those memories with new ones—fake ones."

"They can do that?"

"They can and they do. It happens more than you think."

Andy leaned back into his chair. "I remember this one time during our first war with Iraq."

"You were in the CIA then, right?" Livingston asked.

"I was. I was part of a task force responsible for turning prisoners of war into weapons against their own countries. There was this one prisoner in particular. Let's call him Joe."

"His name was Joe?"

"Of course it wasn't Joe; it was a traditional Iraqi name. I just can't remember it, so we'll call him Joe. Anyway, Joe was not only willing to die for his country—he desired it. He wanted to become a martyr; he wasn't scared of death. He was in our custody for about four months. During that time, we stripped him of his identity. Through the process of reprogramming, we managed to send him back to his country as a U.S. operative. We programmed him to shoot anything and everything when he heard his national anthem. We let that hypnotic suggestion sleep inside of him. He was released, unable to remember any of his time in captivity. Instead, he remembered hiding out, picking off U.S. soldiers one by one.

"Naturally, we had to install the suicide response. Dead men can't talk. They can't be reprogrammed. We programmed Joe to kill himself after he went on his shooting spree. We couldn't take the chance that the Iraqis would retrieve any information using their own reprogramming and hypnosis techniques."

Livingston looked intrigued. "Do you think they do that here? In America, I mean? Do you think they can program a person to assassinate someone without memory of what they've done?"

"They can and they do."

"Do you have any examples? I'd love to include that on the site."

"I have many examples. Better than that, I know men who were responsible for programming mind control slaves. I know one man in particular who found God and strives everyday to forgive himself for the sins he helped perpetrate on his own soil. I bet he'd be willing to give you his story." Andy then walked to his kitchen drawer and pulled out a computer flash drive. He tossed it to Livingston. "Keith dropped this off before he went to New York. It has interviews from Jacinda, the maidservant, and Carl. Carl talks about the sacrifice, but we'll have to wait until Keith gets back to see the video. He didn't have time to upload it from the glasses before he left."

CHAPTER 22

Keith walked down the long hallway leading to Chyanne's room. It had been exactly three months since they'd arrived. In the course of his stay, he'd witnessed unspeakable evil. He watched as they clipped Chyanne's upper and lower eyelids open, preventing her from blinking for over twenty-four hours. As cruel as that act was, it was perhaps the least cruel thing he witnessed at the facility. A wicked energy flowed throughout the building. He was unable to escape it, even when he was alone in his room. He wondered if the black cloud that hung over the facility would follow him once he left.

Earlier, Keith had met a woman named Nurse Fee in the coffee lounge. According to Nurse Fee, Chyanne was broken and vulnerable enough to start the next phase: insertion. The torture phase was complete. It had served its purpose. Chyanne was a shell of the person she was when they'd arrived. He never would have believed someone could be driven to a state of insanity in three months, but there was no question—Chyanne was now insane. She spent a lot of time talking to herself. Sometimes she talked to the walls and other inanimate objects. There were times she didn't even notice she had visitors, and she simply stared into space and hummed a tune that had been playing in her room for a month straight. Although the tune no longer played in her room, it was clearly still playing in her head.

Keith documented much of the torture and transformation with the camera in his glasses and watch. Keith wondered if he, himself, was becoming wicked. The first day they'd tortured Chyanne, he'd become physically ill. However, with each new day, his stomach grew stronger and stronger. He began to witness more and more without experiencing a visceral reaction. By no means did he enjoy the torture; he just wasn't as fazed by it as he had been in the beginning.

He wondered how it was possible to feel less and less affected while watching someone be tortured and violated. Then, he wondered if he would have lasted the entire three months if he remained as affected by the torture on day ninety as he had been on day one. Was he becoming apathetic? Was he becoming as wicked as his environment? He pulled himself out of his own head as he approached Chyanne's door.

Jenni and Lori were already in Chyanne's room when Keith arrived. Keith had become surprisingly close to Lori. She insisted all of this was in Chyanne's best interest, and that she'd finally be able to live out her dreams. She said all things worth having required sacrifice. It was a twisted perspective, but in a way, she had a point.

In a normal setting, Keith and Lori never would have gotten along. But this wasn't a normal setting. It was almost as if they were trapped on an island— Terror Island. If they hadn't talked to each other, they would have gone as crazy as Chyanne. Sure, the staff was in and out, but Lori was the one constant during Keith's stay.

Jenni and Lori were seated at a small table in the corner of the room. The women were drinking coffee and taking about something that didn't seem to pertain to Chyanne. Chyanne was sitting in her bed, hugging her knees tightly against her chest. Her emaciated body rocked back and forth as she hummed the tune that would haunt Keith forever. Chyanne had thin when she'd arrived at the facility, but now she was little more than skin and bones draped in a hospital gown.

Keith joined Jenni and Lori. "What's the plan?" Keith asked, as he sat at the table.

"Nurse Fee will come get her for a room change any minute. Fee is responsible for building her back up, as we like to say in the business. No more torture for Miss Chyanne," replied Jenni.

"She's the good witch," Lori said, making Keith wonder if she'd overheard his and Chyanne's earlier conversation.

"I met Fee earlier," Keith said. "She seemed nice." *Even though she's evil,* he thought to himself.

"Fee is fabulous," Jenni said. "She's really the best there is. We've had our fair share of programmers come through this facility, but nobody has been as good as Fee."

Lori softened towards Keith as the months went by. Each day, Keith worked harder and harder to earn her respect. While he needed to earn her respect and trust to gain vital information, deep down he knew that's not the only reason he longed for her approval. He wondered what kind of depravity this place unleashed in him, that he would even desire the respect of someone like Lori. He'd felt such a sense of triumph when she'd called him Keith instead of Intern Boy. Was this how it happened? Was this how evil was born? Was anyone capable of evil when placed inside the right environment?

Keith looked up to see Nurse Fee walk through the door. "Hello, everyone," she said in a singsong voice. "Out with the old, in with the new," she sang with a thick, Cajun accent. She walked over to Chyanne. "Look at you, baby doll. Don't you look pathetic? Don't you worry about a thing, you hear? Nurse Fee is going to get you back on your feet and better than ever." This was the second time Keith had heard Fee refer to herself in third person. The first time had been early that morning when they'd met in the coffee lounge.

"Nurse Fee is about to turn that little girl around," she'd told Keith, as she poured sugar into her coffee.

"The first thing we've got to do is get you out of this depressing room and into somewhere a spirit can bloom. Yes, ma'am." Fee continued talking to Chyanne, although she never once got a response. "I see they successfully crushed your spirit, child. Well, that's okay, baby doll. Nurse Fee is going to build you better than ever."

A man pushing a wheelchair entered the room. Nurse Fee effortlessly swept Chyanne into her arms. "Darlin', you can't weigh an ounce over a feather," Fee said, moving Chyanne to the wheelchair. She focused her attention on Lori and Keith. "Are you two ready? Say adios to the little shop of horrors," she said, as she wheeled Chyanne out of the room. "That room just gives me the heebie-jeebies every time I go in there. I get a tingle up and down my spine every stinkin' time. Yes, I do. Nurse Fee does not like the chamber room. No, she doesn't. No, she does not, baby doll."

As soon as Nurse Fee wheeled Chyanne out of the room, Keith turned to Jenni. "Does she always talk like that?"

Jenni smiled. "I'm afraid she does."

"Please tell me you're kidding."

"I wish I was. You'll spend two weeks with her. If you aren't careful, you'll leave here speaking in third person, too."

"You're not kidding, are you?" Keith asked Jenni.

"Not entirely, no. Jenni is not kidding. No, she's not, baby doll," Jenni responded as she followed Keith out the door.

CHAPTER 23

Lyla rushed through the house, doing last minute straightening before Carl returned home from work. She effortlessly settled into the role of homemaker. Over the past three months, Carl had taught her a lot of life skills. He'd taught her how to drive, grocery shop, and do laundry. She took pride in the mundane tasks that most people dreaded. It wasn't that she found the chores exciting; she simply felt a sense of satisfaction in knowing she could accomplish such feats as conquering a load of laundry.

Carl had also taught her how to use the internet. Her parents had forbidden computers, fearing knowledge would lead to dissent. Lyla's new life skills empowered her. She found joy in the simplest of things. Kyler was still her number one source of happiness, and God her number one source of joy.

She read her Bible daily. Each day, she felt closer and closer to Him.

She spoke to God often. She prayed He would keep Jacinda safe. Carl told her that Livingston suspected The Brotherhood in her disappearance. She knew in her heart he was right. After all, if she wasn't dead or being held captive, she would have returned months ago. At the very least, she would have called to check on Kyler. Lyla made a promise to God that she would love Kyler as her own until the day she died. She hoped and prayed Jacinda would return, but would gladly become Kyler's permanent keeper if she didn't.

Tossing the last toy into the toy box, Lyla heard the garage door open. Lyla's heart began to race, knowing Carl was home. She missed him when he was gone, and always watched the clock excitedly as she anticipated his return. Lyla walked into the living room as Carl came through the door.

"Where's Kyler?" Carl asked.

"He's asleep. He missed his afternoon nap, and then just zonked out about thirty minutes ago."

Carl looked nervous. It was a look that gripped Lyla's heart with fear. What if he wanted her to leave? What if he was tired of them? Even worse, what if Jacinda was dead? She couldn't wait another second.

"What's wrong?" Lyla asked. Carl didn't answer. Lyla's eyes reflected the panic in her heart. "Carl, what's wrong? Did something happen? What are you holding?"

Carl held up a folder. "These are your new documents." Lyla pressed her hands to her heart. "Is that all?"

"What do you mean, 'is that all'? You have a new identity. I'd say that's kind of a big deal."

Lyla squealed as she reached for the folder. "What's my new name? I hope it's something beautiful like Summer Day or Meadow Rain."

Carl laughed. "Then you're going to be sorely disappointed."

"Why?" Lyla asked, opening the envelope. "What's my new name?" Lyla pulled out a document and flipped it over. "It's a birth certificate. Jenna Roach? My new name is Jenna Roach?" Lyla stared at the document, attempting to process her new name. "Jenna Roach," she said over and over, before looking up at Carl. "Jenna is a beautiful name. I love it, but Roach? Why Roach?"

"I didn't pick the name. It's actually a real person

who was born the same year you were. Sadly, she's passed away. She was a floater. It means she didn't have any friends or family. She had lived in a shelter, and from what I understand, died of natural causes. When someone without roots or loved ones die, their information is put into a system, and they become floaters. That way, someone can take on an identity that's real. It just isn't their own."

Lyla pulled a Social Security card out of the envelope. "Oh, good. Something else with the name Roach on it," she said, only half kidding.

Carl nervously put his hand in his pocket before dropping to one knee. "I'm hoping you'll only have to use the name Roach to obtain a marriage license. I'm so bad at this. What I mean is, would you do me the honor...? Would you consider...? Will you marry me?" Carl opened a small, velvet box. Inside was the most beautiful diamond Lyla had ever seen.

Lyla dropped to her knees and embraced Carl. "Of course I will! Nothing would make me happier!" Carl removed the ring from the box and placed it on Lyla's delicate ring finger. Lyla held out her hand to admire the gorgeous ring. "I just can't believe it. I'm shocked. I'm happy. I'm just so surprised!" Lyla couldn't stop rambling. She never took her eyes off the ring. "It's the most beautiful thing I've ever seen."

Carl stood up and pulled Lyla into his arms. Holding her close, he said, "So, then it's a yes? You'll marry me?"

"Yes, yes, yes. It's absolutely a yes!" She pulled away from Carl and gave him a troubled look.

"What? What is it?" he asked, fearing she had changed her mind.

"Do we have to get married right away? I mean, Jenna Ward is nice, but I'd like to be Jenna Roach as long as possible."

Carl laughed and pulled her back into his arms. "You know you can keep the name Roach, right? I'm really not all that traditional. I would understand if you wanted to keep Roach. After all, it's your identity, and who am I to ask you to change your identity?"

Lyla buried her face into Carl's neck and giggled. "I can't wait to be Jenna Ward. You've made me the happiest person alive. I hope you know that."

"Truthfully," Carl said, "I can't imagine arriving home without you and Kyler here to greet me."

Lyla's eyes reflected the panic in her heart. "What?" asked Carl. "Did I say something wrong?"

"No," Lyla said, "not at all. I just know Kyler won't be here forever. Will you be just as excited to come home if it's just me?"

"Lyla, even if you are the only person I come home to, I'll still be the luckiest man on the planet."

*****

Andy pulled a sack of groceries out of his trunk. While he usually dreaded grocery shopping, it felt good to have a break from the close quarters he now shared with Livingston. Andy liked Livingston, but he was used to living alone. Having a roommate was an adjustment.

Andy walked through the front door to find Livingston working on the computer. "Still at it, I see," Andy said, before taking the groceries to the kitchen.

"I feel like the site will never be complete. Bryant has helped a lot, but I'm just trying to work all of this information into a format viewers will comprehend. Bryant is a genius. He created the entire website in less than a week. I just wish we had someone equally as brilliant to upload content."

Andy wondered if Livingston was faking modesty. "Come on, you're one of the best reporters in the nation. I have faith you'll create something viewers can connect to."

Livingston didn't respond to the compliment. "How long did Bryant work for the government?"

"I'm not sure," Andy replied. "I know it had to be at least twenty years. If you were impressed by his website building skills, you would have been floored by the government databases he helped design. The man is brilliant."

Livingston pointed to his computer screen. "He set it up to look like a standard news station site. We can post news updates, streaming video, audio, and a secure chat room."

"Chat room?" asked Andy.

"Yeah, he worked his computer magic to scramble the IP address of anyone who decides they want to post and share their stories."

"Do you think people will trust it's secure?"

"No, probably not. Not at first, but once we've proven ourselves, I think they'll come around." Livingston walked into the kitchen to pour himself a cup of coffee. "Have you heard anything about George?" Livingston asked, knowing the answer was probably still no.

"No, but there are some rumblings through the

grapevine about Jacinda."

Livingston looked up from his coffee. "Jacinda? What have you heard?"

"A reliable source confirmed members of The Brotherhood have her. They leaked her captivity to all the brothers in hopes that the news makes its way to Gregory."

"So then, they are just using her to flush him out of hiding?" Livingston asked.

"It appears so," Andy replied.

"What will they do to her if he doesn't return?"

"My source said the plan has changed a couple of times. They're surprised Gregory still hasn't returned. He said it appears Gregory has fallen off the face of the earth."

"Maybe he's dead."

"If he is, The Brotherhood had nothing to do with it, because they believe he's still alive."

Livingston stared pensively into his coffee. "What will they do with Jacinda?"

"For now, there are no concrete plans, but they are considering a programming facility."

"Why? Just to erase her memory?"

"They would erase as well as plant things in her memory. She would make a wonderful addition to the team. She would serve their purposes beautifully in the media as a mind control slave."

"If they do that, re-program her, I mean-- can we de-program her?"

"With the right medicine and hypnotherapy, we could." Andy paused. "Well *we* couldn't, but you know what I mean."

"How long would de-programming take?"

"We could de-program her in a third of the time it would take to program her. De-programming doesn't call for torture to the point of insanity like programming does. We wouldn't have to break her down, just build her back up."

"Would she remember anything?"

"Bits and pieces. Her memories would slowly return."

Livingston took his cup of coffee to the living room and sat on the couch. "I heard from Keith today."

Andy walked into the doorway separating the kitchen from the living room. He crossed his arms and leaned against the door frame. "How is he?" Andy asked.

"The conversation was brief, and, of course, there's a lot he couldn't say. I'm sure he suspects every inch of the facility is monitored. He just acted like he was talking to Fisher. His exact words were, 'It's going really well. They've broken her and we're moving to phase two.' Then, he started talking about school."

"What did he say about school?"

"He never said school. He called it a job. He had told his mother that he wouldn't be returning until the winter because of his new internship."

"That's it?"

"That's it. There wasn't a whole lot he could say. He was probably being watched."

CHAPTER 24

Keith sat in Chyanne's plush new room at the facility. The difference between the insertion room and the chamber room were night and day. In contrast to the cold, sinister look of the chamber room, the insertion room was contemporary and Zen-like. The comfortable room would relax anyone with its water wall and soothing music.

Keith had watched Nurse Fee help program Chyanne for the past two weeks. He'd learned a lot about Nurse Fee. She was originally from New Orleans, and claimed to have cut her teeth on voodoo. Hearing she was from Louisiana didn't surprise him, as he'd already figured as much by her accent. She wouldn't allow Keith or Lori to attend the rituals. She said the rituals were sacred, and the spirits only wanted Chyanne and the coven present.

Nurse Fee had also banned Lori and Keith from hypnotherapy sessions, but always included them in the debrief meetings with Dr. Berg. Handler inclusion in the debriefing session was mandatory. Keith had skipped a meeting or two because of illness, but was there most of the time. The handlers had to learn commands and techniques to control their slaves. Each slave was unique, so the handling of each slave was also unique.

Watching Chyanne transform from an invalid to a diva had fascinated Keith. He'd watched Nurse Fee and Dr. Berg create two alter egos for Chyanne. The first alter they'd installed was named Chy. Chy was quite different than Chyanne. Dr. Berg told Keith Chyanne would start using Chy professionally. Since she'd had a tiny amount of success in the industry, changing her name completely was out of the question.

Keith found Chy to be difficult. She was very demanding, and her over-the-top flirting made him uncomfortable. Chy always insisted on wearing inappropriate clothing, and became irate when he suggested she cover up a little.

The second alter ego they'd installed was named Hugh. Hugh was a rotten, eighteen-year-old British boy with the foulest mouth Keith had ever heard. Hugh snapped and lost his temper if he was interrupted while writing. He wrote a lot. In the week since he'd been conjured, he'd spent hours writing music. Keith was still getting used to the voice that came out of Chyanne's body when Hugh entered. She spoke in a deep, masculine voice. Hugh's words were drenched in a heavy British accent. Keith had learned the hard way not to refer to Chyanne as *her* when Hugh was in control of her body. Keith had made that mistake a few days ago, and Hugh had thrown him across the room.

Keith had no idea how such a tiny girl could possess so much strength, but Fee explained that alter egos came with their own characteristics, and that included strength.

Chyanne's lashes fluttered as she awoke from her nap. "Keith?" she said. "Why are you watching me sleep?" Keith was relieved to hear Chyanne's voice. Hearing Chy and Hugh had never gotten any less creepy.

"I'm not watching you; I was looking out the window," he lied. She looked through the window to the beautiful garden oasis outside. "Can you believe that garden exists on the same grounds as the decrepit parking lot?" Chyanne asked Keith.

"No. It's amazing, isn't it? I'd say this view is much nicer than the one before."

"Before what?" asked Chyanne, sounding confused.

"The first room."

"What first room?"

Nurse Fee walked in just in time to hear the end of their conversation. She shot Keith a conspiratorial glance. "This is the only room she's been in, child." Keith hated it when Fee called him child, but that's what she called everyone. She walked up to Chyanne, pulled a comb off her nightstand, and began brushing her hair.

"Well, look at you. You did a number on your hair, baby doll. You've got tangles for days." Fee continued to brush her hair and hummed the tune that had played in the torture chamber for weeks. As soon as Chyanne heard the tune, she shrank backwards. Within seconds Fee said, "Well, hello, Chy. I'm so glad you could join us."

Keith could tell the transformation had taken place. Chyanne's eyes changed. He now saw Chy staring back at him.

"What are you looking at?" Chy asked, utterly annoyed.

Keith cut his eyes to Nurse Fee. "Nothing, I was just..."

Chy finished his sentence. "Leaving? Good. Bye," she snapped before turning her attention to Nurse Fee. "You said I'd be out of this place already. I hate it here. I ordered a milkshake over an hour ago. Where is it?"

"It's coming, child." Fee said calmly.

"Will you stop calling me child?"

"What would you like me to call you?" Fee asked.

"Chy."

"Okay, I'll make you a deal. You sing me a song, and I'll call you Chy."

Chy rolled her eyes before belting out a beautiful chorus. Carl couldn't believe such a big voice was coming out of such a small girl.

"That's right, Chy," said Nurse Fee. "You go on. Make those angels cry with that voice, child."

"Chy," she insisted.

"I'm sorry. You're right, Chy. I was just checking on you. I see you're all right." Fee took a small object out of her lab coat. It looked like a tiny stapler one could find at any office supply store. It couldn't have even been an inch long.

"What's that?" Keith asked, unable to contain his

curiosity.

"You'll see," Nurse Fee replied.

Fee used her thumb and index finger to press the unhinged side together. "Do you hear that, child?" Fee asked, looking at Keith.

"No," replied Keith.

"Good, you're not supposed to." Fee turned her attention back to her patient. Keith could tell by looking into Chyanne's eyes that Hugh had returned.

"What are you looking at?" Hugh snapped. Fee laughed and pressed the device again. It was clear to Keith that Chyanne was back.

"Hello, Miss Chyanne," Nurse Fee said.

Chyanne looked around the room. "Where's Lori?"

"She's with Dr. Berg, baby doll. She'll be back real soon. Nurse Fee can promise you that much. Is there anything you need, child?"

Chyanne shook her head. "No, thank you."

"Well, all right then," replied Nurse Fee. "If you don't mind, I'm going to borrow Keith from you for a minute. He won't be long. I'll tell Lori you're looking for her."

"Thank you," said Chyanne, totally unaware her body had just been possessed by two alter egos.

CHAPTER 25

A booming voice at the top of the stairs awoke Jacinda from her sleep. "Hello, Mrs. Kilmeade," said the man Jacinda recognized as Agent Asher. "What, you aren't going to tell me hello? Isn't that kind of rude? Come on now, Mrs. Kilmeade. You are the wife of a U.S. senator. You're America's media darling. I would think, with that kind of resume, you'd be a little more gracious." Jacinda refused to speak.

Agent Asher walked down the staircase. "I see," he said as he touched his chin with his index finger. "Well, I've always respected the Fifth Amendment. I suppose you still have a right to remain silent, but why would you? I'm glad you're still alive. I was afraid Mike wouldn't bring you your food. He's afraid of stairs, you know?"

"No, he's not, and how long have I been here?" Jacinda asked.

"Look at that, you can speak. I was beginning to worry they cut out your tongue already. To answer your question, you've been here four months. He's not what?"

"Afraid of stairs. He's not afraid of stairs."

"How do you know?" Asher asked. "Did he tell you?"

"Because nobody is afraid of stairs!" Jacinda screamed. She balled her hands into fists and punched her mattress over and over before she composed herself and looked back up at Agent Asher.

Asher continued, "Lots of people are afraid of stairs. It's called bathmophobia. It's a silly name, isn't it? It sounds more like a fear of taking baths. The whole thing is ridiculous, if you ask me."

"Why? Why are you keeping me here? Why not kill me or let me go? What purpose has it served to keep me locked in a basement for four months?"

Asher looked next to her mattress, noticing a pile of books. "I'm glad Mike brought you those books after all. He's forgetful, especially on rainy days. Rain triggers his memory loss. It's not his fault. I blame the programmer. How stupid do you have to be to program rain as a trigger?"

"What?" Jacinda asked, completely perplexed.

"Nothing. It's not important." Asher continued scanning the basement. He spotted a pile of towels. "I see you found the shower. I was hoping you'd find it. Has Mike been keeping you stocked with fresh towels?" Jacinda didn't respond.

"You know, Mrs. Kilmeade. I just don't get you sometimes. We've given you a comfortable mattress, books, a shower, and three square meals a day, yet you still complain. Are you ever satisfied? It's no wonder Gregory took off." Jacinda jumped to her feet and sprang towards Asher. She had time to dig her fingernails into his throat before he pushed her, sending her flying to the mattress.

Asher touched his throat before examining his finger. "Blood. Look at that, Mrs. Kilmeade. You made me bleed. That wasn't very nice. You're not a very nice person. It really is no wonder Gregory hasn't returned to claim you."

"So then, you haven't found him?" Jacinda asked, her voice fueled by anger.

"I'm afraid not. Apparently, you weren't a good enough reason to return. I hope this doesn't offend you, but I can kind of see why." Jacinda let the insult roll off her.

"I hope you haven't gotten too attached to your surroundings," Asher said, removing a bottle of chloroform and a handkerchief from his pocket. He opened the bottle and saturated the cloth. Before Jacinda could process the danger, Agent Asher rushed towards her, pinning her arms down with his knees. Jacinda squirmed and yelled. Her body never stopped moving. *Don't breathe,* she told herself as Asher pressed the chloroform-soaked handkerchief to her face. *Just don't breathe.*

Jacinda held her breath as long as she could. Agent Asher's face was only inches from her own. Her vision started to blur. Then everything, once again, faded to black.

*****

Andy and Livingston poured over the interview videos Keith had brought back with him from California. Livingston was impressed by how much Keith had managed to document. He really did have a talent for recognizing what it took to make a good story. He seemed to ask all the right questions. Often times, reporters complained about answers during interviews. Most of them failed to realize they weren't asking the right questions. That's what set Keith apart from the average reporter—he asked the right questions.

Livingston had been editing the video for the past twenty-four hours straight. He'd been cooped up in Andy's apartment for four months, and hoped his website would someday ensure his safety in the outside world. He dyed his hair blonde, and grew a beard and mustache in an attempt to disguise himself. Although Livingston's appearance was altered, he wasn't satisfied the new look would mask his identity.

It was election month, but neither Andy nor Livingston bothered to watch the debates. They both knew Jarrod Kabbul would be inaugurated in January. The campaign trail was all for show. To those in the know, there was never any question as to who would win the election.

*****

Keith sat in the small, unimpressive conference room with Lori, Nurse Fee, and Dr. Berg. He looked at each person as they talked, hoping to capture them on video using the tiny camera in his glasses. Keith heard something beep. It felt as if cold ice water had been poured inside of his body. *Was it my glasses? My watch?* he wondered. Becoming totally distracted by the source of the beep, he managed to tune out the conversation.

"Keith?" Lori said, sounding worried.

"Yeah," Keith replied. "I'm sorry, I'm just not feeling well," he lied, not wanting them to know he was distracted by spy equipment. He was amazed the camera had lasted as long as it had. If the beep was, in fact, a camera powering down, it had still lasted an impressively long time. Lori reached over and touched Keith's arm.

"I need you to pay close attention to this part. I'm sure you know the drill, but I can't sign off on you as a Louden handler until I see you know absolutely everything there is to know."

"Of course," Keith replied. Dr. Berg laid two pills on the table. "The colors haven't changed since you were here last," Dr. Berg said to Lori. "She must take the yellow pill daily. Yellow. Daily." He emphasized.

"Got it," Keith said.

"Yellow pill every day," Dr. Berg continued. If she stops taking the yellow pill, her mind is likely to go haywire, and her personalities will fight for power. It's also possible she'll begin to have memories of the chamber room if that portion of her mind isn't sedated with this pill every single day. So. Yellow, once a day. Understand?"

"Got it," Lori said.

Everyone looked at Keith. "I got it too," he assured them.

Picking up the black pill, Dr. Berg said, "I like to call this little guy *the eraser*. A good *mnemonic is to imagine the black one as a chalkboard eraser. Get it?*" he said in his thick German accent. The old man always looked so pleased with himself. "As I said," he continued, "yellow pill everyday. Black pill only when you want to wipe her memory clean of the past twenty-four hours."

"Only twenty-four hours?" Keith asked.

"Well, I don't know. It could be twenty or it could be twenty-seven, but I recommend you play it safe and give her the pill immediately after an event you don't want her to recall."

Dr. Berg looked at Nurse Fee. "Did you give them the summoner?"

"Not yet," she said, stuffing her hand into her lab coat pocket. "Here you go, child," she cooed, handing the device to Lori. Lori examined the object before handing it to Keith.

"Does it still work the same?" Lori asked.

"Yes," replied Dr. Berg. "Just hold the two ends together. Just like always." Keith examined the object. It really did look like a miniature stapler. One side was hinged together and spring-loaded, while the part that would dispense staples, if it had been a stapler, simply contained two metal circles.

Keith's curiosity was at an all-time high. "I've used something similar to this before. How exactly does this one work again?" He asked, regretting the question as soon as it came out of his mouth.

"It's a summoner, Keith." Said Lori. It works like every other summoner." Keith hoped his face didn't reveal his embarrassment.

"I know what a summoner does, Lori. I simply wanted to know the science behind it."

Dr. Berg smiled. He was all too willing to answer Keith's question. "It's simple. When the two metal plates connect, the summoner produces a sound in a frequency that human ears cannot detect."

"Then, how does it work?" Keith asked, looking puzzled.

"That too is quite simple. Although human ears can't detect the noise, the human subconscious is able to pick it up. As you well know, the *subconscious is a magnificent thing, Keith. Once it has been trained through hypnosis, it can be triggered at will. Therefore, once the summoner's pitch is detected by the slave's subconscious, it allows for an alter to take over, while notifying the spirit that it's needed."*

Lori nodded. "I don't know how you're used to doing things. But at Louden, we give our artists the freedom to invite the spirit into them before a performance. It lets them feel as if they are in control. You'll have to use the summoner regardless. We just like to let the talent feel empowered."

*****

Lyla looked lovingly on as Kyler kicked a ball around the backyard. "I kid it!" he'd say with each kick. He was growing in leaps and bounds. It seemed as if he learned a new word each day. While Kyler used to call Lyla *me*, because that's how she referred to herself, he now called her Lya. He was a little parrot, and repeated almost everything.

"I hope he never stops calling me car," Carl said, before taking a drink of soda. "It's just so cute. Car. I like being Car."

Lyla laid her head on Carl's shoulder. "I try not to think in terms of always and forever with Kyler."

"Why?" Carl asked, putting an arm around her shoulder.

"Because I don't know what the future holds. Jacinda could come and take him away forever. They might have to hide or leave the country. We just don't know."

"I suppose that's true," Carl agreed, "but I have a feeling Jacinda will always let you play a role in Kyler's life."

"I hope so," she said, wrapping both arms around his waist. "I just wish we knew something. Anything. We haven't even heard from Jill."

"Did I not tell you?"

"Tell me what?"

"That Jill came to the bank."

"Your bank?"

"Yes, my bank."

"When?" asked Lyla.

"About a week ago. I could have sworn I told you."

"No," Lyla assured him. "I'm pretty sure I would have remembered."

"Sorry. Okay, I'll tell you now. Honey, Jill came into the office to open an account."

"Did you talk to her?"

"No, she acted like she didn't know me. She did wander into my office, pretending she was lost. She asked, 'Where do I go to open a checking account?' and slipped a folder on my desk."

Lyla's eyes widened. "What was in the folder?"

"I honestly don't know. I looked through the papers, but they didn't make much sense to me. There was a list of names, addresses, and email exchanges. I recognized a few of the names on the list."

"Well, it's got to mean something. She wouldn't have risked being seen at your bank if it wasn't important."

"I know," Carl agreed. "I called Rob Livingston. He told me to scan the information and email it to him. I went to the copy shop down the street, scanned it, sent it, and forgot about it."

"Why did you go to the copy shop?" Lyla asked.

"I'm not scanning that into my work computer. No way do I want that traced back to me."

"Aren't you worried the information can be found on the copy shop's computer?"

"Not really. I deleted it. Nobody is going to look for it there. Even if someone finds it, there's really no way to trace it back to me."

Lyla relaxed. "What did you do with the originals after you emailed the information to Livingston?"

"I threw them in the dumpster behind the grocery store."

Lyla straightened her back. "Shouldn't you have burned them? What if someone finds them?"

"I'm telling you, nobody could make heads or tails of the information. It's not something anyone would see value in. Plus, I guarantee you that The Brotherhood isn't dumpster diving behind the Shop and Save."

Kyler crawled onto the bench, and wedged himself between Carl and Lyla. "I bonna go da bark."

"The park, huh?" Carl said, as he fluffed the toddler's hair with his fingers.

"I told you it wouldn't take long to learn Kylerese,"

Lyla said with a wink.

"I *am* getting pretty good," Carl admitted. "I'm probably like fourth-level proficient, wouldn't you say?"

"Oh, at least," Lyla agreed, gleefully playing along. "I'd go so far as to say you're an expert."

"Really?" Carl asked. "I wouldn't classify myself as an expert. I mean, I can understand the language pretty well, but I still haven't mastered the writing portion."

Both Lyla and Carl laughed. "Could you imagine if an outsider heard our conversations? They're always so ridiculous," Carl said.

"I love our ridiculous conversations," Lyla responded, kissing Carl's cheek.

"I lub bark," Kyler added, refusing to allow his request to be ignored.

CHAPTER 26

Keith, Chyanne, and Lori walked to the luggage carousel once they arrived in New York City. Keith was relieved to be free of the programming facility. There were so many things he'd missed during his four-month stay at Three Ocean Rehabilitation. He'd missed his family. He'd missed his freedom. He'd missed fast food and crowds of people. He'd missed the hustle and bustle of city life.

He was surprised Chyanne wasn't any different flying home than she had been in flying to Florida. She just seemed like the same girl he'd met four months earlier. Of course, he knew all that would change with one click of the summoner. It baffled him that she didn't remember the chamber room. He had spoken with her the entire way home. Listening to her tell the story, you'd think she'd spent four months with a vocal coach in a beautiful mansion. He was amazed at the capabilities of mind control. She really didn't remember a thing. At least, she didn't remember anything that had really happened. *It's probably for the best,* Keith thought. Nobody should have to remember that kind of torture and abuse.

Keith couldn't wait to get back to his high-rise apartment and upload all the video he'd captured on his watch and glasses camera. Keith hadn't dared to start uploading video at the facility. He'd feared there were cameras in his room, which probably wasn't that much of a stretch.

Lori tied her long, blonde hair into a knot before grabbing her luggage off the carousel. *Yup,* Keith thought. *A lot has changed in four months.*

"Is that one yours?" Lori asked, pointing to Keith's suitcase.

"Yeah, I'll get…" Before Keith could finish his sentence, Lori pulled Keith's luggage off the conveyor belt. Keith looked at Lori in shock.

"Did you just get *my* suitcase?" Lori smirked and threw the suitcase back on the conveyor belt, forcing Keith to run after his own luggage.

Once their luggage was collected, they walked outside to find the limousine Louden had sent to fetch them. They crawled into the luxurious automobile, leaving their bags for the chauffeur to load. Lori untied her hair, and let it fall around her shoulders. She grabbed her purse, looked at Keith, and said, "You want to see something funny?"

"Sure," Keith said. "Humor me."

Lori fished the summoner out of her purse. "Watch her," Lori said. Chyanne's body twitched. Her entire demeanor became different. "Can you tell which one it is?"

"Which what?" Keith asked.

"Which personality?"

"Not really. I can tell Chyanne's gone, though."

Lori looked at the small girl sitting across from her. "What's up?" Lori asked her.

"I'm starving. We need to get something to eat, and I'm not talking about nasty food, either. I want lobster or filet mignon."

"Chy," Keith and Lori said in unison.

"Reverto," Lori said. She placed the summoner back in her purse once she felt confident it was Chyanne peering at her through baby blue eyes.

"So, that's it?" Keith asked.

"What?"

"That," Keith said, pointing towards Lori's purse. "Get it back out." Lori once again removed the summoner. "Change her," Keith demanded.

"Change me?" Chyanne asked. Her beautiful face mirrored her confusion. Keith held out his hand and pressed his index finger and thumb together as if he were operating the summoner.

"Push it," Keith demanded. Lori pulled the summoner back out and squeezed the ends. Keith instantly recognized Hugh.

*****

Lyla, Carl, and Kyler sat in an airplane en route to Hawaii. Two days earlier, Carl and Lyla had been legally married at the Justice of the Peace. Carl wanted to give Lyla a fairytale wedding, but knew that was impossible. Women who were hiding for their lives didn't have the luxury of large weddings. Besides, Carl knew it wasn't her style.

"You know, that was the hardest two weeks of my life," Lyla said.

"When?"

"The sixteen days that I had to be Jenna Roach."

Carl laughed. "It wasn't that bad of a name. It could have been worse."

"Maybe, but no name could be as wonderful as Ward."

Carl pulled her hand to his mouth and kissed it. Carl lovingly looked at Kyler. "The rug rat is doing pretty well for such a long flight."

"Bly," Kyler said, clearly enjoying his airplane ride.

Carl had also secured Kyler a phony birth certificate. "Roach," Lyla said, shaking her head. "I can't believe you let them put the name Roach on that precious baby's birth certificate."

"Roach is your maiden name. What else was I supposed to put?"

"I don't know. What if he had his father's last name?"

Carl played along. "That could have worked, but who would his father have been?"

Lyla thought for a moment. "President Clinton, perhaps."

"You sell yourself way too short, you know that?"

"Okay, fine. Maybe his father was royalty. His birth certificate could have read Tyler of Wales."

Lyla giggled. "I'm glad you didn't change his first name too much."

"There really was no need," Carl explained. "Nobody will be looking for a two-year-old named Tyler."

"At least we got married before I got my driver's license," Lyla said. "The DMV was horrible. I wouldn't go back there a second earlier than I needed to, not even to get the word Roach off my license." Carl laughed at her dramatic tone.

Lyla hugged Kyler close and lovingly held Carl's hand. "The only thing I regret is not getting married in front of a preacher," Lyla said softly.

"There's plenty of time for that. I promise. We'll make that happen soon."

Lyla sprinkled Kyler's face with kisses. "How many two-year-olds do you think get to tag along on honeymoons?" Lyla asked no one in particular.

"Moon," Kyler said. "I lub moon."

"Oh, you love everything," Lyla reminded him.

"I've never been to Hawaii; what's it like?" Lyla asked Carl.

"It's beautiful. We'll touch down in Honolulu, then

take a charter plane to Maui."

"Can we just lay on the beach all day long and pretend we don't have a care in the world?"

"All day and all night," Carl said. "I booked the nature package. We'll be camping out in tents."

Lyla looked less than pleased. "I've never slept in a tent. Won't it be uncomfortable? Where will we shower?"

"We won't need to shower. We'll have an entire ocean!"

"What about food? Will the dining experience at least be civilized?"

"That's the great part! Once we check into the beach campground, they'll issue us two coolers full of food and drinks to last the entire five days."

"A cooler? So, like, hotdogs and sandwiches?"

"If we're lucky," Carl said with a wink.

Lyla felt a sense of dread. She'd never been to a beach, and had been beyond excited when she'd heard about the honeymoon, but something about camping simply didn't appeal to her. *At least Kyler will enjoy camping,* Lyla thought, as she tried to find the silver lining.

"I hope I packed enough," Lyla said. She worried she'd forgotten something important.

Carl shrugged. "If you forgot anything, we can always pick it up there."

"Won't we be at an isolated campground?" The very word campground made her cringe.

"I think they have a bus that runs to town once a day. It'll be fine. Stop worrying," Carl assured her.

Lyla studied her engagement ring. "This really is the most beautiful ring I've ever seen," she said to Carl.

Carl touched the ring with his finger, "I promise to get you a wedding band soon."

"Oh, that's not necessary," Lyla assured him. "It's perfect just the way it is."

The pilot's voice boomed from the overhead speakers. They approached their destination. "We're here!" Lyla said excitedly, as she strapped Kyler into his seat.

"Not yet," Carl reminded her. "We still have to catch the plane to Maui, but it won't be long."

As the plane touched down, passengers began to fidget. The flight attendant reminded everyone to stay in their seats until the fasten seat belt sign had been turned off. The plane came to a complete stop, prompting the *ding* that indicated passengers were free to move about the cabin.

As Lyla, Kyler, and Carl exited the terminal, they were greeted with Hawaiian leis. "Aloha," said the beautiful woman who gave them the leis.

"Aloha," Carl replied. Carl had his hands full with Kyler's car seat, so Lyla was carrying the toddler on her hip.

Kyler closely examined the lei around his neck. "Blowers!" exclaimed Kyler. "I lub blowers!"

*****

Keith was certain Hugh had been summoned into Chyanne. Even before she opened her mouth to speak, it was clear Hugh was in control. Her stare became wicked and menacing. "Reverto," Keith said, expecting to see Chyanne return. Still, Hugh stared at Keith through Chyanne's eyes.

"What?" Hugh asked defensively. "What?"

Keith looked to Lori for help. "Why isn't she changing?" A sly smile tugged on one side of Lori's mouth. She was clearly enjoying this game. "Change her!" Keith begged.

"Change her, *please,*" Lori said, happy to have the upper hand.

"Change her, *please*," said Keith, never taking his eyes off Chyanne.

"You mean, say Reverto?" Lori said, before watching Chyanne regain control of her body.

"What are you guys talking about?" Chyannne asked. She looked as if she'd entered the room in the middle of a conversation.

Keith ignored Chyanne. "Why doesn't it work when I say it?"

"Because she's programmed to return to the sound of my voice. It's a safeguard. Not just anyone can run around saying 'reverto,' waking everyone from their sleep."

"Sleep? Does that particular word choice help you feel less guilty?"

"Guilty about what?"

Keith didn't want to appear inexperienced. He worried he'd already blown his cover.

"I've just never had my talent trained to respond specifically to my voice. It seems inconvenient. I don't want to have to hover over them twenty-four hours a day. I enjoy the security of knowing I can take a vacation without personalities running amok."

Lori found Keith amusing. "I can take a vacation, I just can't do it when Chyanne has to perform. She'll get to know her personalities. Eventually she'll have to learn how to share her body with both of them."

"I haven't met them," Chyanne said, sounding more childlike than ever. "What are they like?" Keith wondered if the summoner suspended reality. He couldn't believe what he was hearing.

"Wait," Keith said to Chyanne. "You know?" He looked at Lori. "She knows?"

"Of course she knows," Lori said. "You have absolutely zero experience as a handler, don't you?" she said, while giving Keith a knowing look that only served to confuse him. *Could she tell? Was it that obvious?* Keith knew continuing his charade would only lead to failure. Instead, he decided to play on her ego.

"No," Keith admitted. "I lied to get this internship. I have absolutely no experience, but I want it more than anything. It seems like every door keeps getting slammed in my face and every opportunity falls though for one reason or another." He looked at Lori with pleading eyes. "I know you're the best. You have the most incredible reputation. Look what you did with Tyla. You're at the top of your game, and I wanted you as a mentor. Please help me. I beg you, please don't tell Mr. Fisher that I have no idea what I'm doing. Let me learn from you. I promise, I won't let you down."

"You have no idea how happy that makes me," Lori said, ruffling his hair with her fingers as if he were a child. Keith immediately smoothed his hair back into place.

"Why?"

"Because, I thought you were just the worst handler I'd ever met. I mean, I like you, but you're absolutely clueless."

"Thanks," Keith said sarcastically.

"No, that's a good thing," Lori assured him. "You're bad, but it's not because you don't have talent. You're just inexperienced. You have to learn to hone that talent, and you'll be incredible. It's like anything else--the more you do it, the easier it becomes."

Keith leaned back in his seat. "So, you'll teach me?"

"Of course I will, but you have to come into this business with both eyes opened. You have to know who you serve."

"Who's that?" Keith asked.

"The keeper of the light. Our lord. The fallen angel, Lucifer," Lori replied. Her face beamed when she said Lucifer. Keith's chest tightened. He could actually hear his own heart beating. It was true. Everything Mitch had said was true. This woman had openly told him that Satan-worship was a prerequisite for the job.

"About that," Keith said, pausing, not for dramatic effect, but out of absolute necessity. Words were failing him. He wanted to choose the right words, as he desperately needed to understand her frame of mind. "What about the devil would you say interests you?" Even as he said it, he wished he could take it back. It sounded so lame.

Lori laughed. "Here we go. Devil worshiper. You're picturing horns and a tail, aren't you?" Keith shrugged. "It's not like that at all," Lori said. "He truly cares for humankind. Christians would have you believe he's the source of all that's evil, but he's not. Evil is a part of human nature, not his. Humans are evil, not angels."

"If he's not evil, why was he kicked out of

Heaven?" Keith challenged.

Lori shook her head from side to side. "No, that was a misunderstanding. Lucifer hated the way God treated humans. He got kicked out of Heaven for disobeying God, but God was merciless. Lucifer loved humankind more than he loved himself. He gave up Heaven so that he could be here on Earth with us. He chose to be here to guide and protect us."

Keith was speechless. Lori was clearly passionate about her beliefs. She defended Lucifer with the same conviction his mother spoke with when she talked of Jesus. He wondered how one person could be so misguided. How could Lori believe Lucifer loved humans after witnessing the torture inflicted on Chyanne? How could Lori have witnessed the kind of horrors that took place at Three Ocean Rehab and believe that Lucifer had any love for humankind? Jesus would never stand for such evil being perpetrated in his name. No loving entity would ever condone such wickedness. Even if Keith didn't believe Christ was his savior, she could never convince him that Lucifer was good and merciful. Where had his mercy been in the chamber room? Chyanne was only able to find mercy through escape—through disassociation.

Keith believed programming through torture was

nothing short of sick and sadistic. "So, you believe Satan cares about you?"

Lori shook her head. "You sound like one of those Christians. Satan is a name used in the Christian religion. It has a negative connotation attached. His name is Lucifer. He isn't red. He doesn't have a pitchfork. He's beautiful. He's so beautiful you can't look directly at him without burning your eyes. He would never reveal himself directly. That would be cruel. Humans are incapable of processing that kind of beauty. Instead, he reveals himself through music and art. He reveals himself in the chorus of your favorite song. He speaks to us through music."

"What about symbols? Keith asked. "I thought he communicated using symbols." Lori rolled her eyes. "No, men communicate using symbols. Lucifer communicates though song. Think about the energy behind music. A single melody can make you cry. Another melody might make you smile. Melodies speak to our spirit, Keith. Don't you find comfort in music?"

Chyanne's silence didn't go unnoticed by Keith. He turned to her. "What about you? Do you believe Lucifer cares about you?"

Chyanne looked down. "I know he's the way," she said softly.

"The way to what?" Keith asked, trying his best to understand.

"He's the way to fame. He's the way to money and respect. Why would he spoil his followers with everything their hearts desired if he didn't love them?"

"Do you really believe that?" Keith asked. Chyanne shrugged her shoulders, but refused to meet his eyes. "I don't know. I mean, I guess. It's worth a try."

"It's worth a try?" Keith mocked, hoping she'd recognize the ridiculousness of her flippant response. "What if you're wrong?"

Chyanne tilted her head as if she was having a hard time hearing him. "What?"

"What if you're wrong?" Keith asked.

"Wrong about what?"

"Wrong about Lucifer caring about you."

Chyanne shrugged. "She's not wrong," Lori insisted.

"No?" Keith responded. "I want to hear this from Chyanne. What if you're wrong about Lucifer caring about you?"

"What has God ever done for me?" Chyanne asked, sounding like a spoiled child. "I've given God twenty-one years to prove He cared about me. What has He ever done for me?"

Keith couldn't believe what he was hearing. "What has He ever done for you? What have you ever done for Him?" Chyanne looked confused by Keith's question.

Keith realized Chyanne wasn't evil—she was reckless. She wasn't aligning herself with Lucifer because she believed he deserved her worship. She was aligning herself with him to increase her worldly possessions and status. "That's pathetic," Keith said.

"What's pathetic?" asked Chyanne, becoming increasingly defensive.

"Your reasoning. I mean, at least Lori believes what she's saying. At least she has some kind of loyalty to someone other than herself. Don't get me wrong, she clearly believes a lie, but at least she has conviction. You only care about yourself. It's your *what can I get out of it mentality* that's going to lead you to places you don't want to go."

Keith surprised himself with his own passion. After all, was he any different than Chyanne? He'd always had a *what can I get out of it* mentality. But somehow, it all seemed so wrong now. Words flowed through him like electricity. He was simply a conductor of the message.

Keith continued, "I've learned more about light and dark in the past five months than most people will learn in a lifetime. I've spoken to people who were saved by the grace of God after a life of despair on the dark side. They'll tell you they've never experienced true joy until they found the Lord, but it's never the other way around, is it? Have you ever noticed that? I've yet to meet one single person who would testify that their life improved after meeting Satan. More stuff? Perhaps. Famous? Maybe. Happy? Absolutely not! God would never force a spiritual death on you—ever! He would never require you to be tortured and harmed."

Lori spoke, "Really? Wars aren't fought every day in the name of God or Allah? Notice no war was ever waged in the name of Lucifer."

"Are you kidding me? Lucifer wages wars on souls! Sure, misguided people have killed in the name of God, but it wasn't because God demanded it. Satan would like people to believe God was responsible, but men wage those wars, not God."

"So your loving God just sits back and watches all the suffering in the world without action? Why would a loving God let people be slaughtered in his name?"

"Because, Lori, He gave us free will. He gave mankind the right to choose. What good is love if you demand it? He wants us to choose to love him. Satan creates all the evil. He's the one behind the slaughter and wickedness. Think about it. Have you ever met *anyone* who knew true joy after turning their lives over to Satan?"

The limousine rolled to a stop in front of Keith's apartment building. He looked over and noticed tears in Lori's eyes. "I'm not going to work tomorrow," he told her honestly.

"I know," Lori said, as she wiped the tears with her sleeve.

"I really do want more for you, Lori. You deserve more." Lori remained silent. Keith looked at Chyanne before exiting the limo. "Do me a favor, Chyanne. Go talk to Tyla. Ask her how the whole Lucifer thing worked out for her, will you?"

CHAPTER 27

After landing in Maui, Carl, Lyla and Kyler headed to the campground in a taxi. "I'm so excited," Carl said. "The brochure said this place is as primitive as it gets."

Lyla cut her eyes sideways. "Exactly *how* primitive?" she asked. Please tell me there will be restrooms. There *will* be restrooms, won't there?"

"Honey, why would we need restrooms? We've got an entire ocean, remember?"

Lyla wondered if she could fake excitement. Of course, just being in the presence of Carl and Kyler brought her a tremendous amount of joy, but the vacation she had looked so forward to was beginning to sound less and less appealing.

"Are we almost there?" Lyla asked Carl.

Carl looked around. "I doubt it. This area is pretty built up. The campground is in the middle of nowhere."

"Perfect," Lyla said sarcastically.

"What's wrong?" Carl asked.

"Nothing. You did say there was a bus that runs to town every day, right?"

"I think so," replied Carl as he checked his watch.

"Why do you keep checking your watch? We're on vacation."

"Campground check-in is at three o'clock. I just don't want to miss it."

"Won't someone be there in case we are a little late?" Lyla asked.

"I don't know. I don't want to take the chance."

The taxi slowed and turned into the most beautiful resort Lyla had ever seen. She looked at Carl. "No?"

Carl grinned. "What?"

"Are you serious? No. Really? Is this where we're staying?" she asked with a smile that stretched from ear to ear.

"You didn't really think I'd take you camping on our honeymoon, did you?"

The cab pulled to a stop in front of the luxurious entrance. Carl helped unbuckle Kyler's car seat, and handed the driver a fifty-dollar bill. As usual, Kyler sat, perched, on Lyla's hip. Carl carried the car seat in one hand and grabbed Lyla's hand with the other. He pulled her towards the front entrance.

"What about our luggage?" Lyla asked.

"They'll bring it in. Come on." It was clear that Carl couldn't wait to get inside. Lyla wanted to stand and admire the beautiful grounds, but followed Carl towards the door. The doorman placed leis around each of their necks. "More bowers," Kyler squealed in delight.

As they walked through the doors, Lyla was struck by the resort's elegant décor. It was breathtaking. "I decided my new bride wouldn't get a star less than five," Carl said, as he pulled her hand up to kiss it. "There's more."

"More?" asked Lyla. "Nothing could beat this."

"Oh, I disagree. I think something will excite you more than just a gorgeous resort."

"What?"

"She's over there." Carl said. Lyla looked across the lobby. There, next to the elevator, stood Marlene. Both women lost all composure when they saw each other. They ran through the lobby, meeting in the middle. Lyla had never hugged anyone so hard in her life.

*****

Keith stood in the lobby of his apartment building. He waited for the elevator, and tried to calm himself after the heated exchange in the limousine. He worried he he'd been too hard on Chyanne. Calling her pathetic was cruel, and cruelty had no place in his message. A good Christian would have approached her with kindness, and would have led with love, not insults.

Lori didn't know Keith's real identity, and he had been careful not to reveal any personal information. It would be possible to leave New York, disappear, and forget, but he couldn't. He couldn't forget. He knew his profession of faith destroyed any chance he had at remaining at Louden Records, but even if it hadn't, what was the point of continuing? He wanted to be a reporter, not a talent handler. He already had the story. What else could he possibly need to know? He had not only witnessed torture and mind control, but he was sure he had captured plenty of audio and video as proof. Sure, he could have filmed the temple room rituals later, but that's the last place he wanted to go.

He felt certain either his watch or glasses had recorded the conversation in the limousine. Even if the watch had died when he heard it beep, he still had the audio and video captured with the glasses. He had witnessed talent entering the machine, and had spoken to Tyla, who had come out the other side. He wished he could speak to someone who had completed the entire cycle—someone who'd entered the machine and had been spit out the other side, but he knew that was impossible, because they were all dead. You either found your way out, or you died. Period.

He stepped on the elevator and pushed the button to his floor. He knew it was time to leave. Where would he go next? Should he just return to Washington D.C? It was already November. The internship at *Your Nation Now* was over. It was over, and he wouldn't get credit for completion.

Should he go back home to Austin? The fall semester was almost finished. He would never graduate on time, and hoped the University would let him pick up where he had left off. Was he foolish to take such an assignment? Was The Brotherhood already looking for him because he had helped Jacinda find Kyler?

Keith felt so lost and alone. The once arrogant, self-assured reporter-in-training questioned not only himself, but also everything he had ever wanted. He had learned that news was not only sanitized for the public, but also hand-picked by the elite to serve their purposes. Truth-seekers had no place in mainstream news.

*****

Jacinda slowly regained consciousness, but found her eyelids too heavy to open. She searched her memory, desperately trying to recall what had happened. She remembered a mattress and an old staircase leading up to a metal door. A tray. She remembered the tray of food the man had left on the top step. He was afraid of something. What was it? Asher, she remembered. Agent Asher was there.

Was she on a boat? She felt as if her body was rocking or swaying as if by wind or water. Where was she? Stairs. The man was afraid of the stairs. That was ridiculous. Nobody was afraid of stairs. What technical term had Asher labeled the fear? *Who cares*, she thought. *It wasn't real.* Was there any truth to anything Asher had said? Had they really found her precious son?

Her head throbbed. It hurt even worse than it had months ago when she'd awoken to find herself in a basement. Where was she now? Was she still in the basement? She desperately searched her memory, looking for anything that might reveal what had happened. It was then that she remembered Agent Asher pulling out the cloth and bottle. *It was chloroform*, she thought. Just like the first time he'd knocked her out in his car.

Fighting against the drugs in her system, she willed herself to open her eyes. Her eyelids felt so impossibly heavy. She tried moving her hands, but could feel the bindings around her wrists. Where was she? Finally, her eyelids parted to reveal a hospital room. *Thank God,* she thought. *I'm in a hospital. They found me. I'm going to be okay!*

She looked around the room to discover a chair with wires and a metal helmet. It looked like a torture device. Her eyes moved to the wall where she saw shackles. To her right, she saw a tank of water. The realization shot through her like a like a bullet ripping through her flesh. She wasn't in a hospital. She was in a torture chamber.

*****

Keith walked into his high-rise apartment and went straight to the sliding glass door. The view was breathtaking, but it didn't bring him the same joy it once had. He'd spent the last four months witnessing evil. He, himself, had started to become desensitized. How was day ten easier than day one?

How was day thirty easier than day ten? The torture had progressed; it hadn't relented. Shouldn't he have become increasingly horrified, not increasingly more comfortable?

What did that say about him? Was he capable of evil? Maybe Lori was right. Maybe evil was a human condition. Maybe we were all capable of evil, but wasn't that the point? Wasn't that why God gave us free will? We were all born sinners— none of us saints. We had to choose the light over the dark. The darkness could swallow anyone whole. Wasn't that why his mother read her Bible every day? She always talked about the importance of staying connected—of not straying. Maybe she realized how easily one could fall into darkness.

Keith felt two lifetimes older than he had when he'd arrived in Washington D.C. He had arrived an ambitious, greedy intern. God and the devil, Heaven and Hell—they had been nothing more than abstract theories five months ago. He was now positive that both existed. Maybe he had never experienced God, but he had experienced Satan, and he'd felt his spirit being crushed. If Satan crushed his spirit, and God was the opposite, wouldn't it also be true that God would build his spirit? After all, light was the opposite of dark. Everything had a polar opposite.

So what if he'd never truly experienced God? If the experience was the polar opposite of the slow death of his soul over the past four months, God would be the one to breath life and hope back into him. He knew that now. He'd spent the past four months in darkness. Although he'd left the programming facility behind, he was unable to leave the darkness in Florida. It had followed him. It hovered over him. He felt depressed and hopeless.

"I need you God," he said out loud, before dropping to his knees. He began to cry, not whimper, but sob. The longer he cried, the better he felt. He felt as if the tears were washing away the evil—washing away the darkness. "I'm so sorry, God. I'm sorry I stood by and let them hurt Chyanne. I'm sorry I put my role as a reporter ahead of my role as a Christian—as a human." But had he ever been a Christian? His mom was, but was he? He'd never felt moved by the spirit, not until that very moment.

Suddenly Keith felt as if weight had been lifted. He felt hope return. Hope. How he'd missed hope. Goosebumps covered his entire body, and he knew God was there. For the first time ever, he knew what it meant to experience God. He'd never looked for God before. He had to experience darkness before seeking the light. Maybe that was true for everyone. He was exhausted. He moved to his bed and continued to pray. He prayed for safety.

He prayed for those he loved. He prayed for answers. He prayed until he fell asleep.

CHAPTER 28

Keith awoke to his cellphone ringing. "Hello," he said, sleep still present in his voice.

"Keith," Andy said. "What happened?"

Keith rubbed his eyes. "What do you mean, sir?"

"I just talked to Fisher. He said his top handler quit this morning. She didn't say why; she just quit. What happened in Florida?"

Keith didn't understand. "Did she quit her job, or just quit working with Chyanne?"

"She quit her job. She's been with Louden forever. She didn't even give a notice. She just quit. What happened in Florida?"

"Nothing happened. I mean, a lot happened, but it was all stuff she's done a million times. She'd never given me any indication that she was going to quit. Yesterday, she made it sound like she had the most amazing job in the world."

"When was the last time you saw her?"

"Yesterday evening, when I got out of the limo. Wait…" Keith thought back to the moment he had exited the limousine. Lori had been crying.

"When I got out of the limo, she and Chyanne were still inside. I was the first to be dropped off. She was crying, but I wasn't sure why. I mean, I thought maybe she was sad I was leaving, but, looking back, that doesn't make much sense. We got along, but it's not like we were so close she'd cry if I left."

Keith thought about the last time he saw her. Why was she crying? Why did she look so defeated? Keith heard a knock at his door. "Someone's here," said Keith.

"What? Who?" Andy asked.

"I don't know. Let me call you back." Keith ended the call with Andy, and made his way to the door.

He looked out the peephole to see Lori. She looked anxious. Keith opened the door. Lori pushed her way past him, removed his watch, and tossed it to the ground. Without saying a word, she grabbed his sleeve and pulled him into the bathroom. She closed the bathroom door and pulled her phone out of her pocket. She used her phone to play music, and turned it up as loud as it would go.

"You have to leave," she told Keith.

"I am. I already told you I was leaving. Did you quit your job? Why are we in the bathroom?"

"No, I mean you have to leave now."

"Why? Why are we in here? What's going on? How did you know my apartment number? Did Fisher tell you?"

"No," Lori responded, "This is Fisher's apartment; one of them, anyway. He told me you would be staying here. The whole apartment is bugged. He can hear everything you say. The bathroom is the only place without a listening device. He's not interested in anything that happens in here. The watch recorded everything. It's a remote listening device. It allowed Fisher to hear everything. I'm pretty sure I heard the battery die when we were talking to Dr. Berg, but I didn't want to risk it, so I took it off."

Keith tried to wrap his brain around the situation. Why was Lori here? Why had she quit her job?

Why was she so insistent he leave?

"Look," Lori said, "he knows you were never a handler." Keith began to understand.

"He does?" Keith asked, but he knew Fisher knew the truth.

"Yes, he knows you never had any intention of being a handler." That particular statement threw Keith for a loop.

"Wait, he told you that? He told you I never wanted to be a handler?"

"He's not who you think he is, Keith. It was all a ruse. You were supposed to get caught up in the apartment and the lifestyle. You were supposed to stay long enough to get swept away by the glitz and glamour. You weren't supposed to quit on the ride back from programming. Nobody would be enticed by programming. You were supposed to become enchanted by the money and parties. You were supposed to meet celebrities. But that was supposed to be later. First, he wanted you to experience the ugly side of the business. After that, there would be no more surprises."

"That makes no sense," Keith said. "Why wouldn't he have won me over with the glamour and glitz before sending me to hotel hell?"

"Because, he thought you would stick it out. He worried you'd fall in love with the glamour associated with the business, and become disenchanted once you'd realized there was also a grittier side—that it wasn't all champagne and strawberries. Andy told him you were coming, so he checked you out. He went to school with your journalism professor, so he gave him a call. Your professor said you were the most ambitious kid he'd seen come through his program in all the years he'd taught at the university."

"He said that? Dr. Kris?"

"I don't know which one. I just know it was one of them. The original plan was to program you in Florida. You were supposed to be in the hall with the sleepers."

"The sleepers?" Keith asked.

"Yes, the people who aren't there voluntarily. The people the government brainwash. We call them *sleepers*, because their alter ego hides, or sleeps, until it's time to be used for the government's purposes. They're used for assassinations, acts of terror, or just a million other reasons. That's not important right now. What's important is that you were originally supposed to be programmed against your will, but after talking to your professor, he had a change of heart. He wanted you to willfully serve

Lucifer, not just become a robot. He heard about your ambition, and figured you'd agree to sell your soul to achieve success. He saw something in you."

Keith leaned against the bathroom counter. He didn't trust his legs to support his weight. "Why are you telling me this?"

"Because," Lori answered, "as soon as you told me you weren't coming back to work, I knew what his reaction would be. I knew he wouldn't just let you walk away after seeing firsthand how we did things. I knew once you made your choice, and you didn't choose Lucifer, he'd find a way for you to serve against your will."

"Why didn't he do that in the first place?"

"I already told you. He wanted your soul!"

"Who wanted my soul?"

"Lucifer."

"I thought we were talking about Mr. Fisher."

"Mr. Fisher simply does Lucifer's bidding. Last night, Fisher heard you pray. Lucifer heard you pray. They both knew they had lost. Fisher couldn't just let you walk away after everything you'd witnessed. He either had to kill you or program you. Killing you would be pointless. After all, you could reveal so much about The Resistance."

"You know about The Resistance?"

"Of course I do. Just like The Brotherhood has moles, so does The Resistance. Fisher never turned his back on The Brotherhood. He never turned his back on Lucifer."

"What about Tyla? Why did he introduce me to her?"

"She never stopped serving Lucifer either, Keith."

"But she told me how horrible programming was. She said once she got out, the industry turned their back on her."

"No, that's not true. She just grew tired of the spotlight. She still works very closely with Louden talent."

Things started to make sense to Keith. It was all part of the act. If he understood the evils of the business, but chose it anyway, he would have turned his back on God. *Free will*, he thought. *Lucifer wanted me to willingly turn my back to God.*

"So," Keith continued, "the plan was for me to choose. I just didn't make the right choice. Now they either want me programmed or killed. So it really wasn't a choice at all. Why are you telling me this, Lori? Yesterday, you couldn't praise Lucifer enough."

"Humanity, Keith. I still feel compassion. Lucifer is supposed to be compassionate, but there was nothing compassionate about programming you against your will or killing you. That wasn't compassion. That wasn't the lord I serve."

"So, you don't think Lucifer has anything to do with this."

Lori closed her eyes. "Yes. I know he had everything to do with this. What you said in the limo about me believing a lie—it struck a chord. As soon as it came out of your mouth, I wondered if there was truth to it. I never even considered it might be a lie. But you were right. Your words made sense. I hear Christians talk about their lives after finding God. They always seem so happy. We're not happy, Keith. We're miserable. We're always looking for that *thing* that will make us happy. That's what keeps us going—discontent. We are fueled by discontent. There's got to be more to life than what I was led to believe. What you said just made so much sense. I can't describe it, but I couldn't *un-hear* what you said. Once I began to question my beliefs, it snowballed. I can't put it into words, but the harder I tried to convince myself I was right, the harder it became to believe it." Lori's body crumbled to the floor. She began crying hysterically. "I'm sorry. I'm so sorry. I'm sorry." Keith didn't know what to do. He bent down and put his hand on her back.

"It's okay."

"I'm so sorry," Lori said.

"Stop saying that. I know you're sorry; it's all right."

Lori refused to be comforted. Nothing Keith said could even begin to ease her pain. "I'm sorry," Lori continued to repeat. "I am so, so sorry." Keith suddenly realized she wasn't talking to him. She was talking to God.

CHAPTER 29

Lyla, Marlene, Carl, and Kyler ate breakfast at a table overlooking the ocean. "It's so beautiful," Lyla said. "I still can't believe all this is happening."

Marlene couldn't stop kissing Kyler's head, but he refused to sit still. Every time she picked him up, he squirmed back out of her lap.

"Wim," he kept insisting. "I wanna wim!" Kyler had had so much fun playing in the waves the day before. They were exhausted from the trip, so they didn't spend a lot of time at the ocean, but they did find time to swim.

"Are we going to build sand castles today? Carl asked Kyler.

"San Bassles!" Kyler squealed.

Lyla laughed. "He has no idea what you're talking about."

Marlene agreed, "No, but he is enthusiastic, isn't he?"

"You have no idea," Carl said. "He's always game for anything."

"I just can't believe how much he's grown since I've seen him last. He's growing into a little boy."

"A little boy who loves everything," Lyla said.

"Does he still love spaghetti?" Marlene asked.

"Oddly enough, no," replied Lyla.

Marlene smiled with both her lips and her eyes. "I have to get used to your new name."

"Eh," Lyla said, "it's only the third name I've had this year." Lyla had told Marlene a fake name when they had met, and had never fully forgiven herself for lying.

"Jenna Ward," Marlene said, placing her napkin on her breakfast plate. "I love it."

Lyla had missed Marlene so much. "Okay, how did you pull all this off?" Lyla asked Carl.

"It was easy. Once you told me about her, I called

every cab company in Oklahoma City until I found a Marlene. I caught her up to date and asked her if she'd meet us here."

Marlene smiled. "I wouldn't have missed it for the world. Besides, you two needed someone to help with Kyler. You can't be chasing a toddler on your honeymoon!"

"Thanks again for watching him last night. It's the first time Carl and I have ever been to dinner alone."

"It was my pleaure," Marlene assured her.

Carl glanced at his watch. Something flashed in Lyla's eyes. "Wait, that's why you kept checking your watch yesterday, wasn't it? We were supposed to meet Marlene in the lobby at three o'clock, weren't we?" Carl just smiled. Lyla beamed. "Mission accomplished," she said. "It was the most amazing gift you could have given me. Now we're all together, and it's time to stop obsessively checking your watch."

Marlene smiled at Carl. "Should we tell her?"

"Tell me what?" Lyla asked.

"It's about that time, but why don't we just show her." Carl looked around the table. "Is everyone finished?" Everyone nodded. Kyler crawled into

Carl's lap. Carl lifted him over his head.

"Bly!" Kyler said between giggles.

Carl looked at Lyla. "Marlene is going to take Kyler back to her room, and I want you to come with me." Lyla wasn't ready to leave Marlene. Breakfast had passed entirely too quickly.

Marlene stood and lifted Kyler from Carl's lap. "Come on, little fella. Let's go see the new toy I bought you."

"Doy," Kyler said, happily laying his head on Marlene's shoulder.

Lyla followed Carl to the elevator. "I still feel like I'm dreaming. This was perfect, Carl. It was absolutely perfect." Carl pulled her in for a hug. "I'm not done yet."

"What do you mean?" Lyla asked. "What more can you possibly do?"

The elevator stopped on their floor and he grabbed her hand to lead her out. "Just one last thing. I promise, no more surprises after this."

Lyla followed Carl to their hotel room. Carl handed her the key card. "Go ahead, open it." Lyla fumbled with the card, clumsily sliding it into the slot. She opened the door to find the most beautiful wedding dress she'd ever seen. She looked at Carl.

"Are you serious? Here? We're going to have a real wedding *here*?"

"You didn't think we could have a wedding without Marlene, did you? I promised you a minister, and we're going to do this right."

"But how? How did you get the dress?"

"I can't take credit for picking out the dress. That was all Marlene." Carl looked down at his watch again, "All right, beautiful, you have exactly forty-five minutes to get dressed, ready, and onto the beach. We don't want to keep the minister waiting."

CHAPTER 30

Jacinda squirmed and pulled against the shackles that bound her to the small hospital bed. She screamed until her throat was raw, but nobody came to her rescue. Her throat was parched. She continued to look around the room, and wished she had at least some idea where she was. Her thoughts turned to her son. She prayed Asher was lying. She hoped Kyler was safe. She would never tell them where her child was. She would die first. If they thought torturing her would result in her telling them where her son was, they were wrong. *Please God,* she thought, *please let Kyler be safe.*

Her mind, still foggy from the drugs, was racing. She desperately wanted to know where she was. She let out one last scream before a woman entered her room. The woman was tall with long, dark hair. "Where am I?" Jacinda asked. The woman responded in a language that sounded like German to Jacinda. "What?" Jacinda asked. She had no idea what the woman had said.

"I'm just messing with you," the nurse assured her.

"Messing with me? Where am I? Am I in a hospital? Did you find me? Was I rescued?"

The nurse didn't answer. "Please," Jacinda begged. "Please tell me where I am." The nurse busied herself with the chair that resembled an electric chair. "I'm so thirsty," Jacinda said. "Can I please have a drink of water?"

The nurse looked at Jacinda.

"So many questions. First of all, I'd like to introduce myself. I'm Nurse Lisa. You'll be seeing a lot of me. Secondly, get used to being thirsty. Last, but not least, you should know that your room is soundproof. You can scream all you want, but nobody will hear you."

A sense of dread washed over Jacinda. "Where am I?"

Lisa smiled. "So inquisitive. I can tell you're a reporter."

"Please help me," Jacinda begged. Two men who looked like orderlies entered the room. Nurse Lisa looked up from the electric chair. "I've got it ready. I just need you to transfer the patient and we'll get started."

Without saying a word, the men released the restraints around Jacinda's wrists and tightly grasped her arms. Jacinda fought against them with all her might, but even if she wasn't so weak from months of malnutrition and foggy on drugs, she never could have overcome two grown men.

Jacinda was shoved into the electric chair. One man pinned her arms to the chair while the other worked quickly to lock the metal cuff restraints around her wrists. Nurse Lisa held Jacinda's head against the back of the chair, while one of the orderlies locked a metal neck restraint into place. "What are you doing to me?" Jacinda screamed. The two orderlies never said a word. They moved quickly, as if they had done this a hundred times before.

Once the men secured Jacinda's legs to the chair, one man finally spoke. "Flip the switch."

*****

Keith sat on a plane en-route to Washington D.C. Following Lori's warning, he had left immediately. He had begged Lori to come with him, but she'd refused. In a way, he understood. Her entire belief system had just been rocked. She was confused, angry, and scared. He knew Fisher would review the surveillance cameras and see Lori pull him into the bathroom. He feared for her safety, but she assured Keith she'd go somewhere safe. Nonetheless, Keith had given her his safe phone number.

A million thoughts competed for Keith's attention. He knew there was no place in mainstream news for him. Not after everything he'd learned. He knew he couldn't return to school. He knew he had a target on his back. After all, he had witnessed what went on in the programming facility. He was officially a threat. There was no way The Brotherhood would let him live. In a way, he was still in shock. Somehow, a simple internship in Washington D.C. had led him into the heart of a well-organized, wicked conspiracy that had changed his life forever.

His eyes were now opened to an evil he never would have believed existed. He found it ironic that, while God gave us free will, Satan had to first destroy a person's will before he could fully submit. Before he could completely be indoctrinated, his spirit and will had to be crushed, then rebuilt to suit Satan's agenda. He'd heard about demons his whole life, but was more convinced than ever that demons used human hosts. Through human hosts, demons perpetrated unspeakable acts of cruelty.

He thought back to all the horrible stories he'd ever heard on the news. He wondered if all the mass murderers were somehow possessed by demons to carry out such evil atrocities. Keith had so many questions, and such few answers. He would go to Andy's as soon as he arrived in D.C. Hopefully, Andy would help Keith sort things out. He needed someone to help him make sense of the past four months. He prayed they would find a way to keep him safe.

His mind drifted to Chyanne. He wished he could save her, but knew she had chosen the darkness. She didn't want to be saved. Keith knew his life would never be the same. He had seen too much. It's as if someone had switched on a light and he was able to see the world for how it really was. He understood spiritual warfare was very real. He knew Satan was constantly fighting for souls. Satan lured people in with false promises of love, and enticed them with material wealth and fame. Four months ago, Keith had wanted to take on the news industry. Now, he wanted to take on the evil forces that were gaining such a stronghold in this world. He had been transformed into a warrior.

*****

Livingston and Andy watched Jarrod Kabbul's interview on *Your Nation Now*. The interview promised a glimpse into the presidential candidate's home life. Kabbul's charm was undeniable, except, of course, to those who saw right through it. Men like Livingston and Andy were able to see him for the wicked man he was. "How can anyone buy anything he says?" Livingston asked Andy.

"Their eyes haven't been opened," Andy replied.

Paula Strong sat across form Kabbul and his wife, Ellie. Ellie held their son, Raider, in her lap, as Kabbul looked on lovingly. Paula focused her attention on Jarrod Kabbul. "As you know, a prankster thought it would be funny to run a story saying BARAchip was the Mark of the Beast," Paula said.

Kabbul laughed. "I can find humor in that," he said. "You have got to be able to find humor in everything, but the fact is, BARAchip is invaluable technology that was designed to keep our children safe. Now, more than ever, you see horrible stories about child abductions on the news. I certainly wasn't taking any chances with my son. We didn't leave the hospital until we were certain he had BARAchip securely implanted in his hand. My wife and I watched as they inserted the safeguard. It was so easy and painless. Raider didn't even cry. As a responsible parent, who loves my child with all my heart, I knew it was my responsibility to do everything in my power to keep my child safe. I'm so grateful for such advances in technology."

Paula looked at Ellie. "What about you, Mrs. Kabbul? How do you feel about BARAchip?"

Ellie smiled. "I'm a mother. I think it's great. What kind of mother would I be if I didn't take every precaution possible to protect my son?"

"Indeed," Paula agreed before turning her attention back to Ellie's husband. "One of the issues that has been so fiercely debated this year is gun control."

Kabbul's expression became serious. "I don't think of it so much as gun control as I do murder control. Every time you turn on the news, there's another mass shooting. It's so senseless and avoidable. My hope is to make this great country of ours as safe as I possibly can. Let's remove the weapons that make mass killings so common. Let's safeguard our children by implanting them with a chip that will tell us their whereabouts if they are ever abducted. It all seems so obvious to me. Who, aside from murderers, want the mass shootings to continue? Who, except sick child predators want missing children to be untraceable? Are the people who oppose gun control and BARAchip condoning and promoting terror? I just can't comprehend who would oppose measures taken to secure the safety of Americans."

Livingston looked at Andy. "I can't watch this anymore."

Andy shrugged. "What did you expect? You knew how this interview would go."

"I know, but it sickens me. There's no point in watching this. We already know the agenda. We know he will be put in power. We know BARAchip will eventually be required for everyone who wants to work, purchase groceries, obtain a driver's license, and function in society. It's been decided, and America will fall for it, hook, line, and sinker."

There was a knock at the door. "I'll get it," Andy said. He stood and flipped off the television. He too had heard enough. He looked out the peephole and saw Keith. He opened the door and stood back so Keith could enter. Andy thought Keith looked different somehow. He looked exhausted, but determined. Keith walked into the living room and tossed the glasses Carl had given him onto the table.

"It's all there," Keith said. "The birth of the anti-Christ, the sacrifice, and everything I witnessed at the programming facility. It's all recorded on the camera inside the glasses."

Livingston picked the glasses off the table. "How do we retrieve it?"

Keith opened his suitcase and pulled out a cord. "You can use this to upload everything onto your computer."

"Have you seen the footage?" Livingston asked.

"No, I haven't had the chance. But I'm dying to see it."

*****

Jacinda pulled at her wrist restraints as she stared at the ceiling above her bed. Having endured hours of electrocution, her body was still twitching. *I won't let them,* she thought. *This is how captors break down their victims. They torture them until their spirit is crushed. Once they crush their victims' spirit and will, the victims become sympathetic to their capturers. Not me. They won't break me.* She thought of Stockholm Syndrome, and all the stories of children who were kidnapped, only to be broken down and re-shaped by their capturers. *Not me,* she assured herself.

She looked at a table by the foot of her bed. There was a live rat inside a cage. She wondered what they would use the rat for. Would they let the rat feast on her? She didn't know, but felt certain they'd use it as some form of torture. Her throat was dry and sore from screaming. Her head throbbed, and the constant twitching was uncomfortable, but she refused to let them break her spirit. She prayed. *God. Please keep Kyler safe. If I don't make it out, please let him know how much I love him, and please don't ever let him find out how I died. I don't want him to know I suffered.*

Her prayer was interrupted, when the door to her room flew open. Standing next to Nurse Lisa were two brute-looking men. Their eyes mirrored their evil intentions. Lisa smiled at Jacinda. "I'm afraid you won't enjoy what you're about to experience."

Jacinda glared at Lisa. "I don't care what you do to me. You'll never break me. You might be able to kill me, but you'll never break me."

Lisa smiled at the two men and retrieved a pair of scissors from the drawer.

"She's feisty, isn't she?" Lisa said to nobody in particular.

As Nurse Lisa began cutting the front of Jacinda's hospital gown, one of the men approached her and punched her in the face as hard as he could. Excruciating pain caused her to see only blackness for a few seconds, but she never lost consciousness. Jacinda, almost in a state of delirium, began to laugh.

"Is that all you've got? My husband was killed.

My baby was stolen from me for over two years. *That* was pain. There is nothing you can do to me that will even come close to that kind of torment."

"We'll see about that," replied Nurse Lisa.

CHAPTER 31

While Keith, Andy, and Livingston reviewed the video captured by Carl at the grove, Keith's safe cell rang. "Hello," Keith said nervously. He noticed the call was from an unknown number.

"Keith, it's me—Lori."

"Lori, are you okay?"

"I'm fine. But I just talked to Jenni."

"Jenni?"

"Yes, you remember Nurse Jenni from the programming facility."

"Yes, I remember," Keith replied.

"She didn't know I'd quit Louden. We've been friends for years. She called, very excited that they had admitted Jacinda Kilmeade. She's obsessed with the Kilmeades like some people are obsessed with the Kennedys."

Keith looked horrified. "They have Jacinda?"

"Yes. Jenni isn't working with her, because Jacinda is in the wing where people are sent against their will, but she was excited to have such a high-profile patient at the facility."

Keith pulled his phone away from his face and whispered, "Jacinda is at the programming facility. I know where it is." Keith then spoke to Lori. "How long has she been there?"

"Only a day or two, I'm really not sure."

"What about you? Are you okay? Where are you?"

"I can't tell you that, but I'm safe. Don't worry about me. Save Jacinda. Security is minimal, because nobody knows what goes on there, except for the people who condone it, of course. But there are a few armed men. The whole building is outfitted with cameras." With that, the phone went dead.

"Lori," Keith said. When there was no answer, he tried again, "Lori?" Keith dropped his phone. "They have Jacinda, and I know exactly where it is. They have a few armed guards and cameras, but you wouldn't believe what goes on in that place. We have to save her."

Andy picked up his phone. "Where is it?"

"It's in Verra, Florida. It's called Three Ocean Rehabilitation. There is a sign out front, so I imagine there is some kind of listing."

Andy could see the panic in Keith's eyes. "We'll save her, Keith. There are quite a few ex-military, special-forces soldiers within The Resistance. They were sent on missions to create terror on U.S. soil, and cast blame on terrorists. Many of these men feel an enormous amount of guilt for following orders that killed Americans. They will do anything they can to try to atone for their actions. They'll get her out. Don't worry."

Andy dialed a telephone number and walked to the other room to have a private conversation.

Livingston wasted no time focusing his attention back to the video in front of him. "This is amazing," he said. "Carl managed to get the entire sacrifice and birth on video."

Keith looked at the computer screen in awe. "It's all so clear. I mean, the picture. I expected it to be grainy and low quality, but it's so clear."

"Amazing, isn't it?"

"It really is," Keith agreed. "I can't wait to see how the programming center video turned out. What are you planning on doing with all the evidence?"

Livingston pulled up the website he had created. "I'm putting all the proof on our new website. It's going to function just as a mainstream news website. We'll have stories, video, and even live interviews."

"Aren't you worried they will track you?" Keith asked nervously.

"Not at all. It's all been set up to send anyone who tries to find the source on a wild goose chase. It can't be shut down."

Keith's eyes were fixed on the computer. "So then, you're still going to be a reporter?"

"I don't know how to be anything else," Livingston admitted.

"What is weather modification?" Keith asked as he read the screen.

"Since the year 2000, the government has worked on programs to manipulate natural weather patterns. For instance, they did this in China during the Olympics to assure there was no rain during the games. But that was just the beginning. The government plans on creating droughts and mass destruction with hurricanes and tornadoes. They need the world to be in a state of disorder, and for the people to be dependent on the government to rebuild their communities."

Keith looked unconvinced. "They can really do that?"

"They can and they do."

"So then, you're just using this site to inform the public of everything the government is planning?"

"I am. Information is power, and the American people need to take as much power back from the government as possible."

Keith looked intrigued. "I want in."

CHAPTER 32

Tears filled Lyla's eyes as she hugged Marlene goodbye at the airport. "You'll never know how much this has meant to me," Lyla said.

Marlene smiled her kind smile. "I wouldn't have missed it for anything in the world. I'll never forget how beautiful you looked, standing there on the beach in your wedding dress." Marlene picked Kyler up. "I will miss you with all my heart," she said, before she kissed his little face. She walked over to Carl and pulled him into an embrace. "I couldn't have asked for a better man for Lyla. Please take care of her. Thank you so much for including me in such a special event."

Carl smiled. "I'll always take care of her. Always. Kyler, too. We'll never give up hope that Jacinda will return, but if she doesn't, I will always treat him as my own. I love both him and Lyla more than anything in the world."

Carl and Lyla watched as Marlene boarded her plane. They only had a one-hour wait to board their own plane back to California. Lyla leaned her body against Carl's. "I can't believe it's over. Can we just stay here forever?"

Carl smiled. "That would be nice, wouldn't it? We'll come back. I promise. This is just the first of many vacations."

Lyla snuggled her head on Carl's arm. "I love you, Carl."

"I love you, too, Jenna Roach-Ward."

Lyla laughed. "I still can't believe you couldn't have found an identity that didn't include the creepiest bugs alive."

*****

Jacinda wasn't sure how long she'd been at the facility, but she guessed it had at least been a week. She refused to detach from reality. She refused to be broken. She'd endured the torture with an almost supernatural inner strength. It was obvious the staff had become annoyed by her inner strength, but she knew exactly what they were trying to do, and refused to let them win. The sensory deprivation chamber actually brought her peace. She used the time to pray and build her strength for the next round of torture she was sure she'd have to endure. Her hunger pangs had subsided. She was given a tablespoon of water daily, but drank the water in the sensory deprivation chamber until she was sure she was finally re-hydrated.

She lay, shackled to her bed, and wondered what bizarre form of torture they'd use next. She heard what sounded like gunfire, and wondered if she was hallucinating. Her door flew open, and she saw a man with a gun and bulletproof vest.

"In here," the man screamed, as he rushed toward Jacinda. A man entered behind him and pulled a knife out of his pocket. As the man with the gun stood guard, the second man cut the restraints that bound Jacinda to her bed.

Everything happened so quickly; Jacinda didn't ask questions. She didn't feel scared, just confused. Who were these men? What were they going to do with her? Why was there so much commotion in the hallway? The man who had freed Jacinda from her restraints scooped her into his arms and screamed, "Let's move!"

Once they made their way out of the room and into the hall, Jacinda saw two nurses on the floor. They were both bleeding profusely. She wrapped her arms around the neck of the man carrying her, and looked over her shoulder. She saw men with guns kicking down doors and carrying other prisoners out of their rooms.

She heard a man scream, "Seven minutes!" before she was carried outside. She looked around and saw five vans. Men with guns were guarding the vans and keeping a close eye on their watches. The man carrying Jacinda handed her to a man standing by the van before he turned to re-enter the building. The man climbed into the van with Jacinda in his arms.

"Go!" he screamed at the driver. "Go!"

The driver hit the accelerator as Jacinda looked back towards the facility. She saw other prisoners being carried to vans. Like her, she knew they were all too weak to walk. She hadn't eaten in a week. That, combined with the physical abuse, left her weaker than she'd ever felt in her life. "Who are you?" she asked the man sitting beside her.

He studied her face, "You *are* Jacinda Kilmeade, correct?"

"Correct," she answered.

"You just look so different," he said.

She did look different than when she'd disappeared.

She had been a prisoner for over four months, first in the basement, then at the facility. She was gaunt. Her hair was tangled and knotted. Her eye was blackened where the orderly had punched her in the face. She looked nothing like the beautiful, healthy woman who was affectionately known as America's sweetheart.

They drove for miles before pulling to the side of the road. "One minute," she heard someone say through a walkie-talkie. Again, she looked behind her. She saw the other vans close behind. "Thirty seconds," said the same voice.

"All clear," said a man whose voice was deeper than the one who had been counting down. A loud explosion vibrated the van as fire and smoke filled the sky where the programming facility had once stood.

"What about the others?" Jacinda asked. "Did you save the others?"

"We did, ma'am."

Jacinda felt overcome with emotions. She began to cry. Her tears weren't from joy or sadness. They simply poured down her face as she tried to process what had just taken place. Her eyes grew wide. "My son! Is he okay? Please tell me he is okay."

"He's safe, Mrs. Kilmeade."

"Take me to him. Please, take me to him!"

CHAPTER 33

Carl walked through the door to find Lyla playing with Kyler. His face beamed, and she wondered what had happened. "What?" Lyla asked. "What happened?"

"Jacinda's safe!" Lyla jumped to her feet. "She's safe? Are you sure?"

"Positive. She was rescued a couple of weeks ago. She's been resting at a doctor's home. She was pretty emaciated and beat up, but she's going to be just fine."

"Why a home? Why not a hospital?"

"She never would have made it out of a hospital alive. There are too many members of The Brotherhood there. They would have killed her and made it look like she didn't survive her injuries. Of course, they would have lied about where she got the injuries in the first place, but she's safe. She's on her way."

Lyla threw herself into Carl's arms. "She's coming here to our house? She will be so excited to see Kyler! Oh, thank God she's alive!"

Carl's expression turned solemn. "Have you watched the news today?"

"No, why?" Carl didn't know how to break the news to Lyla.

Although Lyla resented her father, he wondered how the news of his death would affect her. "Lyla, I don't know how to say this, but your father was found murdered today."

Lyla's eyes grew wide, and she placed her hand over her mouth. "How? How was he killed?"

"He was found shot in his bed. The news is speculating that it was a robbery gone wrong, but I don't have to tell you that's probably not what happened."

"No," Lyla said quietly. "They killed him."

"Are you okay?"

"Yes, I'm just a little shocked. That's all."

"That's not all, Lyla. That happened late last night.

Apparently, Gregory heard about his father's murder and turned himself in at the border of Texas and Mexico."

"He turned himself in? What? Why?"

"I have no idea. He said he couldn't hide forever, and he was willing to accept any punishment he had coming."

Lyla thought for a moment. "If he turned himself in this morning at the Mexican border, then that at least proves he was nowhere near my father when he was murdered."

Carl nodded. "True, but he'll have to face charges for kidnapping, not showing up to his court date, leaving the country, and a string of other crimes. I'm not a lawyer, but I'd guess he's looking at a pretty stiff prison sentence."

"What was he doing in Mexico?"

"I have no idea."

"Does Jacinda know?"

"Honey, I'm not sure. I just know she's on her way here. Livingston, Andy, and Keith are also on their way."

Lyla looked surprised. "Here? Where will everyone

sleep?"

Carl shrugged. "We'll figure all that out later. Have you checked Livingston's website?"

"No. Kyler and I have been busy all day. Why?"

Carl sat on the couch and picked up his laptop. He typed in the website address and said, "Let's see what he has to say about all of this."

Lyla joined Carl on the couch. The headline read: **Jacinda Kilmeade found alive after months of imprisonment.** Below the headline and accompanying story was a video. The video contained all of Jacinda's interviews documented by Keith. There was also a video of Jacinda lying in her recovery bed discussing her time in captivity, and outing Agent Asher as one of her kidnappers.

"I can't believe this is all happening so quickly," Lyla said.

"I know. Livingston said there have already been over two million unique visitors to the site." Lyla and Carl listened to Jacinda talk about her time in the basement and the programming facility.

Tears welled up in Lyla's eyes. "She's been through so much already. Now this. How much can one woman take?"

Carl wrapped his arms around her. "You of all people should know how resilient the human spirit is. Hope is a powerful thing." Carl looked regretful. "I shouldn't have mentioned anything. The last thing you need right now is stress."

"You had to tell me. I would have found out anyway."

Someone knocked on the door. Lyla looked at Carl. "Could that be her already?"

Carl shrugged. "I don't know." He made his way to the door and peered out the peephole. He turned towards his anxious wife and smiled. "It's her!"

Carl opened the door to find Jill and Jacinda standing on the front porch. Jacinda embraced Lyla.

Lyla cried, "I didn't know if you were dead or alive. I was so worried about you. I'm so sorry for everything that happened. Are you okay?"

Jacinda didn't answer. Instead, she asked, "Where is Kyler?" Within seconds of Jacinda asking about his whereabouts, Kyler poked his little head around the corner. Jacinda collapsed to her knees. She held out her arms and said, "Baby. I've missed you so much!" Kyler slowly walked towards her. He was acting shy, but Lyla knew his act wouldn't last longer than a few minutes.

"See my deep!" Kyler said, as he pulled her hand. "Your what?" Jacinda asked, looking at Lyla as she stood.

Lyla smiled. "His pride and joy. He'll show you." Kyler happily led Jacinda to the backyard. He plopped himself into the driver's seat of his toy Jeep and beamed at his mother with pride.

"My deep!" Kyler said, hoping his mom would be as excited as he was about his toy.

Jacinda laughed, "Your very own Jeep! You learned how to drive while I was gone?" Kyler just giggled.

Lyla followed Jacinda into the backyard and closed the door behind her. Jacinda put her arms around Lyla. "I can't thank you enough for taking such good care of him while I was away. For taking such good care of him his entire life."

Lyla's eyes once again filled with tears. "I'm going to miss him so much."

"What?" Jacinda asked. Lyla immediately worried that her statement sounded selfish. "I just mean that I'll miss him. He's your child, and I know you've missed him terribly. I know he belongs with you. I'll just miss him."

Jacinda smiled. "You won't miss him that much; I'm moving down the street." Lyla threw her hands over her mouth. "What? You are? When?"

"I saw a house for sale on my way over. All my family is gone, Lyla. Jill is the closest thing to family I have. I want to live close. Plus, it would be cruel to take Kyler out of your life. You've raised him like a son. I want you two to maintain a relationship. I just think it would be best for everyone if we all lived close together."

Lyla wrapped her arms around Jacinda. "You have no idea how happy that makes me! I have news for you, too, but you have to promise not to tell anyone."

"You have news?"

"I do." Lyla put her hand on her belly. "Carl and I are having a baby!"

Jacinda's face lit up. "Congratulations! Why can't I tell anyone? You should be telling everyone. It's so exciting!"

"I'm not far enough along yet. We just found out. I wasn't going to tell anyone, but I just couldn't keep it in any longer."

Jacinda hugged her again. "What a lucky baby to have you for a mother," she said.

Lyla and Jacinda sat at the picnic table and watched Kyler drive around the backyard. Jacinda looked towards the back door. "Where are Carl and Jill?"

Lyla smiled, "I think they're giving us time to talk and you time to see Kyler." Lyla's smile turned to a look of concern. "Have you heard about Nicholas and Gregory?"

Jacinda nodded. "I have."

Lyla cast her eyes to the ground. "I'm sorry, Jacinda."

"Don't be sorry. You didn't do anything wrong. Something I never told you or anybody else was that I sent Gregory to a mission after I saw him in D.C. He was so contrite and broken that I wanted to keep him safe. I had no intention of ever taking him back, but I saw how shattered he was, and I couldn't help but feel compassion for him. Father Garcia runs the mission. I talked to him today. He said Gregory accepted Jesus. That alone made me cry. Gregory heard about his father's death and confessed everything to Father Garcia. He insisted on going home and taking responsibility for the kidnapping and skipping bail. He also said he was going to grant me a divorce and wanted me to keep the money from his inheritance." Jacinda paused. "I'm so sorry. I didn't even think that half of that inheritance should be yours. You are Nicholas' daughter."

Lyla waved her hand, "I don't want a penny of it. It's all blood money."

Jacinda nodded. "I agree. That's why I intend to put every penny towards educating people about the Illuminati and the New World Order. Livingston, Keith, and Andy are all going to need a salary to survive. Since our full time jobs will be informing the public through alternative sources like the website, that money will keep us and the website afloat."

Carl and Jill joined Lyla and Jacinda in the backyard. Carl hugged Jacinda and said, "Since I didn't get to hug you earlier." Jacinda happily returned his hug. "Did Lyla tell you the big news?" he asked.

Jacinda placed her hand on Lyla's belly. "She did, but said I wasn't supposed to tell anyone." Carl cut his eyes to Lyla. "She's just sharing all kinds of news, isn't she? I was talking about us getting married."

Lyla giggled, "Oh, yeah, that happened too!"

Jill looked confused. "I really missed a lot, didn't I?"

*****

Lyla, Jill, Jacinda, and Carl stayed up all night talking. Everyone had so much to share. Kyler made it as long as he could, but eventually passed out in his mother's lap.

Carl said, "It's already three o'clock. I should probably get some sleep. I have to go to work in the morning, but you guys feel free to stay up as long as you want."

Jacinda flipped on the television. "I just want to see what's on the news. I'm curious as to how they'll handle Gregory's story." Jarrod Kabbul's face was plastered all over the news.

"All right already!" Jill said. "We get it, he won."

"He didn't win," Jacinda corrected her. "He was placed."

"You know what I mean. We all know he'll be inaugurated in January. I wish they'd stop rubbing it in."

Lyla stood up to retire to the bedroom. "I thought Keith, Livingston, and Andy were coming tonight."

"I did, too," Carl said. "Maybe they'll be here tomorrow. It's too late to call now, so we'll get it all figured out in the morning."

Everyone was exhausted and fell asleep quickly. It

seemed they were only asleep minutes when they were awakened to the sound of the doorbell. Lyla opened her eyes and noticed Carl wasn't beside her. She looked at the clock, and realized it was already eleven. She sprung out of bed to check on Kyler, briefly forgetting Jacinda was there. She walked into the living room to see Jacinda open the door for Livingston, Keith, and Andy.

Keith looked at Lyla. "Hello, stranger."

Lyla smiled. "Hi, Keith."

Keith instantly noticed her wedding ring. "Are you married?"

"I am," Lyla said with a smile. Lyla swore she saw a flash of disappointment in Keith's eyes, but he quickly said, "Congratulations! That was fast. Who's the lucky guy?"

"Wow, it has been a while, hasn't it?" Lyla asked. "Carl."

"Carl, Carl?"

"Yes, Carl, Carl," Lyla said with a smile.

Everyone made their way to the living room. Lyla put on a pot of coffee. Keith picked up the remote control. "Do we even want to watch the news?"

"Why bother?" Jacinda asked. "We already know Kabbul will be all they're talking about. I do wonder if they'll mention Gregory, though." Jacinda's phone rang. She looked at the caller ID. "It's my divorce attorney. I didn't expect to hear from him so soon."

Jacinda excused herself and stepped into the backyard so she could talk privately with her attorney.

Within minutes, Jacinda returned from the backyard looking absolutely shocked. "What happened?" Lyla asked, fearing the worst.

"My attorney just got off the phone with Gregory's attorney. As promised, Gregory is granting me a divorce. He's giving me everything. Gregory's divorce attorney already contacted the attorney of Nicholas' estate. Nicholas was worth 100 million dollars. It was all willed to Gregory. Gregory requested that it all be given to me."

Keith looked shocked. "Wow."

Jacinda nodded. "I knew they were wealthy, but I had no idea they were worth 100 million. Do you have any idea how much good we can do with that kind of money?" Jacinda turned to Livingston. "I'm buying your news site. You and Keith will be put on salary as reporters, and Andy will be put on salary for helping to coordinate the resistance."

Andy waved his hand. "That's nice of you, but I already draw a retirement. I don't need the money."

"I need the money!" Keith said. "After New York, I had no idea how I was going to survive financially. I can't go back to school. I can't go back to mainstream news. I just had faith everything would work out. This is perfect!" Jacinda smiled.

Livingston was also smiling. "I guess The Resistance is no longer just ex members of The Brotherhood. It's now an entire movement. With this kind of funding, we can dedicate all of our time and resources to educating the public about what's to come. They need to know the government will cause what will look like natural disasters by tampering with the weather. They need to know how the government facilitates terror right here in our own country to further their agenda. It will take a while to convince people to wake up, but hopefully, with enough education, people will become proactive and we can change the course of this country."

Jacinda nodded. "It won't be easy."

"No, it won't," Livingston agreed. "We need to put reporters on different beats. Keith, I want you to cover the music industry. It's important that Americans learn that Satan uses popular music to desensitize and spread his message. I'll cover the mainstream media's influence. I have video of George admitting to following the Illuminati's agenda for years."

Keith interrupted, "Speaking of George, where is he?"

Livingston shrugged. "I don't know. He left a note saying he was going to Thailand to find his daughter. I haven't heard from him since."

Hope electrified the living room of Carl's house. "So, we're really going to do this?" Keith asked.

Jacinda smiled. "Yes, we're really going to do this. It will be a series of battles, and things won't change overnight. But yes, we'll fight the New World Order every step of the way."

Lyla wished Carl had been home to see the hope that burned in the eyes of everyone involved. Hope really was a living, breathing thing. As long as there was hope, nothing was impossible. Keith picked up the remote control. Turning it to the news station, he saw Jarrod Kabbul exiting the voting booth in the same video they'd been playing since Election Day. Kabbul placed an *I voted* sticker on his lapel and waved to the media. His wife, Ellie, and son, Raider, accompanied him to his makeshift press conference after he no doubt voted for himself.

"What did they name that kid?" Keith asked. "It was something weird."

Livingston rolled his eyes. "Raider Maylot."

"Huh? Keith asked.

"Raider Maylot. R-A-I-D-E-R-M-A-Y-L-O-T."

"That's a horrible name," Keith said. Keith's mind seemed to be spinning. Something about the name woke up the part of his brain obsessed with puzzles. "I need a pen and paper," Keith demanded.

Lyla handed Keith a notepad and pen. Keith wrote down the letters of the baby's name. "Raider Maylot is an anagram," Keith said. He held up the paper. "The soon-to-be First Baby's name is an anagram for LORD MAITREYA."

To be continued...

Marked III Summer 2014